The Consequences of Murder

The Consequences of Murder

A 1920s Mystery

MICHAEL SINCLAIR

CHAPTER ONE

November 1928

George Latimer sat in a first-class carriage on the 20th Century Limited and irritably wondered why he and his sister were returning to Albany, cutting short their trip to New York City, having just arrived yesterday for what was supposed to be a three-day holiday.

As the locomotive picked up speed, leaving Grand Central Station on its way northward, he glanced at his younger sister, Sue, sitting next to him. She was absorbed in reading the latest issue of *True Confessions* magazine, quite popular with young women her age. George hardly acknowledged such nonsense. For him, it was the classics, Bronte, Dickens, Chaucer, Shakespeare. He had taken out a hardcover copy of *Pride and Prejudice* from his suitcase. It was open on his lap, but he wasn't reading. Even Jane Austen's fine prose couldn't occupy his mind. He was too preoccupied to concentrate.

George Latimer was twenty-five years old, a graduate of Union College, and employed at the Home Savings Bank in downtown Albany. He was of medium stature, with a slim build, short-cropped brown hair, and green eyes. He was somewhat serious and rather brusque in manner but pleasant enough. He strongly disfavored the drinking and parties' people his age attended to in droves.

His younger sister, Sue, looked up from her magazine and smiled. Like her brother, Sue Latimer was a Union College graduate and worked in the business office at the Ten Eyck Hotel, also in downtown Albany. Sue was quiet and reserved, at twenty-three, she was resolved to work until she found the perfect man to marry. Not for her the flapper lifestyle, the late-night parties, or the endless drinking or smoking cigarettes. No, Sue had never been interested in such immoral and inappropriate behavior. She thanked her Aunt Sophie and Uncle Arthur for her good upbringing.

Brother and sister had gone to New York City to see a show, *An Enemy of the People* by Henrik Ibsen, a favorite author of George's, which had recently opened on Broadway. They had only arrived at the hotel yesterday, Thursday, and were planning to return Sunday. After spending Friday morning at the Metropolitan Museum of Art, they arrived back at the hotel for lunch when a messenger boy stopped them in the lobby and handed George a telegram.

Sue had looked at her brother wondering what it was about. George quickly ripped it open, not knowing what to expect. It was from their Aunt Sophie. She told them to return to Albany at once, as something dreadful had happened to their younger brother, Thomas. She added nothing more. Returning to their room, George called his aunt (and worried about the long-distance charge to the hotel bill) and told her he and Sue would return this afternoon. He asked her to explain more about it. She abruptly but calmly told him she'd explain after they arrived.

George looked out the train window, at the frozen Hudson River. The train was soon approaching Yonkers. He had discussed with his sister what she thought the telegram could be about. Their younger brother, Thomas, was always getting into trouble of some sort. More than once he was involved with brawls in speakeasies and dance halls.

Unlike me, George thought positively as he abhorred such behavior. He glanced at his sister who had dozed, the magazine open on her lap. And thank goodness Susan had also known the difference between right and wrong. But his younger brother Thomas was a different story altogether. He wondered what his aunt and uncle had to tell them about Thomas. He sighed and settled back for the train ride upstate.

The 20th Century Limited from Grand Central Station, on route to Chicago, unceremoniously pulled into Union Station in Albany, albeit later than its projected 5:50 p.m. arrival. After a signal failure at Poughkeepsie of at least a half-hour, the delay and cold weather created uncomfortable travel conditions, to say the least. It was close to six-thirty and as the train came to a screeching halt, weary passengers were eager to disembark. Porters beckoned help in earnest, carrying suitcases for those already loaded down with bags and some with screaming children in tow. Others managed to exit the train quickly and hastily made their way to their destination.

George and Susan gathered their bags from the overhead rack, exited the train, and followed the crowd along the platform. Inside the busy station, people were eagerly making plans. The extreme cold, not unusual for Albany in November but still a surprise, nevertheless, added to the frustration of exhausted travelers waiting at the infor-mation desk and ticket counters. Even the policeman on duty in the waiting area appeared dismayed at the chill that permeated the station.

"Should we walk?" Sue asked her brother as they made their way out of Union Station and to the entrance on Broadway. Their aunt and uncle's house, on Lancaster Street, was within walking distance of Union Station but upon exiting, it was clear that walking was not the best option.

They crossed Broadway and hopped onto the first trolley that pulled up. George was glad it wasn't too crowded. He noticed an elderly woman and her female friend chatting amicably, a rather tall, thin middle-aged woman with her little son, who was enjoying the whistle he was playing with and blowing it at times, startling and even annoying the conductor and a younger man, absorbed in a newspaper, who occasionally sent disapproving glances at the boy and his mother.

George sat at a window seat, still too preoccupied with his aunt's telegram. He looked out the window as the trolley started its journey through downtown Albany. As it turned onto State Street, he thought again of his younger brother, Thomas. He also thought of the Ibsen play he wanted so much to see, having purchased advance tickets, but in returning to Albany earlier than planned, going to see it was now out of the question.

"What do you think happened to Thomas?" Sue asked her brother, settling in the seat next to him. "For Aunt Sophie to send a telegram it must be something really bad!"

George agreed. "Whatever it is, we'll have to get through it, as we've done before."

The trolley seemed to take forever in reaching Washington Avenue. It was the usual Friday evening crowd. Office workers erupted out of city hall, the state capital, and the state education building and were waiting patiently to board on each corner, along with people out for the evening.

"There's the boys' academy," Sue pointed out to her brother as though he wasn't aware of it. "Aren't they having an alumni dance soon?"

"I don't know," George replied, looking at people getting on at the intersection of Washington Avenue and Hawk Street. "I haven't been up to date with the alumni recently." George was a proud graduate of the Albany Boys Academy but even alumni dances were far from his mind right now. He wondered if his sister was making small talk to take her mind off of Thomas and the impending doom of learning what had happened to him.

The trolley crept up Washington Avenue and then turned abruptly left onto Lark Street. It passed State Street and Chestnut Street before finally arriving at the corner of Lark and Lancaster. Brother and sister gathered their bags and disembarked. As they walked along in silence, their thoughts were worrisome, confused, troublesome. They wondered what news awaited them as they made their way to the brownstone house on Lancaster Street.

"Sophie, tell me the whole story. It can't be true!"

Mrs. Henry Olmstead, a small, compact woman in her middle seventies, with a fine head of white hair and vivid blue eyes, stood in the front doorway of the Drake home on Lancaster Street. Her cheeks red from the cold, she looked at her long-time friend, Sophie Drake.

It was a quarter after six on the evening of November the ninth. Sophie and her husband Arthur were awaiting the arrival of their nephew and niece. When the doorbell rang, Sophie, thinking it was George and Susan, quickly went to the front door, expecting to see them.

Instead, Marjorie stood before her. Sophie smiled at her old friend. Marjorie Olmstead and Sophie Drake had been friends for over half a century. They were native Albanians and graduates of local colleges, Marjorie at the Albany Nursing School, and Sophie at the State Teachers College.

And through the years, Sophie and Marjorie maintained their friendship, through marriages and the birth of Marjorie's daughter, who was grown and living in Jamestown. As Sophie and Marjorie lived in the same Albany neighborhood, Marjorie often dropped by with homemade baked goods, jam, casseroles, and even knitted sweaters and scarves for Sophie, her husband Arthur, her niece, Susan, and her nephews George and Thomas. Marjorie marveled at Sophie's tenacity to maintain a busy household with her niece and two nephews living with her and Arthur. She knew Sophie, being childless, welcomed their presence and never complained. Until Thomas got older and started to get into mischief.

Marjorie repeated her flustered comments to Sophie while standing in the doorway, oblivious to the cold. She exclaimed she first heard about it from a neighbor at the corner market and then read it in the evening edition of the newspaper when she got home.

"I came as soon as I unpacked the groceries," she continued as Sophie stood aside permitting her friend to enter. "Is it true, Sophie? Tell me what happened!"

Sophie Drake sighed, smiled wanly, and ushered Marjorie into the living room. She took her coat, hat, and scarf, left them on a hallway chair, and then motioned her to an armchair. She offered coffee but she refused.

Marjorie always enjoyed Sophie's pleasant brownstone house and her spacious living room, looking around at the appearance. The fireplace on the far wall warmed the room comfortably and the furniture was agreeable and inviting. There were paintings of landscapes on the walls, two large bookcases on each side of the front windows, and a rather large radio console near the doorway.

"Is it true, Sophie? Thomas is dead?" Marjorie's voice rose but her frustration was further compounded by the apparent calm demeanor of Sophie, who sat opposite her and simply looked at her, expressionless. "I couldn't believe it when I read it in the paper! Henry showed it to me, and I was in shock, of course." She paused. "He didn't believe it, either."

Henry Olmstead, Marjorie's husband of over fifty years was always skeptical about what appeared in the press, Sophie knew. Unfortunately, what he read in the *Albany Evening News* this time was indeed the truth.

Sophie sighed. "Yes, it's true, Marjorie. We heard from the police this morning. Thomas was killed last night, on South Pearl Street." She paused. "There'll be an inquest, of course."

Marjorie was shocked into silence. She knew Sophie always held her emotions intact. But Sophie, Marjorie also knew, at times allowed her pent-up feelings to get the best of her. She looked carefully at her friend. She was still pretty at seventy-five and certainly didn't look her age. Her sparkling brown eyes were now downcast, her pretty gray hair rather tousled and disarrayed. Even the blue dress she wore was wrinkled, which was unusual for Sophie. Her decorum was always of pristine neatness and sophistication.

"Please tell me what happened, Sophie," Marjorie practically begged her.

Sophie sighed again. "The police told us Thomas was found lying on the sidewalk on South Pearl Street, where he had left a speakeasy." She paused and swallowed hard. "Arthur is upstairs, resting. The doctor was here this afternoon after the police left and gave him a shot of morphine to calm him."

"Oh, those horrid speakeasies," Marjorie lamented. "They should all be shut down!"

Sophie coughed and then continued. "He was stabbed, in the stomach." Before Marjorie could interject, Sophie continued. "He was taken to Albany City Hospital, but he died without regaining consciousness."

Marjorie sat back on the armchair and was silent. She stared at Sophie, incredulous, unable to speak. There was a moment or two of silence before Sophie spoke again. She tried to maintain her dignity as she was unaccustomed to tears. From her mother, she learned a Victorian firmness that carried her throughout her life. Although at the moment, Sophie wondered if even the Victorians would break down upon hearing of murder.

"What more did they tell you?" Marjorie asked, finding her voice to speak.

"They plan to investigate, of course. They asked us if we knew of anyone who might have wanted to kill Thomas. We didn't have to mention his previous criminal record as they appeared to be aware of it already." She paused. "I don't know how to break this to George and Susan. They should be here any minute now."

"What can I do to help, Sophie?" Marjorie asked.

Sophie smiled, again wanly. "Just being here helps, Marjorie." She paused. "I told Thomas not to go out last night, especially in the cold weather. Arthur and I warned him about those speakeasies. Bad things happen in those places, you know. I read about them in the newspaper and hear it on the radio, too."

Marjorie agreed. "But who would want to kill Thomas? He may have enjoyed his nights out but that doesn't mean he…"

Sophie interrupted her friend. "Thomas had been in trouble over the years, Marjorie. He could have gotten into a fight at the speakeasy." She sounded despairing.

"Will the police come back to speak with you again?"

"Yes, tomorrow morning, after George and Susan return tonight.

Arthur was too upset by the news earlier and will be more fit to speak with them tomorrow."

"But how are *you* holding up, Sophie?"

"I can't talk too much anymore, Marjorie, dear." Sophie wiped away a few tears. "I'm waiting for George and Susan to arrive. They went to the city for a few days, but I sent a telegram to the hotel, telling them to return at once."

Marjorie tried to speak, to comfort her friend but found her words had little effect. Just then the doorbell rang. Both women looked towards the living room entrance, somewhat startled, as though dreading the anguish of what lay ahead. But it was inevitable. George and Susan had to be told. Marjorie started to get up, but Sophie told her to stay. She walked out of the living room and to the front door. She paused a moment as though trying to regain her inner strength. She then opened it slowly and looked at the two young people on the doorstep.

"Aunt Sophie," George said pleasantly but by her demeanor, he could tell something was wrong. Sue, next to her brother, had never before seen such an expression on her aunt's face.

Sophie stepped back allowing her nephew and niece to enter. She looked at them gravely but did not speak. Marjorie entered the hallway just then, breaking the uneasy silence, and greeted George and Susan cordially. She helped Sophie with their coats and luggage.

It was after George and Sue were settled in the living room, with cups of hot chocolate that Sophie and Marjorie prepared in the kitchen, that Sophie started to speak. But before she could explain what she knew, Sue boldly asked about Thomas. Even George wanted to know what was happening. And why they ended their trip earlier, too, he added regretfully.

Casting a furtive glance at Marjorie and looking at the fireplace as it emitted a fine glow and plenty of warmth, Sophie's gaze then returned to her nephew and niece. She took a deep breath and began to tell George and Susan about, Thomas; something they would never have imagined and ultimately did not want to hear.

CHAPTER TWO

Mr. Reginald Donaldson, attorney-at-law, sat at his desk in the living room of the brownstone house he shared with his step-daughter on Chestnut Street, looking at affidavits. His stepdaughter, Laura Dupont, encouraged him to put papers aside for now, after all, it was Friday evening and the weekend was upon them, but Reggie was always involved with his work.

Reginald, or Reggie as most people referred to him, was a tall, but rather stocky sixty-five-year-old, with a full head of grayish hair with leftover black streaks visible throughout, large brown eyes, and an obstinate chin. He was a widower having lost his wife to the flu pandemic in 1918. Rotten luck she caught the virus and fell ill. His stepdaughter, his wife's daughter from her first husband whom she divorced and then promptly married Reggie, lived with him in the Chestnut Street house. Laura didn't know her mother had been involved with Reggie before divorcing her husband.

Over his long legal career, he had assumed a variety of roles; director, trustee, and arbitrator before striking out on his own and opening his firm fifteen years ago. He was a native of Albany, a graduate of Albany Law School, and was a partner in several area law firms before deciding to open his own office. His business prospered and he never regretted it. As dedicated as he was to his work, Reggie found his attention drifting. He was forgetful at times, but he knew he could always rely on Mrs. Mary Olson, his assistant. Of course, Mrs. Claire Palmer was also officially an assistant but the working relationship between them had often been strained and Reggie wondered if she should continue with the firm. He didn't have a basis to dismiss her as her work was meticulous.

He took off his glasses and rubbed his tired eyes. It was true what Laura told him. He needed to get out and socialize. He knew Laura was fond of dance halls and speakeasies and attended them often. Perhaps too often, he thought irritably. He realized he had little if any control over his stepdaughter. Of course, she was twenty-five years old and far from being a child, but Reggie found her behavior at times appalling. His stepdaughter was a flapper, as she proudly proclaimed herself, one of the "modern girls" who danced the night away at dance halls and jazz clubs. Fast cars, fast friends, young men. Laura was a good time girl, enjoying cocktails and maybe more. Reggie sighed and shuffled a few papers, deep in thought.

He lit a cigarette and exhaled a fine trail of smoke toward the ceiling. He loosened his tie, removed his vest, and got up to put on the radio to listen to the evening news. He'd finish reviewing the documents before him as he returned to his desk and then call it a night. He'd read the new Zane Grey western he had borrowed from the library before going to bed. He drew heavily on his cigarette, while in the background from the radio he heard advertisements for shampoo, soap, milk, and even new Fords and Chevrolets when the news suddenly began. Still reading the affidavits, his cigarette in hand, he was arrested by what he now heard. He looked at the radio in silence, his face frozen, as he listened to the radio announcer.

Last evening Mr. Thomas Latimer, twenty years old, who resided on Lancaster Street in Albany, was found stabbed on South Pearl Street. Mr. Latimer was rushed to Albany City Hospital, but he died without regaining consciousness. Police have questioned bystanders and anyone who was in the area at the time. So far, they have no leads. Detectives from the Albany Police are investigating this apparent homicide. Anyone with information is asked to contact Albany Police.

He got up from his desk chair, went to the radio, and turned it off. He was about to return to his desk when his stepdaughter entered at that moment, smiling and full of life.

"Hey, Daddy! What's cooking? What are you up to? You look like you've seen a ghost!" . She got no reply from her stepfather. She had the evening paper with her, which she placed on the coffee table, then went to a large wall mirror where she applied fresh lipstick and rouge.

Laura Dupont was a pretty twenty-five-year-old, with shiny blonde hair and very bright blue eyes. She was tall and alluring and most men found her charm and wit quite appealing. While she worked at the Ten Eyck Hotel, she met many men and often enjoyed their company. She shared her work duties with Sue Latimer, who, in Laura's opinion was a goodie-two-shoes and who should learn to loosen up. With her excessive make-up, Chanel No. 5 perfume, and high heels, it seemed to Reggie that Laura was ready for another night on the town.

"You look like you've seen a ghost!" Laura repeated.

When Reggie didn't answer but just stood by the radio, she knew something was troubling him. He continued his silence and walked slowly back to his desk, unable to speak. Laura, on the other hand, continued to flounce around the living room, telling her stepfather of her evening plans.

"Oh, I should check to make sure what time the show starts." She grabbed the paper from the coffee table, unfolded it, and looked at the theater section, oblivious to the troubled expression on her stepfather's face. In turning the pages, her eyes fell on a small article in the city section. Laura gave a small cry and sank on the couch, confused, and dazed. Reggie looked at her, realizing that she must have read what he just heard on the radio.

"It says here Thomas Latimer was stabbed last night, downtown," she said, looking at the article in the paper. "Who'd do such a thing?"

Finding his voice, Reggie coughed, swallowed with difficulty, and addressed Laura. "I heard it on the radio just now. They don't know what happened or who was responsible."

"Well, this won't stop my evening plans," Laura said, determined to enjoy herself no matter what. "I can't leave my date waiting for me, you know."

Always the selfish Laura, Reggie thought irritably. He wondered how his wife raised this wild young creature. He had married her mother twenty years ago and while Laura, who was five years old at the time, seemed a precocious child, she grew up to be a reckless, irresponsible young woman. Thank goodness her mother wasn't alive to see her, he thought.

"I should call Sophie and Arthur," Reggie said. "They must be devastated by this news."

"Not this evening, Daddy," Laura advised. "I'd wait if I were you. It only happened yesterday. Why don't you call them tomorrow?"

Reggie agreed with his stepdaughter, thinking for once Laura sounded calm and rational. Reggie and Laura were acquainted with Sophie and Arthur Drake as well as George and Susan Latimer, their nephew and niece. Their house on Chestnut Street was a block from the Drake's house on Lancaster so it was convenient to quickly visit, although that was something Reggie hardly ever did.

"Do you need me for anything, Daddy? I'm meeting Mark at Keelers for dinner, then we're going to the Paramount to see Mary Pickford's new film. And then, who knows?" She giggled and flashed her shiny white teeth.

"Perhaps you should be in touch with Sue. She must be upset over this news."

Laura agreed and then brushed his remarks aside with a wave of her hand. Contacting Sue Latimer was the furthest thing from her mind.

Reggie ignored her superfluous attitude and asked her for the paper. She got up and handed it to him, pointing out the article on Thomas Latimer. He realized Laura was speaking to him.

"…a night on the town! You need it, Daddy! Why don't you get out and go to a nice restaurant? There's always the Capital Club, you know."

Reggie forced a short smile. "Thanks, Laura, but not tonight."

Laura shrugged. "Suit yourself, Daddy." She went to the hallway, put on her fur coat and cloche hat, said goodbye from the living room doorway, then banged the front door behind her.

Reggie continued to sit at his desk, perplexed, thinking of Thomas Latimer. He returned to the radio, turned it back on, moved the dial to the station he wanted. He settled in his favorite armchair to listen to *The Atwater Kent Hour* and the classical music that he so much enjoyed.

As the relaxing symphonic music filled the living room, Reggie's thoughts turned again to Sophie, Arthur, George, and Susan, too and the turmoil they must be going through. Sophie and Arthur asked his advice for helping Thomas out of some predicament he got himself into. He wondered how George and Susan, so well-mannered and intelligent, could be totally unlike him.

His mind drifted to his clandestine activity and with the money he earned from it, he could afford a new car and trips to the beach every summer. Of course, he knew he shouldn't continue with it, but it did help with expenses, as though that justified his devious endeavors. The headquarters was on lower Broadway, which no one paid attention to. If it was known that Reginald Donaldson, Attorney-at-Law was involved with illegal activity, it'd ruin his law practice, especially if it was printed in the local papers.

But no one knows, not even Laura, so Reggie told himself he needn't worry.

Mrs. Mary Olson stood at her kitchen sink, filled a tea kettle with water, and then lit the gas stove. She turned on a burner, set the kettle on top, and waited for the water to boil. She then looked out the kitchen window above the sink, at the small city garden she and her husband had worked so hard to maintain. This time of the year it was covered in snow.

Mary shivered and drew her shawl closer around her shoulders. She had been sick for two days with a head cold and found aspirin and chicken soup the best remedies, handed down from her mother and grandmother years ago. The kettle soon started to whistle. Mary drained the hot liquid into the cup and dunked the teabag a few times.

While looking out the kitchen window, her thoughts turned to her employer, Mr. Donaldson. She called Reggie to tell him of her desire for a few days of rest. It was rather exciting being a legal assistant, Mary thought and smiled. She had been at it for twenty-five years and although she grew tired from time to time, she still felt the thrill of legal work, especially in Albany.

Gratefully she sipped the hot tea and found it restored some vitality. She sat down at the kitchen table and opened the evening paper the newspaper boy had delivered about an hour ago. She glanced at the wall clock and saw it was close to six-thirty. Her husband, James, was upstairs changing his clothes, having arrived home from work only fifteen minutes ago.

At fifty-five, Mary Olson was quite pretty and had a pleasant disposition which most people found pleasing. She was tall and slender, and although she adhered to the dress styles and flapper appeal, she wasn't all too concerned about her appearance. Her brown hair was tastefully worn in a fashionable bob, her brown eyes alert and intelligent. She tried different shades of lipstick and new hats, too, but her overall dress was conservative, which suited her fine. She and her husband were deciding what to do for Thanksgiving, but with the way she was feeling, Thanksgiving was far from Mary's mind at the moment.

Mary unfolded the paper, wiped her nose with a handkerchief, and read about the recent election of Herbert Hoover as president. She glanced at his picture and shook her head. A Republican. Well, Governor Smith should have won, she thought somewhat bitterly, he was the only man for the job. But either way, it was thrilling to vote, she thought. This made the third time she had voted since women finally earned that right eight years ago. She continued turning the pages until her eyes rested on a small article in the city section. She was about to call out to her husband when James Olson appeared in the kitchen doorway.

Having been married to Mary for almost thirty years, James knew his wife well. Just by her expression, he could tell something was wrong. She started to speak before he could ask.

"Th-there's a write-up here," she stammered, her face ashen and James thought she'd faint.

"What is it?" he asked, horrified at his wife's expression.

"Thomas Latimer was found dead last night on South Pearl Street! The police are investigating it as a homicide!"

James approached the kitchen table and sat next to Mary. He put his hand over hers and tried to calm her, although he too was shaken by what she told him. She merely pointed to the article and James read it for himself.

James Olson, at sixty, was a distinguished, well-groomed gentleman, rather soldierly in appearance. Quite tall at six foot three inches, his brown hair was streaked with gray and his green eyes, usually brilliant and alert, were now full of worry and even indignation.

James was employed at the Delaware and Hudson Railroad Building in administration. He had been with the railroad since graduating college. From a conductor to foreman and now vice president, James had worked his way up the D & H ladder and had prospered, enabling him to purchase a beautiful brownstone on Dove Street. It was a charming house, with a large living room and kitchen on the first floor, two bedrooms on the second and three rooms on the third floor, one which Mary used as a sewing room and James used another as an office.

"I can't believe it," Mary said, looking at her husband. "Sophie and Arthur must be beside themselves. And poor George and Susan, too."

James agreed. "But Thomas was a troublemaker, Mary. Even Sophie and Arthur couldn't handle him. Wasn't there a time when Sophie locked him out of their house?"

"Well, she said she did," Mary replied. "Sophie's too good to do something like that." She paused. "On the other hand, George and Susan weren't too fond of him, either."

James agreed. "He made life hell for Sophie and Arthur. And I suppose George and Susan, too. Didn't they bail him out of jail?"

"Yes, more than once. Sophie told me several times about his escapades. Poor Arthur had to pick Thomas up at the city jail."

James shook his head. "George and Susan are such fine young people. It's always a pleasure to talk to them. But Thomas…" He paused. "He's just the opposite!"

"Well, I'll start making dinner," Mary said trying to sound cheerful. "Meatloaf and a tomato salad. I bought a pumpkin pie for Thanksgiving, but we can have it a little earlier."

"Mary dear, if you're still sick, you shouldn't be working in the kitchen," James almost scolded her. "You have to get better! You've missed two days of work."

"Well, I'll be much better for Monday. I've had tea, aspirin, and plenty of chicken soup for lunch. I'm feeling better already!"

There was a strange silence between them, rare in their marriage. They then started to talk of trivial things; of a vacation, shoveling the front steps, tending next spring's garden, dinner at the Capital Club, and then Thanksgiving, and finally deciding to stay at home for the holiday. Childless and with no other relatives, the Olsons preferred their holidays at home, with a few friends as guests rather than a busy restaurant. Mary often invited Sophie and Arthur Drake and George, Susan and even Thomas would come, too, neighbors they had known for years, for coffee and dessert after Thanksgiving dinner. Mary believed in having people visit, especially during the holidays. And it was great they all lived within a relatively short distance of each other.

James entered the living room, turned on the radio to the station playing the *Atwater Kent Hour* and the wonderful symphonic music that he and Mary enjoyed. But they found it did little to alleviate their chaotic thoughts.

After the meal, Mary made coffee and cut two pieces of the pumpkin pie. James helped his wife clean up the kitchen and then relaxed in the living room with a book. Mary went upstairs to work on sewing.

Nothing more was said about the murder of Thomas Latimer, until the weekend when the police came to see them.

"Well, he finally had his day," Mr. Henry Olmstead said out loud, comfortably ensconced in his favorite armchair while listening to the news on the radio. He was alone in the comfortable brownstone he and his wife lived in on State Street, a block north of the state capital building. He listened carefully to the news on the radio and at the same time read the article on Thomas Latimer in the *Albany Evening News*. Henry was not in the least bit shocked or dismayed at what he heard or read. Almost as if he expected it.

Henry Olmstead, at seventy-seven, kept a fit and busy lifestyle. He was of medium stature with a full head of gray and white hair and large brown eyes. He took an active interest in the Capital Club and the local church. He was on the board of several companies downtown. Professional and intolerant of immaturity or nonsense in others, Henry was always ready with a smile that was genuine and meaningful, and his demeanor was of gentility and friendliness. Except when it came to Thomas Latimer.

Henry and his wife Marjorie had had run-ins with Thomas Latimer over the years. Henry considered him to be a loser, who'd never amount to anything. Marjorie, on the other hand, tried to be upbeat probably because of her friendship with Sophie Drake. But she also knew the problems they had had with young Thomas.

Henry looked at the clock on the mantel, to the fire dancing brilliantly in the fireplace, and then his glance went to the long windows overlooking State Street. Henry was retired from the New York State Department of Labor, having graduated from the State Teachers College, and then joined the service before returning to Albany. He and Marjorie met and married soon after. They enjoyed spending time with Sophie's nephew George and niece Susan. And Sophie and Arthur were two of their closest friends.

Marjorie had come home from the market, her hands full of groceries when Henry showed her the article in the paper about Thomas. He thought she'd peel over from worry. He understood her friendship with Sophie, but it was only Thomas, after all, and he had what was coming to him. Why the big surprise? Henry didn't say that to his wife, of course, but she knew there was no love lost between Henry and Thomas Latimer.

Not one to brood on the past, Henry stared into the crackling fire and could not but think of the misery he and Marjorie went through because of young Thomas. Several years ago, when the Drakes were visiting, George and Susan were also present, along with Thomas. While Henry and Marjorie were busy entertaining Sophie and Arthur, George and Susan were engaged in a lively bridge game. Thomas also played but wound up wandering the Olmstead's house and thought nothing of taking a valuable ceramic vase and putting it in his jacket pocket.

It was an heirloom, handed down to Marjorie from her great-grandmother. It went unnoticed until Henry happened to visit an antique shop in Schenectady and there it was on display. Henry tried to get what information he could from the clerk on duty, but it didn't help. When he got back home, he was furious. He told Marjorie who promptly told him it couldn't be the same, after all, how would it get there? Upon searching for it, she didn't find it anywhere. Then her thoughts mirrored those of her husband: Thomas took it and pawned it.

Henry shook his head in anger. He didn't want to think of the rest; the confrontation at the Drake's house, the police probe, the denial by Thomas who had a smirk to his face and Henry had all he could do not to wipe it off himself. In the end, Thomas admitted taking it as he claimed he "needed the extra money" and agreed to make restitution, which included buying it back from the pawnshop in Schenectady. Marjorie, being a good-hearted soul, decided not to press charges.

Over the years, Henry had heard of others in the neighborhood who had trouble with Thomas. Sophie and Arthur bailed him out of jail more than once. What kind of idiot was he? George and Sue were pleasant. He could tell they didn't have much love for him.

Well, now he's dead, good riddance, Henry thought, looking again at the paper and then at the clock again wondering when Marjorie would return from seeing Sophie.

Henry wondered what kept Marjorie. Of course, she and Sophie always talked endlessly. The war had taken its toll on Marjorie, as a nurse she had so many sick and wounded patients at Albany City Hospital. And then the flu pandemic, an extra burden to them both, as hospital beds filled and people in his office became sick and some even died. Reggie lost his wife to the pandemic, which devastated him but didn't seem to affect Laura too much.

Henry sighed tiredly. But now it was 1928, and ten years had come and gone, light years away it seemed from those events. Albany had changed, like the rest of the country, but Henry didn't think it was all for the better. Flappers, like Laura Dupont, acting luridly, smoking, and drinking in speakeasies and dance halls. A good time girl, like so many in the city. Herbert Hoover winning the recent election. Henry opposed his bid for the White House and strongly favored Al Smith, their governor. But to his shock, Hoover won in a landslide, and Smith was defeated.

Henry's reverie was broken when the front door opened, and Marjorie entered. He heard her take off her coat and hang it in the hallway closet. She entered the living room, smiled, and seemed glad to see her husband. She approached him, kissed him on the cheek, apologized for being so long, and then turned abruptly to the kitchen to prepare dinner.

Well, so much for news with the Drakes, Henry thought rather irritably. Usually, his wife was one for relaying news. Eventually, she'd tell him what she and Sophie discussed.

Henry got up, turned off the radio, and entered the kitchen. Marjorie was busy cooking stew and potatoes and finishing chopping lettuce and placing it in a bowl. She smiled when she saw her husband.

"Hungry, dear? The stew looks delicious. Lots of beef, potatoes, and carrots, too. And the gravy is simply fine." She rambled on and on about the stew until Henry finally interrupted her.

"What did Sophie say about Thomas?"

Marjorie had a ladle and was serving up the stew into plates. "Well, dear, she didn't say too much. She was in shock like I was, of course. She doesn't know anything more about it."

She put the plates with the hot stew on the table, along with rolls and plates for salad. "George and Sue had just come home from New York City. Sophie sent them a telegram at the hotel to come back earlier. We told them about Thomas." She paused as though for dramatic effect. "They were in shock, too, of course."

"Of course," was all Henry found he could say at the moment.

The Olmsteads ate in comparative silence, Henry admitting the beef stew was excellent and even the salad with the tomatoes and basil sprinkled on top was perfect. To his surprise, Marjorie asked what he thought happened to Thomas. She knew what her husband thought of Thomas Latimer, but she asked his opinion anyway.

"Well, he must've gotten involved with something pretty bad. He was always going to speakeasies and hanging around a bad crowd. Those speakeasies downtown can be pretty raunchy, from what I've heard. Laura Dupont goes to them as well. Didn't she date him a few times? She's in with that party crowd, too. I don't know how Reggie handles her."

Marjorie agreed. She finished her salad and sat in silence. "Didn't Arthur say once that Thomas had threatened him?"

"That sounds like Thomas," Henry said. "He'd threaten anyone who got in his way."

"He threatened you once, dear, don't you remember? Over the vase. I'll make tea for us. Why don't you go in the living room and listen to the radio?"

Henry offered to help clean up but as always Marjorie considered the kitchen her domain. He walked to the living room and was about to turn on the radio again when the memory struck him, so sharply that he leaned on the radio console for support.

He straightened himself, looked toward the kitchen, heard Marjorie making the tea. A long-forgotten and unpleasant memory came hurtling toward him. He had forgotten the time Thomas had threatened *him*, over the missing antique vase. Nothing came of it, and he didn't think Thomas would have ever harmed him, but he still did make a threat. He had said it in a heat of anger, of course. Henry had thought of telling the police at the time, but he never did.

Did it really matter now? Henry thought as he relaxed with the soothing music filling the room. He stretched his legs comfortably and stifled a yawn. The young bastard was dead, and he couldn't disturb them anymore, or anyone else for that matter. It was all best buried and forgotten.

CHAPTER THREE

At five minutes to five, in the law office of Mr. Reginald Donaldson on lower State Street in downtown Albany, Mrs. Claire Palmer finished typing the last letter of the day. With a sigh of relief, she put the letter on top of the "inbox" on the corner of her desk so Mr. Donaldson would see it first thing upon arriving Monday morning.

If he arrives, Claire thought contemptuously. She butted her cigarette, placed a few files in the bottom left drawer, and then as always locked the drawers, testing each one to be sure they were secure. Claire smiled to herself. She believed in accuracy and confidentiality.

Sometimes she wondered how her boss maintained a business with his absent-mindedness; his often-late arrivals, his anti-social behavior, his forgetfulness, his foolish stepdaughter. He insisted she call him Reginald or even Reggie, something Claire was reluctant to do. Over time, she relented and resorted to Reggie.

She looked around the empty office. She glanced at the desk of Reggie's other assistant, Mrs. Mary Olson, a middle-aged woman, who, like Claire was competent and trustworthy to her boss. But not to me, Claire thought wryly. There was no love lost between the two women. Although Mrs. Olson had been with Reggie for several years, Claire personally found her to be incompetent and lacking motivation. More than once and without Mary knowing it, Claire had looked through her desk—even the garbage—but to her disappointment, she didn't find anything of interest, nothing to present to Reggie to convince him to dismiss her. She found Mary's old-fashioned sensibility and her dog-like devotion to Reggie absurd.

She glanced again at Mary Olson's desk. She was out today. Upon arriving this morning, Reggie had told Claire that Mary was sick and wouldn't be in today. Oh, poor doll, she thought sarcastically. She hadn't been in for the last two days. He then holed himself up in his office all morning and only came out to go to court. He reminded her he wouldn't return and would see her on Monday.

Claire turned off the banker's lamp on her desk. She glanced out the windows overlooking State Street and noticed a few snowflakes. She was reminded of her hometown of Elmira, New York; graduating from Elmira College and promptly making the biggest mistake of her life; marrying Samuel Palmer. Good ole Sam, the neighbors called him and she, too, thought her husband-to-be had desires of making it big as an accountant and in the stock market. Well, that dreamboat sank years ago, she thought. It wasn't long before Claire realized what a fool she'd been; her husband's career was going nowhere, that he'd never be successful in his work, with no ambitions. She stayed in her unhappy marriage, hoping her husband's accounting career would prosper. But Claire was restless in Elmira and even more so with her useless marriage.

After nearly twenty-five years and three miscarriages, Claire figured out that charming, debonair Sam, was cheating on her, with a woman he met in Ithaca. One day he admitted it all and told her he planned to divorce her. Well, I beat him to it, Claire thought with satisfaction. Of course, Claire had a past, too, but that was buried long ago in Elmira. She divorced her husband and moved to Albany to make a new start.

She pushed back her desk chair, stood, and stretched. She smoothed the sides of her dress, taking a moment of satisfaction feeling her waistline. When they were dating, Sam had often told her she'd make a great model, with her head of fine black hair, long shapely legs, and sensitive brown eyes. Well, a lot of good that's done me, she thought rather bitterly. She didn't worry about her figure as so many women did. Claire fought tooth and nail for everything she had.

She had always played her cards right and was known to the best people in Albany and frequented the best dance halls and restaurants. How else would she learn things about her employer? At fifty-five Claire was determined to make a better life for herself. Parties, speak-easies, politicians! She always enjoyed the company of rich, successful people. And with her charm and flirtatiousness, it hadn't been difficult to meet rich men in Albany. She reached for her pack of cigarettes on her desk when the phone suddenly rang.

Before answering, Claire wondered if it was irritating Mary Olson deciding to check up on her, to see if she was still in the office. Well, I don't answer to her, she thought. But then she knew Mary and Reggie were confidants and if Claire were to slip up, dear Mary would babble it all to dull-witted Reggie in a heartbeat. And he'd believe her, too.

"Mr. Donaldson's office," Claire said in her most professional tone although she wondered who'd call for an appointment at this late hour.

It was not a business call but for Claire herself. She listened and then hung up with satisfaction. Grabbing her fur coat from the coat rack, she affixed her cloche hat firmly on her head and with a glance in a wall mirror, was rather pleased with her appearance. She then opened the office door and almost collided with the cleaning woman who was just getting ready to vacuum. Claire brushed past her on her way to the elevator and the evening ahead of her.

It was a quarter after nine on Friday evening. It seemed like a long day to the inhabitants of the brownstone house on Lancaster Street. Sophie, George, and Sue were in the living room, finishing their hot chocolate and trying to find solace in each other's company. George brooded moodily that what started as a holiday for him, and his sister would be ruined by his reckless brother, who got himself killed Thursday night. Of course, he didn't say that to his sister and aunt. Like Sue, he was confused about this mysterious death and wanted to know all of the details.

"I don't know everything yet," Sophie told them. "Only what the policemen told us this morning. They'll conduct an inquest. They'd want to speak to you, too."

George nodded but admitted he did not look forward to it. "Did they say what happened?"

"We don't know that yet, dear," Sophie tried to sound consoling while understanding her nephew's frustration. "Your uncle and I have been most distressed over this."

At that moment a tall, elderly man entered the living room, walking with a slight limp. He greeted his wife warmly and did likewise with his nephew and niece. Arthur Drake was a retired businessman, at eighty, he was pleasant and professional and dedicated to his family. He had gray hair with a bald patch in front, green eyes, and the glasses he wore lent an air of knowledge and even power. He was a proud graduate of Union College and encouraged George and Susan to study there, too. Like his wife, Arthur Drake disapproved of flappers and drunken parties. A member of the Democratic party and the Capital Club, Arthur was conservative to the extreme and passed that conservatism to his nephew and niece.

"Are you feeling better, dear?" Sophie asked him as he sat next to her on the couch. Her eyes, brimming with concern, looked at him carefully.

"It's been a shock," he said, attempting to maintain his dignity. "I wasn't fond of Thomas or his lifestyle. But he didn't deserve an end like this."

"I think we all feel the same," Sue said.

"After the police are here," Sophie said, "they will figure out what happened."

"But we don't know anything!" Sue spoke, clearly agitated. "What can we tell them? George and I saw him yesterday morning before leaving for Union Station, remember George?"

George nodded. "Yes, he didn't say where he was going or what he planned to do." He paused. "I tried to get him a job at the bank, but he wasn't interested."

"You're a good brother, George," Arthur said and smiled at his nephew. "We tried to help Thomas, but he was intent on spending his money foolishly on drinks and parties."

"What money?" Sue interjected. "He didn't work, so how did he even have any money?"

Sophie smiled tiredly at her niece. "Sue, sweetheart, we know the lifestyle of Thomas was not something we adhered to. But we have to face the reality of his death, prepare for his burial, and get on with our own lives."

She looked at the young people seated before her. "Why don't we get a good night's sleep. We'll be better prepared tomorrow when the police come to see us." She hesitated. "We'll attend the inquest, so you won't have to."

It was agreed that Sophie and Arthur would attend the inquest, whenever it takes place. Sophie and Sue went to the kitchen to clean up while Arthur stoked the remaining logs in the fireplace. He drew the curtains on the windows, turned off the living room lights, locked the front door, and then said goodnight to his nephew. Slowly he climbed the stairs as though the news of Thomas's death deprived him of strength in his legs. He arrived at the second floor and entered the bedroom he shared with Sophie.

George retreated to his room on the third floor, although rather moodily, wondering what the police would say to them tomorrow, what he should reveal about Thomas. And what he should keep hidden.

Claire Palmer arrived at her apartment on upper Madison Avenue. She had taken the trolley from downtown and had gotten off at the intersection of South Main Avenue. The street was practically deserted now. She glanced at her watch and saw it was nearly two in the morning. And she felt wonderful! She had danced the night away at a speakeasy and thrilled to the great jazz music, the liquor, and the adoration of several gentlemen, one, in particular, she made plans to see soon. She felt light-headed and carefree. That's what evenings are made of indeed, she thought jubilantly.

Entering the spacious apartment, she kicked off her high heels, took off her fur coat and her cloche hat, and threw them on a nearby chair, and then realized she had left the evening paper on the doorstep.

She retrieved it and closed and locked the door. She then settled in her living room, lit a cigarette, turned on a light, and unfolded the paper.

The usual headlines: the stock market doing well, Herbert Hoover getting ready for his inauguration in January, President Coolidge making plans to leave the White House, predictions for 1929. Locally the new DeWitt Clinton Hotel boasted the best accommodations in Albany, most with their own bathrooms. It mentioned its convenient location across from the state capital to allure politicians there rather than the Ten Eyck, the Kenmore, or the Hampton.

It was as she turned the page and glanced at the city section that she noticed the small article on Thomas Latimer. She read it several times, her eyes narrowed, her expression a tight frown, making sure she understood it and its implications. Thomas Latimer, dead, murdered on South Pearl Street? Claire knew of a speakeasy on South Pearl that had quite a notorious reputation. Most likely Thomas had been there. She turned to the next page and wondered if Reggie knew about it.

She folded the paper and tossed it on the coffee table in front of her. She always thought it odd that George and Susan were so well-mannered and Thomas a wild, irresponsible youth, almost as if he wasn't related to them. Strange how siblings could be so far apart in manner and temperament. She was sure Sophie and Arthur made a good home for them, nevertheless.

And Mary Olson would undoubtedly mention Thomas's murder Monday at the office. She'd ask if Claire read it in the newspaper, trying to squeeze information out of her. Nosy woman, what else does she have to do, except be inquisitive? Well, that inquisitiveness could get her into trouble someday, Claire thought contemptuously.

It never hurt to ask questions. She was an expert at that, in her kind, innocent, nonchalant way, especially with men. With her friends at the various dance halls and speakeasies, she'd find things out soon enough.

She butted her cigarette in an ashtray on the coffee table. Rather exciting to have murder in our midst, even thrilling. Maybe more mysterious deaths to come, too.

She would later realize how unfortunate her thoughts proved to be.

CHAPTER FOUR

T he following day was one of the most troublesome George had ever experienced. It was close to ten o'clock on Saturday morning. After breakfast, he had retreated to his bedroom on the third floor and found solace in smoking cigarettes and reading Jane Austen.

He closed the cover of *Pride and Prejudice,* glanced out the window overlooking Lancaster Street and realized there wasn't much to see; the milkman dropping off bottles to each house, the mailman delivering mail, a few children playing stickball in the snow, two elderly women walking and engaged in conversation, a young woman with a lively Doberman, being pulled by the animal's exuberance.

Like his sister, aunt, and uncle, George was waiting for the police to arrive. He glanced at his watch. Well, it was still early, but Aunt Sophie said they'd be here in the morning. What could he tell them about Thomas? That he was a lousy, lazy drunk who rarely held down a job, never finished college, and had been involved in illegal activities? The police would know that already, of course. There were plenty of times that George had made excuses for him, even paid his bail, and helped get him out of unsavory predicaments. But what good did his efforts do? And despite the reprimands from Uncle Arthur and Aunt Sophie, he continued his nefarious lifestyle. George wondered if Thomas had been involved with gangsters. There were plenty of underworld characters in Albany and many found the speakeasies as their havens. Since Thomas frequented those establishments, he might have been involved with something that George, his sister, aunt, and uncle were unaware of, something worse than his previous brushes with the law. But what could it have been? George shook his head. He couldn't begin to fathom a guess.

Breakfast over, Sophie decided to clean her spotless kitchen, with Sue helping. They polished silverware, stored unused plates and cups in the basement, and wrote a grocery list for items they needed at the local market.

In the living room, Arthur sat brooding, the newspaper open on his lap, but he wasn't reading it. His thoughts turned to his nephew, Thomas, who was lying in the hospital morgue. What the devil could have happened to him? And then came the guilt knowing that Thomas went out Thursday night and that neither he nor Sophie stopped him. Almost as if they were glad, he was out of the house, which, of course, was the truth. Even if they tried to stop him, it wouldn't have mattered as young Thomas was used to doing whatever he wanted. What could have happened within the last ten years that Thomas turned out so bad?

The doorbell rang at eleven o'clock. In the kitchen, Sophie stopped writing the grocery list and looked at her niece. Sue, her eyes full of worry and remorse, maybe even fear, looked at her aunt as though for help. Sophie managed a smile, patted her hand reassuringly, and then left the kitchen on her way to the front door.

It was the police as she expected. She had never had any contact with the law much less had them present at her home. They asked if she was Mrs. Arthur Drake and having received a positive reply, Sophie then beckoned them into the house.

They followed her to the living room, where Arthur was listening to the news on the radio. He looked up at his wife and the policemen with her. There was an awkward silence before Sophie invited them to sit down and offered them coffee, which they refused.

"I'm Lieutenant Taylor and this is my partner, Inspector Harris," Lieutenant Taylor said, introducing himself and his colleague. "We're here to ask you about your nephew, Thomas."

Sophie nodded. She continued standing, even though Arthur encouraged her to sit on the couch. They were different policemen from yesterday. They looked more official and, in some ways, frightening. While they were speaking to Arthur, Sophie took a better look at them.

Lieutenant Taylor was a shortish, stout, middle-aged man with a firm, no-nonsense manner about him, who came directly to the point when speaking. Inspector Harris, on the other hand, was more subtle, tall, and athletic for a man of about fifty with fierce, determined brown eyes.

"I'm afraid that's all I can tell you," Arthur concluded his discourse. "My wife and I didn't see Thomas at all Thursday after breakfast. We didn't know where he went. He did have a few job interviews pending, although given the lies Thomas would tell us, I don't know if I believe him."

Inspector Taylor turned to Sophie. "Mrs. Drake, would you tell us about your relationship with Thomas? Do you have any idea who would harm him?"

Sophie nodded, her face a mixture of fear and remorse. "Thomas was my nephew, my brother's child. My brother Max died during the war and his wife, Lydia, died during the pandemic. I told my sister-in-law that Arthur and I would take in her children, as they were under twenty-one and couldn't live on their own. They moved in with us and things went well." She paused. "I don't know of anyone who'd want to harm Thomas. If he had enemies, I wasn't aware of them. He enjoyed going to dance halls quite often. He dated several girls, one of them was Laura Dupont, a neighbor of ours."

Lieutenant Taylor mentioned his previous run-ins with the law. "Did you say anything to your nephew to discourage his behavior?"

"We tried, Lieutenant," Sophie said rather tiredly. "But he was like a son to us. Arthur and I have no children and we've doted on George, Susan, and Thomas. We've loved them as though they were our own." She paused. "I promised Lydia I'd take care of her children. And I haven't gone back on that promise."

Inspector Harris managed a small smile. "What was he doing downtown Thursday evening? Did he usually go out on weeknights?"

"I'm afraid Thomas did whatever he wanted," Arthur said. "We don't know what he was involved in, but he was a frequent visitor to the speakeasies downtown."

"Like many people," Inspector Harris remarked dryly. "We've attempted to shut down most of them, but new ones open right up. It's rather a frustrating endeavor."

Lieutenant Taylor asked about George and Susan. He mentioned their input on the movements of their brother was invaluable.

Sue entered at that moment from the kitchen, looking forlorn and tired as though she hadn't slept for nights. She wore a comfortable dress of light blue, with a string of pearls and extraordinarily little make-up. She sat next to Sophie on the couch and looked at the policemen.

"This is Lieutenant Taylor and that is Inspector Harris," Arthur said as though making a social introduction. "They'd like to ask you about Thomas."

Sue looked at the uniformed policemen curiously. Like her aunt, Sue had never had dealings with the law. Unlike Sophie, she was not in the least intimidated and looked them squarely in the eyes and asked what she could do for them.

"We'd like to know more about your brother Thomas," Inspector Harris began. "What he was like, what he did during the day and night."

Sue coughed. "I think he was involved with bootleggers, although I can't say for sure. He also had been arrested for drug smuggling." She paused. "Thomas and I weren't especially close. I didn't approve of his lifestyle, although he wasn't particularly rude to me. My brother George and I tried to change him, but people don't change," she added rather bitterly.

Just then everyone's attention was turned to a young man who stood in the doorway to the living room, taking in the scene before him. His presence was captivating as though he exuded intelligence and authority. Inspector Harris figured this was George Latimer, the victim's older brother. He judged him to be about twenty-five which, after questioning him, proved correct.

"What my sister just said is the truth," George said equally bitterly as he entered and sat on the couch alongside Susan. "Thomas was always getting into trouble. He was especially unkind to me. He took money from me more than once and thought nothing of it."

"What exactly happened to Thomas?" Sue asked the policemen.

"He was found lying on the sidewalk, on South Pearl Street. A man and woman, who were out for the evening, found him and called the police. This was quite late, after one in the morning. An ambulance took him to Albany City Hospital. On examining him, it was found he was stabbed. He died at the hospital without regaining consciousness."

"Where were you on Thursday?" Inspector Harris asked George.

"My sister and I went to New York for the weekend," George said. "We left Thursday morning. We went to see a show and to visit a few museums. We stayed at a hotel and planned to return on Sunday. Aunt Sophie sent us a telegram Friday morning, telling us to return at once."

"Do you have photographs of Thomas?" Inspector Harris asked.

"Of course, Inspector," Sophie said, surprised.

"We'd like to use them in our inquiries. Businesses on South Pearl Street may provide some information." He paused. "There will be an inquest. The coroner will contact you."

Sophie nodded, then cast a reluctant eye to her husband, who nodded as though telling her it was all right to give them a few photos of Thomas. She then went to a desk against the far wall and opened a drawer, extracting a rather large photo album. She returned to the sofa and started to flip through the pages. She removed two recent photos of Thomas.

Inspector Harris took them and together with his partner looked carefully at the photos. The first showed a rather playful, mischievous young man looking directly into the camera, taken during a bright sunny day, in what appeared to be Washington Park. The second was also of a rather high-spirited young man on Lancaster Street, looking away from the camera, but still exuding a mischievous aura. The lieutenant asked if they could keep them for a while. Reluctantly Sophie agreed. There followed an awkward silence until the policemen stood to leave.

"We'll be in touch, Mr. Drake," Inspector Harris said and stood. "Thank you, Mr. and Mrs. Drake and George and Susan for your time. We'll let you know what we learn."

"How long will it take?" Sue asked rather impatiently, looking up at them from the sofa. "Somebody killed Thomas and we need to know who and why!"

"Some murder investigations wrap up quickly while others last much longer," the inspector told them. "We'll connect with people who knew Thomas and see what leads we get."

"Our friends the Olmsteads and the Olsons knew Thomas," Sophie suggested.

"They might shed some light on his character," Arthur pointed out.

The inspector asked for their addresses, which Sophie supplied. She thanked them for coming and showed them to the door. After they had gone, Arthur, George, and Sue were speechless, sitting in silence. Sophie came in and sat near Sue, joining in the strange silence. Arthur fiddled with the radio, finding a station playing jazz that seemed to alleviate the heaviness in the atmosphere.

As the day progressed, George, Sue, Sophie, and Arthur did next to nothing, their minds turning over the events of the last forty-eight hours. Sophie and Sue cooked dinner rather absent-mindedly while Arthur took a long walk along Lark Street. George found solace at the Harmanus Bleecker Library on Dove Street and later Sue took the trolley to Whitney's Department Store to shop for a new hat.

When evening arrived, after an uncomfortable dinner conducted mostly in silence, Sophie joined her husband in the living room, listening to the news on the radio. They heard nothing more about Thomas, much to their relief. She took out her knitting, while Arthur was intent on the crossword puzzle in the *Albany Evening News*. Sophie mentioned they'd need to prepare for the burial, but Arthur told her it was too soon to discuss it.

"We'll take a walk tomorrow morning," Arthur said to his wife, with a weak smile. "Clear our minds. We'll ask George and Susan to join us."

"If it isn't too cold," Sophie agreed, although she admitted her nephew and niece liked to sleep late on Sundays. At the moment, Sue was busy chatting with a girlfriend on the telephone in the kitchen, while George was reading his new library book and writing letters to some of his college friends. Despite the recent tragedy, it was a rather placid evening, with the fire emitting warmth and a fine glow to the charming living room.

But as Sophie continued knitting and Arthur concentrated on the crossword, the Drakes had no way of knowing that this recent death and the events leading up to it would soon take a turn for the worse.

Arthur had woken early, as was his custom, to take his morning walk. He and Sophie always enjoyed strolling through Washington Park. They also ventured to the Port of Albany, a favorite place as the view of the river was magnificent. Arthur finished his coffee and was about to clean his breakfast dishes when Sophie entered the kitchen.

"Good morning, dear," she said and helped herself to coffee. Her gray hair was tastefully arranged, the gray dress and sweater she wore appropriate for the cold weather. "I haven't forgotten about our walk," she added with a smile. "I'll just have some coffee."

They hesitated to wake George and Sue but decided to let the young people sleep late. After rinsing the coffee cups in the sink, Sophie and Arthur put on their winter coats and made their way out the door and to the streets of Albany. They continued walking southward toward the river, past the Albany Police Station and numerous theaters, restaurants, and shops.

It was a bright but raw and cold Sunday morning, as mornings usually are in Albany in November. Those who hoped Indian Summer would return were disappointed. The wind blew aggressively from the south, chilling the pedestrians at the Port of Albany. It was especially noticeable as the wind gusted off the mighty Hudson River. There were few people about; a man walking his dog, two women talking animatedly, a couple with their small children.

As they approached the riverfront from Broadway, they saw the Hudson River Day Line steamer *Albany* filling up fast, bringing passengers to Kingston, Newburgh, Poughkeepsie, and eventually to the Port of New York. Sophie and Arthur looked at the cruise boat as it was steadily boarding passengers. Sophie was surprised so many people preferred the cruise lines to the train. She glanced northward and saw Union Station shimmering in the distance.

She linked her arm through Arthur's and together they continued walking, enjoying the crisp air and each other's company. They had taken many such walks around Albany over the years, but things were different now. They tried to put out of their minds the visit from the police and what happened to Thomas. Sophie mentioned that they'd need to plan for his burial soon.

"Let's not talk about that now," Arthur tried to sound reassuring.

Sophie agreed. "We need to clear our heads. It's been too much lately. I don't think I can handle anything more, Arthur." She clenched his arm tighter and leaned her head on his left shoulder out of weariness and confusion.

They felt as though their world was turned upside down, with Thomas's murder. Their lives wouldn't be the same. Sophie felt a deep stab of regret, knowing she had not fulfilled her promise to her sister-in-law in caring for her children. What *could* have happened to Thomas? She loved him as she loved George and Susan like they were her own children. They had many good times over the years; George and Susan graduated from Union College and made fine careers for themselves. But Thomas was different; his personality, temperament, and even his demeanor were in stark contrast to his sister and older brother. At times Sophie wondered where she went wrong. Thomas managed to graduate high school and was accepted at Union but could not maintain a high enough average and dropped out. Since that time, he had made their lives a living hell. Sophie as well as Arthur knew Thomas was too much to handle. She was determined to give Thomas a decent burial and to learn what exactly happened to him.

They continued walking, saying little, breathing in the fresh cold air and looking at the mist off the Hudson River, when Sophie's gaze was alerted to something in the bushes.

"Arthur, look," she exclaimed. "There, behind that trash can."

In the back of the garbage can, Sophie and Arthur saw what they thought was a shoe. Of course, it was just garbage, old shoes being thrown away. But upon closer inspection, they realized it was a shoe attached to a leg. Arthur moved the garbage can slightly and saw more clearly the body of a man, a young man, his shirt front covered in blood, his eyes open and staring into space. A young man who was obviously very dead.

Sophie grabbed Arthur's arm and directly they quickly walked off in the direction of the police department on Broadway, sweating profusely, despite the chilly air. Upon reaching the police station, Sophie and Arthur caught their breath. Arthur told the bewildered policemen on duty about the gruesome discovery behind the trash can at the Port of Albany. The policemen assured them they would send officers to the scene and then asked for their names, address, and phone number.

As she listened to her husband, Sophie wondered if this death, somehow, was related to Thomas. And if it was not the end of a chain of events but the beginning.

CHAPTER FIVE

George stubbed out his cigarette in an ashtray on the kitchen table, peering anxiously through the haze of smoke at his sister, sitting across from him. It was late morning and brother and sister had recently gotten up, dressed, went downstairs and fixed breakfast, and sat in silence. Sue sipped her coffee, while absently eating a slice of toast. George didn't have anything except several cups of coffee and smoked one cigarette after another. Sue glanced at the clock on the wall and frowned.

"Usually, Aunt Sophie and Uncle Arthur are back by now," she said.

"Maybe they wanted to clear their minds," George said resourcefully. "Not altogether a bad thing. Too bad they didn't wake me. I'd have gone with them."

At that moment they heard car doors slam and footsteps near the front door. George and Sue looked at each other apprehensively and simultaneously got up and went to the hallway. They heard the key in the lock and the front door suddenly opened. Sophie and Arthur entered, breathlessly, followed by a grim-faced policeman.

"What happened?" Sue asked, horrified at seeing her aunt and uncle accompanied by a policeman. From their expressions, George and Susan could tell something was very wrong with their aunt and uncle.

"They've had a rather nasty shock," the policeman told them. He was a square-faced middle-aged man, tall and solid with a slight smile and piercing brown eyes. "They found a body at the port. A dead body that hasn't been identified yet." He paused looking from Sophie to Arthur and then George and Sue. He mentioned they'd be in touch and left.

Sophie and Arthur hugged their niece and nephew as though they hadn't seen them for days. Sophie, unaccustomed to such an upheaval in her daily life, told them she'd make coffee, but Sue told her to relax in the living room, that she'd fetch coffee and muffins. George followed Sophie and Arthur to the living room and faced them on the couch as they sat in their chairs by the fire. He waited for them to speak but could tell they were too much in shock. He decided to initiate the conversation by asking them what happened.

Sophie, ashen and disturbed spoke quietly, looking at her husband as though for support. "We walked to the port, as the policeman said," she started slowly. "Everything was fine until I noticed a shoe in the back of a trash can. When we looked closer, it was a dead body."

"There was blood all over his shirt," Arthur added. "Fresh blood, too, like he hadn't been there too long. It may have happened recently."

Sue entered carrying a tray with two cups and a plate of muffins. She set it on the coffee table, handed the mugs to her aunt and uncle, and then sat next to George on the sofa.

"Please tell us what happened," she pleaded to look at Sophie and Arthur.

Sophie related to Sue what she and Arthur told George, the finding of the dead body of a young man near a trash can at the port. It appeared he had been stabbed in the chest. Sue told them she had heard enough and was almost on the point of tears.

Sophie managed a smile, which she reserved even in the most difficult of circumstances for her niece and nephew. "We'll be all right, dear. It's been quite a shock, to say the least. Finding dead bodies isn't something we're used to."

"I wonder who the man was," George pondered. "Of course, there's been a lot of crime in the city recently. It's in the papers all the time."

Sue agreed. "Maybe it was a gangster or one of those bootleggers. I read in the paper that Al Capone plans to visit Albany next year."

"Frankly, I don't care about the new year or Al Capone," her brother said. "My concern is with Aunt Sophie and Uncle Arthur."

Arthur attempted to calm his nephew. "We're just in shock, George. A dead body isn't something we're used to seeing, as your aunt said."

"We'll have to wait until the police identify the young man," Sophie said. "For now, there's really nothing else we can do."

"I don't think it's a good idea for either of you to go out alone," Arthur said, looking at his wife and niece. He paused, turning his attention to George. "And the same for you, George. Young people seem to be targeted. First Thomas and now this young man."

"First, we need to plan Thomas's burial service," Sophie told them as though Thomas had momentarily been forgotten. "I'll contact the funeral parlor tomorrow to make arrangements."

"And the inquest should be held this week," Arthur added.

They finished their coffee, rather relieved by the hot liquid and by the fire warming the room pleasantly. George and Sue then decided to go to the state museum while Sophie started to plan their Thanksgiving meal. Arthur walked to the Capital Club to play billiards and have lunch.

Life returned to normal in the Drake house or as close to normal given the recent tragic events. They had no way of knowing another death was soon to follow and that this time, it would occur much closer to home.

Mrs. Mary Olson poured a cup of coffee and then took the skillet off the stove. She emptied the scrambled eggs onto a plate and brought both items to the kitchen table for her husband.

"Nobody prepares eggs like you, Mary," James said appreciatively.

"Well, thank you, dear." She returned to the stove, retrieved the jug of cream and sugar from the counter. She sat next to her husband, sipping her coffee. Husband and wife exchanged a few words of Sunday morning small talk, nothing more. The silence between them was intense, as though they were mechanically going through the motions of everyday life. The unspoken issue, the murder of Thomas Latimer, was present but neither spoke of it.

It was after breakfast that the doorbell rang. Mary looked at her husband, almost frighteningly. James put down his coffee cup and went to the hallway. He opened the door and saw two policemen, who introduced themselves as Inspector Harris and Lieutenant Taylor.

"Please come in," James said rather seriously and moved aside allowing the men to enter.

Inspector Harris noted the spacious, well-furnished living room and the comfortable husband and wife who sat before him on the couch. They appeared a good-natured couple, the Inspector thought, quiet, subdued, and not prone to trouble. Mrs. Olson wore a dress of light green, with a shawl covering her shoulders to keep warm. Her brown hair was swept back and being Sunday, her coiffure was more relaxed. Mr. Olson was conservative in his blue shirt and the vest he wore kept him warm, along with his corduroy slacks. James and Mary Olson fixed anxious, worrisome eyes on the policemen, wondering what they could say to help.

Inspector Harris cleared his throat. "We're here to ask you about Thomas Latimer. There also was another man found just this morning, at the Port of Albany. The body was discovered by the Drakes."

Lieutenant Taylor cleared his throat. "We don't know if the body found this morning ties in with the murder of Thomas Latimer. We also don't know if we're dealing with a mass murderer. That's why we're questioning people who know the Drakes."

"We didn't see Thomas too often," James said.

Inspector Harris nodded. "Were you acquainted with Mrs. Drake's brother and his wife?"

"I met them a few times," Mary said. "They lived and worked in Utica, where their children were born. That is until Max was called to serve in the war."

"When was the last time you saw Thomas?"

"I think it was about a month ago," James offered, shifting slightly in the armchair. "We were visiting the Drakes and Thomas was there, too." He offered nothing more and Mary kept quiet.

"How was his demeanor? Anything out of the ordinary?"

This time Mary spoke. "Not at that time, Inspector. But I will say he was quite difficult for the Drakes. He was in trouble from high school and flunked out of Union College, where his brother and sister graduated. He couldn't hold a job and was arrested a few times." She paused. "I didn't understand how he could turn out so bad when George and Susan are so lovely."

47

James agreed. "The Drakes didn't know what to do for him. His temperament was the opposite of his brother and sister."

"You said another man was found this morning?" Mary asked.

"Yes, the Drakes were walking near the Port of Albany and discovered the body of a man. An identification has yet to be made but once we know who it is, we will naturally contact the next of kin." He paused and asked the Olsons where they worked in case they needed to reach them during the weekday.

"I work at the Delaware and Hudson Railroad Building," James offered.

"I'm a court reporter and legal assistant for Mr. Reginald Donaldson," Mary said. She gave the policemen the address, in the Douw Building on the corner of State Street and Broadway.

Inspector Harris nodded, made notes, and then closed his small notebook with a snap. He thanked the Olsons for the information and their time and along with Lieutenant Taylor, they made their way to the front door.

"Let us know if you remember anything more about Thomas Latimer that could help," the Inspector mentioned, stepping out of the house onto the sidewalk.

James and Mary watched as they got into their patrol car and started down Dove Street toward Madison Avenue. James closed the door and looked at his wife.

"Poor Sophie and Arthur," Mary said.

"I always said he'd come to a bad end," James said remorsefully.

"He was different, without remorse or conscience. There was something different about him, something I've never understood."

Mary shook her head and headed off for the kitchen, leaving James at the door. He wondered if there were further revelations about Thomas Latimer; perhaps things better kept quiet, in the past, where they belonged.

"Oh, my goodness, the police," Marjorie Olmstead said in a dreaded tone to her husband as she stood by the kitchen window overlooking State Street. Her tone implied it was more like an army ready to invade or gangsters about to break into their house.

Henry Olmstead joined his wife at the window and saw two men getting out of a patrol car and approaching their house. Henry and Marjorie looked at each other. They had never had contact with the police. When the doorbell rang, they hesitated but then Henry walked to the hallway and cautiously opened the front door.

"Mr. Olmstead? I'm Inspector Harris and this is Lieutenant Taylor. We're from the Albany Police. We'd like to speak to you about Thomas Latimer."

Marjorie also came to the front door and with her husband looked questioningly at the policemen. They saw two rather distinguished middle-aged men, very business-like in demeanor and eager to begin inquiries. There was a moment's awkward silence until the Olmsteads stepped back allowing the policemen to enter. They ushered them into the comfortable living room and sat down on the couch. Looking up at them, Marjorie was perplexed and full of consternation.

"Thomas Latimer was murdered Thursday night," Inspector Harris began rather bluntly. "I understand you were acquainted with him as well as his aunt and uncle, Sophie and Arthur Drake."

He looked at the Olmsteads. A comfortable elderly couple, he thought. Well-dressed, even for a Sunday, a charming brownstone house on State Street. He listened to Marjorie as she addressed him, her tone sincere but somewhat cautious.

"Sophie and I have known each other since childhood. She's a remarkable woman. She took in her brother's children after he was killed in the war and her sister-in-law died during the pandemic. She and Arthur have been good parents to George, Susan, and Thomas."

The Inspector nodded. "Did you get along with Thomas?"

Marjorie glanced at her husband. "Well, yes," she hesitated. "We didn't see him too often,"

"Thomas stole an antique vase that belonged to Marjorie's great-grandmother," Henry said bluntly. "I found it in a pawn shop in Schenectady. Marjorie decided not to press charges."

"When was this?" the Lieutenant asked.

"A few years ago," Henry continued.

"He would've been underage," the Inspector noted. "Possibly arrested as a juvenile."

"Any more can you tell us about Thomas Latimer?" Lieutenant Taylor said. "We've spoken to his aunt and uncle and also his brother and sister. They admitted Thomas was involved with the underworld here in Albany." He hesitated, wondering what more this elderly couple could tell them.

"Thomas caused much heartache for Sophie and Arthur," Marjorie volunteered.

"Could he possibly have been in a fight at a speakeasy?" Henry offered. "And the fight spilled out onto the street? Someone could have pulled a knife then."

"A body of a young man was found earlier this morning, at the port of the city," the Inspector said, rather bluntly. "The body was discovered by the Drakes."

"What?" Marjorie exclaimed. "Who was it? How is Sophie?"

"We haven't released the identity of the victim yet. Mr. and Mrs. Drake discovered the body when they were walking earlier today."

Henry and Marjorie were stunned. Another murder in such a short period?

"Those speakeasies are full of gangsters," Henry said. "They should be closed down!"

"We're aware of that, Mr. Olmstead," the Inspector said patiently. "But when one closes another opens somewhere else in the city."

"Why can't you tell us who it is?" Marjorie asked, still shaken.

"The body is at the morgue. After the examination and attempts to contact next of kin are when we usually release the identity of the victim."

"Is there a maniac running loose here in the city?" Marjorie asked, her voice rising slightly. "I've always felt safe walking alone here but now, I don't know!"

"We've increased patrols in the city," the Inspector assured her. "Albany has its fair share of crime and violence. It's part of our job to get to the truth."

"I must call Sophie," Marjorie said urgently and excused herself. She walked to the hall, practically grabbed the phone, and gave Sophie's number to the operator and waited rather impatiently for the call to go through.

Realizing there was little more he could learn from the Olmsteads, Inspector Harris asked Henry if they would contact them at the Broadway police barracks if they should remember anything at all that may be pertinent to the murder. Henry assured them they would and accompanied them to the front door.

"Thank you," Henry said to them, rather awkwardly, and then closed and locked the door. He turned, expecting to see Marjorie, talking to Sophie on the phone. Instead, he heard her in the kitchen, cleaning up. He glanced at her as she was busy washing the dishes.

He returned to the living room, lit a cigarette, and turned the radio dial to a news program. Poor foolish Thomas, he thought, what did he get himself into this time?

CHAPTER SIX

G eorge closed the account book he was writing in and looked at the customers waiting for service in the large bank. It was Monday, and the workday was in full swing. He had already attended to several clients regarding their savings accounts, stocks, shares, bounced checks, safe deposit boxes, overdrawn accounts; issues an assistant bank manager could expect on a workday. He planned to meet his sister at the Ten Eyck Hotel, just across North Pearl Street, for lunch. Glancing at the wall clock, he noticed it was only ten-thirty, so he had quite a way to go until then.

While ushering the new clients to sit in front of his desk, George could not concentrate fully, despite his resolve to do so. His mind kept returning to Thomas and now the murder of an unknown man, discovered by his poor aunt and uncle. Of all things!

He listened and smiled at the elderly couple before him, as they related their business, that of making changes to their savings accounts and their safe deposit box. George spent quite an inordinate amount of time with them, retrieving their safe deposit box, adding more items to it, including a new will and other important documents. He returned the safe deposit box to the safe and thanked them for coming. He was

53

surprised when his colleague approached, telling him he'd take over while he went to lunch.

Grabbing his coat from the staff room, George looked at himself in a mirror. Always the consummate professional, with his hair slicked back and his eyes brilliant and alert. He made his way out of the bank and onto North Pearl Street, where the lunchtime crowd was already filling the streets. Traffic, trollies, departments stores, theaters, and restaurants; it was great to be in downtown Albany, George thought as he joined the throng of people on the sidewalk.

Light snow and a brisk wind added to the harshness of the November day. George crossed at the light and approached the Ten Eyck Hotel. He went through the revolving door and met his sister in the lobby. They entered the restaurant and saw it was busy, but the usual noontime crowd had yet to arrive, which pleased George. They found a table near the front windows, overlooking the street. George lit a cigarette as a waitress approached with menus; they ordered sandwiches and coffee and it was after she disappeared that Sue started to talk.

"Laura's a regular pain, George. She keeps talking about Thomas and what could've happened to him. Why would she mention him in the first place?"

The waitress returned with their orders. While George butted his cigarette and was putting cream in his coffee, Sue was about to start on her sandwich when she looked up and saw Laura just entering the restaurant. She had her fur coat over her arm as though she planned to leave the building.

"Oh no, it's Laura," she exclaimed.

George glanced sideways and inadvertently made eye contact with Laura. Sue almost kicked him under the table. Laura greeted George as though he was the one person in the whole world, she wanted the most to see, as though it filled her cup of contentment to the brim. Neither brother nor sister was glad to see her and did not encourage conversation much less ask her to join them as she began to speak.

"Sue, you left those accounts half-finished, you know. I had to finish them for you. Mr. Nolan wanted them before lunch." She paused as she put on her fur coat and gloves. She was about to turn and leave when Sue spoke up, somewhat harshly and to the point.

"You came here to tell me that? I did finish those accounts, Laura. They were yours from the beginning, anyway. If you weren't so busy flirting with the guys down the hall, you'd have gotten them done!"

Laura smiled. "Well, I wouldn't worry, Sue. I always do my work and Mr. Nolan's been pleased. On the other hand, you don't know very much about flirting, do you?" With that, she turned to leave before Laura could say anything further.

"Forget it," George told her, lighting another cigarette. "She isn't worth your time."

"That's what I have to contend with," Sue lamented.

"Well, she isn't your boss, so don't worry. Besides, we have more urgent things to think about. Such as Thomas's wake and funeral."

"Aunt Sophie's making the arrangements," Sue said, sipping coffee.

"Sue, what do you think happened to Thomas?"

Sue looked at her brother from behind the coffee cup. "What do you mean?"

"I mean, there must be more to it than we know! Was he involved with something we weren't aware of? He was murdered and we don't know by who or why!" He paused. "And that other man found at the port yesterday morning. Too bad Aunt Sophie and Uncle Arthur stumbled upon it. Undue stress isn't good at their age."

Sue agreed. "I haven't had time to think too much, though. With work and contending with Laura in the same office, there's too much going on!" She paused. "Aunt Sophie and Uncle Arthur will attend the inquest. I'm sure we'll know what happened soon enough." They finished their coffee and talked about the upcoming Thanksgiving holiday.

The hour seemed to fly by, and George and Sue realized their lunchtime was nearly over. They paid the check and after leaving the restaurant and before she headed for the elevators, George told his sister he'd meet her to catch the trolley as usual after work.

George glanced at his watch and realized he had all of five minutes left so he decided to walk up North Pearl Street. Usually, the chilly air and the crowds exhilarated him but not so much today. As he crossed the street, he walked past Whitney's and Meyer's bustling with shoppers. But even the mannequins in the windows and the advertised sales didn't interest him.

For ten years, they had been living with their aunt and uncle in Albany. And how well they've treated us, George thought appreciatively. It seemed a long way from Utica, where they were born and spent their early childhood until their parents died so tragically.

He dodged a businessman hastily walking up North Pearl Street and a woman carrying two hat boxes rushing to catch the trolley. Walking as though in a daze, with people brushing past him, he was seeing a rather confusing picture. He had questioned things, of course, with his naturally inquisitive nature but never spoke to his parents or his aunt or uncle. George finally reached the bank. Upon entering the lobby, his thoughts were chaotic, confused. Thomas, Thomas, Thomas…

He couldn't quite put a finger on it, but there was something, definitely wrong.

Henry Olmstead got off the trolley at the corner of Washington Avenue and Dove Street. In a rather strong gusty wind, with intermittent snow-flakes, he crossed Washington Avenue and looked up at the Capital Club. A distinguished establishment, the Capital Club bolstered the social life of its members and enabled alumni of area colleges to mingle, share news and enjoy the sumptuous food offerings in its fine dining room.

Henry and Marjorie had been members of the Capital Club for many years. They enjoyed numerous social events and were well known to the members and the executive chamber. Upon entering, Henry received a warm welcome from the host who ushered him into the reception area where he was further greeted by long-time members, who, like Henry himself, spent time at the club to socialize and to escape the occasional boredom of retirement. Amongst the familiar faces, Henry saw Arthur Drake, chatting with a few members. He made his way over to him.

"Arthur, great to see you," Henry said congenially.

Arthur smiled at his old friend. Henry and Arthur, like their wives, were native Albanians and had been friends for many years.

"Have you had lunch yet?" Henry asked him.

"No, I don't have much of an appetite," Arthur admitted and shook his head. "It's been difficult for us, Henry. Sophie and I are too preoccupied. We're planning the burial for this week, but it was too much for me. Sophie suggested I come here to take my mind off it at least for a while." He paused. "And yesterday morning, when Sophie and I were out walking, we discovered a dead body at the port. A young man, but we didn't know who it was."

They walked over to an area of the reception hall where several armchairs were arranged, along with tables containing numerous ash-trays. Henry took his Lucky Strike cigarettes from his jacket pocket and offered one to Arthur who took it absently. Henry struck a match, lit Arthur's first and then his own, blew the match out, and put it in an ashtray. While Arthur puffed at his cigarette, Henry took a good look at his friend. Arthur Drake was certainly looking the worse for wear, dressed conservatively but looking even older than his eighty years. Indeed, Thomas's death and the discovery of this other dead man at the port had dealt him a blow. Henry wondered how he'd react if such things happened in his life.

Having ensconced themselves comfortably in chairs overlooking Dove Street, Henry and Arthur exchanged small talk but then the conversation took a more serious turn.

"Thomas's wake will be this week," Arthur said. "We hope you and Marjorie can attend."

"Of course," Henry told him. "Now what about this dead body you found yesterday morning at the port? Do they know who it was?"

Arthur shook his head. "Unless they've contacted Sophie today to tell her who it is. I doubt if it's related to the death of Thomas." He spoke as though trying to convince himself that was true.

"There've been crimes here in the city recently," Henry said, butting his cigarette in the ashtray. He looked around and saw the crowds diminishing in the reception area as most had entered the dining room for lunch. "Shouldn't we get something to eat, Arthur?"

Again, Arthur shook his head. "Not yet. My stomach's been in knots since the police came to see us Friday morning about Thomas. Now another dead body we discovered ourselves!"

Henry told his friend, in as polite terms as he could, what he thought of his nefarious nephew and his inappropriate lifestyle. He mentioned the stolen ceramic vase and how Thomas had threatened him. Arthur shook his head, his face a mixture of remorse and anger compounded by fear.

"He was different than his brother and sister. We hoped George and Thomas would get closer, but they never did. And Susan tried her best, too. Thomas always had a mind of his own."

"You and Sophie have done an excellent job in raising them, Arthur. You shouldn't feel any guilt. They've been fortunate to have you and Sophie as parents."

Arthur forced a smile. "They've been with us for the past ten years after Lydia died. They were born, raised, and attended school in Utica, so moving to Albany was an adjustment for them."

"But they were young enough to adapt, Arthur," Henry told him. "And look how George and Susan have prospered in their careers. Do you ever regret taking them in and raising them?"

"No, not at all. Of course, we didn't know what Thomas would be like. He had trouble in school, unlike George and Susan, but we figured he'd change as he matured."

"What do you think happened to him, Arthur?"

"I couldn't say. He may have been involved with something we don't know about."

"He was so young to get involved with things of that nature. You mentioned George and Susan tried to help him?"

"Many times. He was a stubborn youngster at best and believed in having a good time first, then he worried about other things if he ever did at all."

"What do you and Sophie plan to do for Thanksgiving?"

Arthur showed surprise. "I haven't even thought much of Thanksgiving. With the burial this week, I haven't had the time. I'll talk to Sophie; she'd likely plan the dinner."

Arthur glanced at the wall behind Henry where several notices of upcoming events were posted on a bulletin board. One of them caught his eye.

"They're having the annual Thanksgiving meal here," he said as he read the notice as best, he could from his chair. "Maybe I'll mention it to Sophie and perhaps save her the trouble of cooking."

Henry turned and also read the notice about the Capital Club Thanksgiving dinner for its members. He knew the club had had a holiday meal but had never given it a second thought until now. He turned back around and looked at Arthur.

"I'll mention it to Marjorie, too. Perhaps we could all have Thanksgiving dinner. We should be together as much as possible during this difficult time, Arthur."

Arthur smiled at his friend. "Thanks, Henry. You and Marjorie have been like family. It's a good idea to have Thanksgiving dinner here. I'm sure it'd be a dinner we'd never forget."

"Come on, old boy." Henry stood. "Let's have lunch before they close the dining room."

For a long time after Arthur left for the Capital Club, Sophie sat in the living room, beside the dying fire, reading the morning paper. She was still in shock over the two grisly murders. Everything that had happened in the last four days seemed so unreal that its truth had an eerie effect. She had received a call about the inquest. She told the coroner's assistant she and her husband would attend on Wednesday. The ringing of the telephone again prompted her to attention.

Upon answering, she was in shock to hear the voice of the inspector from the Albany City Police. She was unaccustomed to speaking to policemen.

"Mrs. Drake, we've identified the man who you and your husband discovered yesterday morning," Inspector Harris said gravely.

Sophie listened, stunned, incapable of speech. When asked if she or her husband were acquainted with the dead man, she told him she had never heard of him before. She spoke for her husband as well, but the inspector mentioned he and his partner would return soon to speak to them again., although he did not specify when. The inspector also mentioned there were no more leads regarding the murder of her nephew. The inspector continued with information about the dead man and Sophie was too shocked to even say goodbye when the conversation ended.

After a few moments, she slowly replaced the receiver on the candlestick phone and stood motionless next to the table. She then collected herself and returned to the living room, where she turned the radio dial to the local news and looked out the front windows overlooking Chestnut Street. She pushed back some gray hair that had fallen across her forehead. Her dress, a dark gray, seemed to match her mood and her face, usually upbeat and pleasant, was more downcast and troubled.

Szymon Bartosz. Who in the world was he? She had never heard the name and was not acquainted with the last name. He could not have been from Albany. Most likely a refugee, possibly Polish. But why was he murdered? The inspector mentioned it wasn't robbery as his wallet was still in his back pocket, which enabled them to identify him easily. But then, why should she care? Other than discovering the body with Arthur, she had no connection to this Szymon Bartosz whoever he was. Then came a nagging impulse; was this murder somehow related to Thomas? Did Thomas know this Szymon Bartosz?

She returned to her favorite armchair by the fire, listening to the local news and the weather report. It'd be a cold day for the wake, which she had planned for Thursday. The following Thursday was Thanksgiving already and she wasn't even prepared for it. She opened the end table and took out a pad and pencil. She started to jot down items she'd need at the local market for Thanksgiving dinner, but then realized she and Sue had already made such a list, although at the moment she didn't recall where she put it.

Remembering her strict Victorian upbringing, she collected herself, wiped away tears, and arched her proud head high with her usual poise and dignity. She wouldn't want George or Susan to see her in such a state and certainly not Arthur. He also was stressed and found solace at the Capital Club. After dinner, she'd call Marjorie and make plans to meet her before the wake.

Her anxiety caused her to dose, and she did not wake until later in the afternoon. She realized she hadn't started to prepare dinner and that Arthur was not home yet. She got up feeling more refreshed and found the short nap did her good. Before starting to cook the evening meal, she decided to call the Capital Club. Most likely he was talking with friends and playing cards.

She found the number in the city directory and asked the operator to place the call. Upon reaching the club reception, she identified herself and inquired about her husband. The operator mentioned Mr. Drake was lunching and would participate in a bridge tournament shortly. Would Mrs. Drake care to speak with him or to leave a message?

Sophie paused, then said there was no message and hung up, rather disturbed that her voice sounded so hesitate—and frightened.

Claire Palmer finished typing the court agenda for the day. She took the paper out of the typewriter and prided herself on her efficiency. It was Monday and a busy day in the city courts.

She looked across at Mary Olson, also busy at her desk, as she was preparing to return to court this afternoon with Reggie, who, as usual, isolated himself in his office.

"I wonder if they'll identify the man who was found at the port yesterday," Mary commented as though to herself more than to Claire. "I heard it on the radio this morning, while I was having breakfast. What's this city coming to, anyway? So much crime and even gangsters, too."

Claire agreed. She butted her cigarette and inserted a fresh sheet of paper into her typewriter. She glanced up at Mary and the contrast between them was stark. Mary was dressed appropriately but plainly in a black dress, little make-up, and a fashionable but somewhat unkempt bob hairstyle. On the other hand, Claire was fixed to the max; her coiffure was pristine, and her voguish blue dress, high heels, stockings, and mascara accentuated the vibrance of her persona and her alluring nature, especially to men. She mentioned to Mary that Albany was indeed changing and then stopped talking to this irritating woman, hoping she'd take the hint.

Mary finished writing up the court report for Reggie and put down her pen. She picked up the morning paper that Reggie had carelessly left on her desk. Usually, he brought it into his office to read, but he left it with her, which Mary found odd. On the bottom of the first page, she saw the article on the discovery of the dead body at the Port of Albany. She looked again at it and gasped suddenly causing Claire to mistype in her correspondence.

"The Drakes discovered the body," Mary exclaimed as she picked up the paper and scrutinized the article. "The radio didn't mention who found the body. Poor Sophie and Arthur!"

If she expected Claire to say something she was disappointed. She simply ignored her, lit a cigarette, and continued typing. There was an awkward silence while Claire kept at her work and Mary kept reading the article over and over.

"I should call Sophie," she said with concern.

"I wouldn't if I were you," Claire said, putting down her cigarette. "You know Reggie doesn't approve of personal calls during business hours." She looked at Mary who kept her eyes on the paper. "If you're finished with the court report, I'll bring it to Miss Neale for you."

Miss Martha Neale, the assistant to the district attorney for Albany County, worked in an office on the second floor.

Mary blinked. "Yes, thank you, Claire, that would save me time." She got up and handed the court report to Claire.

As an escape from Mary and her lamenting over old Sophie Drake, Claire eagerly took the court report and headed out the office door and to the elevators. The elevator boy, a youth of no more than twenty, smiled when he saw her and admired her perfect figure and the scent of her perfume.

"Second floor, please, Willie," Claire told him. "Off to see Miss Neale again."

The elevator gates closed and shot down to the second floor in no time. Upon opening the gates, Claire thanked him and walked the length of the hallway until she arrived at the office of the district attorney.

"Hello, Miss Neale," Claire said cordially, entering the office. "Here's today's court report."

Miss Martha Neale, known to most of the law community as simply Martha, although Claire was not on a first-name basis with her, was a middle-aged woman who quite literally knew everything about the Albany court system. And quite literally Claire couldn't stand the sight of her. She was a bossy brunette with a boisterous voice, who dressed plainly and whose carelessly applied lipstick always smeared at the corners. She was smoking fiendishly as Claire entered, gulping down the remains of a cold cup of coffee. A small table bearing a typewriter, a candlestick telephone, and a spare chair, was all that comprised this rather dingy office. Some place for the district attorney, Claire thought wryly.

"Is Mr. Donaldson keeping busy these days?" Martha Neale asked between puffs, keeping the cigarette between her lips. She flicked the pages of a calendar book and made little eye contact with Claire, accepting the court report from her without a word of thanks.

"Yes, of course. Mr. Donaldson's services are most in-demand."

Martha gave a slight smirk. "How well you know your boss, Mrs. Palmer? I hear he's quite busy after work. Word gets around, you know."

"What's that supposed to mean?"

Martha continued her sly smirk. "Hear about that body found at the port yesterday morning? Quite a story, isn't it? And just last week that Thomas Latimer was murdered, too."

"I prefer to keep my opinions to myself," Claire remarked coldly. "That's all for now, Miss Neale." She turned before Martha Neale could say anything more and left the office.

As she walked down the dimly lit hallway, Claire decided to take the stairs. She thought of the infuriating woman she just encountered. Now what did she mean by that comment about Reggie, she wondered, slowly making her way up the stairs. Did she also suspect Reggie's involvement with bootleggers? Of course, in Albany, word spread quickly. Fortunately, her contacts with Martha Neale were exceedingly rare. Dear Mary, Reggie's girl Friday, could butter her up for all she cared.

As she returned to the office, she saw Reggie talking with Mary at her desk, quite intimately it appeared as though they were discussing something clandestine that was only between the two of them. She was surprised he even came out of his office. They stopped conversing when Claire entered.

"Am I disturbing something?" she asked deliberately, returning to her desk.

"Mary was telling me more about the body found at the port yesterday," Reggie said, fixing tired eyes upon her. "It was discovered by the Drakes."

"Well, it'd be bound to be discovered sooner or later," Claire said uncaringly. "If it wasn't the Drakes, then someone else would have found it."

Reggie, whose vest, and tie had seen better days, reached for his jacket on the coat rack, along with his winter coat. He smoothed down his hair and adjusted his glasses, which as usual had fallen halfway down his nose. He cleared his throat and told Claire he and Mary were about to leave for court for the afternoon, unlikely they'd return before she left. Claire promised him she'd finish typing the reports for tomorrow and said goodbye to them. And good riddance for today, she told herself.

With the door closed and the afternoon to herself, Claire lit another cigarette and took her time in typing the reports. As she blew smoke and looked out the windows overlooking Broadway, she didn't know who to trust in this rat-race office. Martha Neale was a sneaky bitch, Mary Olson was a goody-goody and Reggie was, well, just what was Reggie?

A man with secrets, Claire thought, smoking furiously, her mind preoccupied. But then, she had plenty of secrets, too. She didn't worry, though, about her past because she knew it was long buried and nothing would ever come to light.

Finishing one page and inserting another sheet into the typewriter, she paused briefly, puffing at her cigarette. At least, she hoped she needn't worry about anything coming to light.

CHAPTER SEVEN

Overlooking the Hudson River and the tracks leading to Union Station, the Delaware, and Hudson Railroad Building, commonly referred to as the D & H Building, is an architectural masterpiece that sits proudly and majestically at the base of State Street hill. On a typical weekday, professionals labored to boost the services of the railroad. Also located in the D & H building were the offices of the *Albany Evening Journal*, with reporters and copy editors rushing about with stories to print and leads to follow up.

An engaging place, James Olson would readily admit as he was usually up to his elbows in work. An administrator for the railroad, James created and enforced rail safety regulations, administered rail funding, and researched rail improvement strategies. At the moment, he was alone in his office, reviewing legal reports, his sharp eyes swiftly scanning the pages. Those requiring his signature, he put in a separate folder. Before signing, James always read the document in full to prevent any future complications.

He and Mary had breakfast early this morning, preparing to leave for work as usual, when on the radio they heard about the murder of another young man, only this time the body was found at the port.

His identity was not yet released. James shook his head irritably, baffled as to the two murders in recent days. Who could this other victim be? Was there a connection with Thomas Latimer? He remembered when Albany was a fine place to live and work. Now, with bootleggers, gangsters, and drug-smuggling, it had changed.

He picked up the phone and impulsively decided to call his wife at Reginald Donaldson's office, which was just across the street on Broadway. The operator asked for the number please, but James hesitated, thanked her, and hung up. He smoothed his brown hair and wrinkled his dark eyes in consternation. Most likely she'd be at court with Reggie Donaldson, a character James could barely tolerate. He suggested to his wife to find a new job with another lawyer, but the salary was excellent, and she enjoyed her work. The few times he met Mary at her office, he found Reginald Donaldson obtuse and not very friendly, a man of few words. His brief exchanges with him were usually restricted to comments on the weather, which suited James fine. After work, he preferred to meet Mary in front of the D & H Building, so they could take the same trolley home.

He lit a cigarette and got up from his desk chair. He strode over to the large windows overlooking Broadway and State Street. Always an admirable view, with the state capital at the top of State Street, but even the view couldn't sustain his interest. He was about to return to his desk when a knock came on the door. It was Leroy Stoddard, another railroad executive standing at his door, holding a newspaper, and looking rather flushed.

"Mr. Stoddard, please come in," James said politely and moved back allowing his colleague to enter. "What can I do for you?"

Mr. Stoddard was a rather young fifty, who, like James, had worked for the railroad for many years. A robust man with a strong voice and powerful personality, he came straight to the point when speaking.

"I just got the *Albany Evening Journal*," he said. "A convenience in having a newspaper publisher in this building; we get the paper before it hits the streets." He paused. "You heard about the body discovered at the port yesterday, didn't you?" He didn't wait for James to answer but continued, clearly exasperated. He held the paper out for James to take and read it. Upon folding back the page, his eyes quickly reviewed the article, his face a mixture of shock and remorse.

Albany Evening Journal
Monday, November 12, 1928
BODY DISCOVERED AT THE PORT OF ALBANY

The body of a man was discovered yesterday morning at the Port of Albany, in back of a trash can along the path near the river. The victim, Szymon Bartosz, thirty years of age of Albany, was stabbed in the chest and died at the scene. His body was found by Arthur and Sophie Drake of Albany, who were walking along the path when they made the gruesome discovery. Further investigations into this homicide are continuing. Anyone with information is asked to contact the Albany City Police.

"Szymon Bartosz? Who in the world?" He stammered, almost at a loss for words. "And the Drakes discovered the body! First, their nephew was murdered, and now this!"

Mr. Stoddard nodded gravely. "Does that name ring a bell?"

James looked up. "No, not at all. It sounds foreign."

Again Mr. Stoddard nodded, puffing away at his cigarette. "Most likely a refugee, Polish or Russian, I'd say. But what he did or how he ended up at the port is anyone's guess."

"I wonder if Mary's seen this," James said, his thoughts turning to his wife. He looked out the tall windows and saw evening fast approaching. It was close to five o'clock and Mary should be done with court by this time.

"It may tie in with the murder of Thomas Latimer," Mr. Stoddard said thoughtfully. "Two murders in less than a week."

James continued looking at the article. "Maybe they knew each other."

"Or they were involved with something that went wrong," Mr. Stoddard said sensibly. "In this city, practically anything can happen." He crushed his cigarette in the ashtray on James's desk and stood. "Since you and your wife are friends with the Drakes, you should tell them to watch out for their nephew, George."

James was shocked. "George? You think he's in danger?"

Mr. Stoddard shrugged. "Two young men murdered in less than a week, not far from each other, either. Perhaps there's a mass murderer around these parts, you never know." He paused. "You can keep the paper. Show it to your wife." He said goodbye and closed the door behind him.

James felt a chill run up his spine. He realized darkness had encroached on the city and that it was past five o'clock. He put the reports and folder in his desk drawer, turned off the banker's lamp, folded the newspaper and put it in his pocket. He then grabbed his coat from the rack behind the door and left the office.

George stood at the corner of State and North Pearl Streets, in front of the Ten Eyck Hotel, waiting for his sister. It was a blustery November evening and as the five o'clock rush hour was in progress, the streets were crowded. He put the collar up on his Mackinaw plaid jacket and pulled his cap lower on his head. George waited for his sister to finish work as Sophie and Arthur did not want them to travel alone. He turned and looked at the traffic and the trollies making their way up and down State Street. As soon as he returned his gaze to the Ten Eyck Hotel, Sue appeared as she exited the revolving doors. She smiled and came up to him.

Brother and sister walked up North Pearl Street to the trolley stop and waited with a sizeable crowd. It wasn't until they were settled in a rather crowded trolley that George asked his sister if she had heard from their aunt or uncle.

"No, I haven't heard from either one. Was I supposed to?"

George shook his head. "I wondered about the inquest on Thomas. I thought of calling her, but I was too busy today." He paused a bit uncertainly as he looked out the trolley window.

"I was too busy to call her." She hesitated. "George, are you still thinking of Thomas?"

"Yes, I can't stop thinking about him. Aunt Sophie said she'd plan the wake for this Thursday." He cleared his throat. "I suppose the burial will be Friday. I'm sure she'll tell us the details tonight. But I can't stop thinking something else about Thomas; his past life, his arrest record."

"We tried all we could to change him, George. You can't blame yourself."

George shook his head. "No, Sue, it's not that."

Sue started talking about Greta Garbo, Joan Crawford, and Colleen Moore, which, George assumed, was similar to the last time; making small talk because she too was thinking of the recent death and didn't want to discuss the impending wake and funeral. He nodded and made a few comments of no importance. She could tell he was not in the mood for chit-chat.

Her brother looked professional as usual, she thought; his cap low on his head as though he wanted to conceal his face at least in part, his plaid Mackinaw jacket fitted perfectly, his brown eyes brilliant and alert. Sue reflected how handsome he was and although he stood only a little over five foot five, his well-groomed appearance and intelligence more than made up for his lack of extreme height. His overall impression was quite debonair.

The trolley turned onto Lark Street and continued until it came to Lancaster Street. They got off, waited at the light for the trolley and cars to pass, then crossed Lark to Lancaster. They were silent as they walked and neither felt much like talking. Upon arriving, George's key in the front door lock, the aroma of Sophie's cooking brought comfort to them as they shook the snow off their shoes and hung their coats in the closet. Arthur greeted them in the hallway.

"Anything new on the radio?" George asked, his face rather ashen and worried. "About Thomas. Have they caught who was responsible?" His voice hinged on slight hysteria.

"Yes, there must be some news by now," Sue said, also clearly perturbed and anxious.

Arthur could sense the strain. "The news is on the radio now."

George and Sue followed their uncle to the living room. Sitting on the sofa in the comfortable room, George and Sue watched as Arthur turned the radio dial to the local news, increasing the volume at the same time. Sophie entered at that moment and greeted her niece and nephew warmly, carrying the evening newspaper. Her black dress with pearls rather matched her somber mood, her gray hair worn tastefully back from her forehead, her brown eyes cautious and concerned.

She sat next to them on the sofa and showed them the article in the newspaper on the murdered man at the Port of Albany. She also relayed to them, as she did to Arthur upon his return from the Capital

Club, the phone call she received from the Albany City Police, telling her the identity of the man. Both George and Sue read the article together and then looked up at their aunt and uncle.

"Szymon Bartosz," George said thoughtfully. "I've never heard of him."

"Neither have we," Sophie said including Arthur who merely nodded in agreement. "It's a foreign name, perhaps he was a refugee."

"Maybe he knew Thomas," Sue suggested as George handed her the paper and she was able to read it for herself. "He knew a lot of people in the city. Maybe their deaths are related." She looked up at Sophie expecting clarification.

"I'm sorry, dear," was all Sophie could say. "I wish I had more information."

"Let's have dinner now," Arthur said. "Your favorite, George, roast beef."

George smiled and followed his aunt, uncle, and sister into the kitchen, where Sophie started to serve the meal. Rich roast beef with sweet potatoes and green beans, followed by homemade vanilla cake and coffee. A satisfying and relaxing meal helped to alleviate the anticipation and turmoil within George and Sue. It wasn't until George finished his second cup of coffee that he mentioned the inquest, the wake, and the funeral.

"The inquest is Wednesday, and the wake is set for this Thursday," Sophie mentioned, looking at her nephew and niece. She felt sorry for them, so young to endure this kind of pain. And now with the murder of this other young man. But then, did that really concern them at all?

"The burial will be on Friday," Sophie continued. "The service will be at St Mary's."

George and Sue announced they'd take the day off from work and then lapsed into silence. George finished his coffee while Sue picked at her piece of cake. There was a rather uncomfortable silence at the dinner table and Sophie wasn't sure how to break it. The awkwardness was broken by the ringing of the doorbell.

Sophie got up, rather glad to escape the silence of the dinner table and entered the hallway. Upon opening the front door, she saw Marjorie Olmstead, carrying a basket and smiling at her old friend. She shook her snowy boots and handed the basket to Sophie. She took off her coat, hat and scarf and left them on a chair, and then followed Sophie into the kitchen where Arthur, George, and Sue still sat in silence.

"Well, hello, George and Sue," Marjorie said pleasantly upon entering the kitchen. "Hello, Arthur dear. I brought some fresh muffins I baked this afternoon," she said brightly.

"Why don't we sit in the living room," Sophie suggested.

Marjorie stayed to help her, while George, Sue, and Arthur returned to the living room, Arthur taking the newspaper with him. He left it on the coffee table and went to the radio. He turned the knob and found a station playing soft jazz music and then a drama program. Sophie entered with a tray with more coffee and Marjorie's muffins on a plate. George and Sue refused more coffee but appeared eager to ask Marjorie if she knew anything more of Thomas.

"Just what I read in the papers and from speaking to the police." She paused. "I hardly ever saw your brother." Her tone implied she was grateful for that.

"What did you tell the police?" George asked, rather boldly taking Marjorie by surprise.

"Well, Mr. Olmstead and I told the inspector we didn't know anything of Thomas's death." She hesitated. "He asked us about our relationship with your aunt and uncle and with Thomas. We mentioned the vase he stole from us some years ago."

"Mrs. Olmstead, did you ever notice anything different or unusual with Thomas?" George asked looking her in the eye.

"What do you mean, dear?"

"Anything about Thomas. The police have gotten nowhere and it's almost a week."

"Well, Mr. Olmstead and I rarely saw Thomas, of course," Marjorie said, fumbling for words. "He wasn't like you, George, or you either, Sue."

"Nothing else?" George persisted.

"No, dear, I'm afraid not. Thomas wasn't very pleasant to be around. He threatened Mr. Olmstead about the stolen vase. I never brought charges against him. I figured it'd be in his best interest not to."

Marjorie mentioned she and Henry would attend the wake and burial. She suggested cooking dinner Thursday evening, but Sophie declined and thanked her friend for her generosity.

Sophie picked up the newspaper Arthur left on the coffee table. She showed Marjorie the article about the dead man they found at the Port of Albany.

"It seems more new people are coming to Albany," Marjorie commented.

George and Sue remained silent, creating an uneasy tension in the living room. To lighten the atmosphere, Sophie suggested a round of bridge, but they declined. Arthur tended to the fire while Marjorie joined Sophie in the kitchen, cleaning up and discussing the upcoming wake and funeral. Sue announced she wanted to iron a few dresses and disappeared upstairs. Arthur attempted to make small talk with his nephew who politely but not wholeheartedly chatted with him. He then told his uncle he'd take a short walk outside, and went for his jacket and cap. Before Arthur could protest, George was out the door and on the sidewalk.

It was even colder than when he was downtown and the harsh air, although invigorating chilled him to the bone. He bundled his coat, lowered his cap on his head and headed north on Lancaster to Lark Street, walking with no particular purpose in mind.

He watched as trollies went up and down Lark Street and people bustled about, heading home to warmth and an evening meal. Disturbing thoughts moved in his mind as he continued walking slowly. He decided it was too cold to continue, so he turned and walked the short way back to the house. He arrived home but paused on the doorstep. Always Thomas…

It was at that moment that he experienced his first real thoughts of incredulousness.

CHAPTER EIGHT

T he next few days passed with agonizing slowness. George and Sue went to work as usual, while Sophie and Arthur got ready for the wake and burial. Marjorie stopped by to lend support and bring more homemade sweets.

The inquest on Wednesday produced few results and many unanswered questions. The coroner concluded that Thomas Latimer died as the result of a stab wound, having never regained consciousness. The verdict was death at the hands of a person or persons unknown.

When Thursday evening finally arrived, it was another cold, blustery night. At the funeral parlor, friends of Sophie's from the church and Arthur's friends from the Capital Club came to pay their respects, cordially and wished them well.

As he sat in the front row of chairs at a distance from the casket, with Sue beside him, George took in the scene before him. The lights were dim, and the air was heavy with steam heat.

Mr. and Mrs. Olmstead, of course, were there practically before they even arrived. Mrs. Olmstead stood near Aunt Sophie, ready to lend support and anything else she could do to help. Looking at faces entering the funeral parlor, he was surprised so many people showed up; the

Olsons and even Laura Dupont and her stepfather Reginald Donaldson. George thought, why in the world would they attend Thomas's wake?

He took a good look at Laura. Like his sister, he was not fond of Laura Dupont. As she entered the funeral parlor, he noticed her manner was flippant as ever, nonchalant, more concerned with her appearance than paying respects to a grieving family. Mr. Donaldson appeared bored and acted as though he couldn't wait to leave. George never understood Mr. Donaldson and how he could tolerate Laura. Of course, she was his stepdaughter but life with her had to be intolerable. He saw how Mr. Donaldson approached Aunt Sophie and Uncle Arthur. He murmured brief words of sympathy before sitting in the back row with Laura.

As the evening wore on, few people remained. George looked at Sue, whose face was a mixture of remorse, anger, and pity. Uncle Arthur sat in a chair to his far-right, his face almost wooden with grief and loss and maybe a touch of anger, too. Aunt Sophie chatted with a few women, including Mrs. Olmstead and Mrs. Olson, before saying goodnight to them and thanking them for coming.

At last, Uncle Arthur rose, and Aunt Sophie glanced at George with a rather whimsical look, as though she knew he hated being there and couldn't wait to leave.

"George, Sue, that's all for tonight," Arthur told them as they put on their coats and hats

George took one last glance at the casket, as though by looking once more he would be able to dispel the chaotic thoughts churning over in his already troubled mind. He then hurriedly left the funeral parlor and followed his uncle to the car where Sophie and Sue were awaiting them.

On Friday afternoon, Claire and Mary were busy in the office, review-ing accounts and writing up court reports for the following week. Mary finished filing numerous letters and other legal documents while Claire typed one report after another, including affidavits and wills.

Mary returned to her desk and looked briefly at Claire. "My hus-band and I attended the wake last evening and the burial this morning." She expected Claire to comment but she continued typing and ignored her. "I felt so bad for Sophie," Mary went on. "And Arthur, George, and Susan, too. It was a lovely service at St Mary's. I'm glad James and I were there to support Sophie. She's gotten on in years, you know. She's almost eighty."

Claire thought she looked more like a hundred but didn't say so. She simply finished the document she was typing and inserted another piece of paper into her typewriter. Her head was bent over a court report she was about to start typing when Reggie suddenly came out of his office.

He cast a glance at both women and appeared to be in a thoroughly bad temper, rather unusual for Reggie Donaldson. Claire thought he'd burst from the strain of not saying something to them, but she kept her eyes on her work and paid him little attention.

Reggie again looked at them as though trying to decide which one to speak to. Mary made a few comments about Thomas Latimer's wake and funeral and to Claire's surprise, he mentioned he had attended the wake, too, with his stepdaughter, Laura. He turned to Claire, almost mocking in his absent-minded nature.

"Did you attend the wake last evening, Claire?"

"No, I didn't feel close enough to the Drakes to attend. But if I see Mr. and Mrs. Drake I will offer my condolences, of course."

That seemed to put him in his place, Claire thought, as though he wasn't expecting such an intelligent answer.

By mid-afternoon, a client, a middle-aged man seeking to divorce his wife, showed up for his appointment to see Mr. Donaldson and was shown into his office by Mary. Nearly an hour passed before the man emerged, quite happily with a satisfied look about him. Following this visit, another client, a husband, and wife appeared for their scheduled appointment to discuss their last will. Claire was called in to take shorthand and to assist, as necessary. It was close to five o'clock by the time the husband and wife left. Claire mentioned she'd type up a draft of the new will and returned to the outer office, where Mary was finishing her work for the day. She closed a file cabinet with finality as though she was exhausted and couldn't go on any further. Looking at her quickly, Claire thought she looked tired, perhaps the wake and funeral were too much for her. She was surprised she'd come to work for half a day in the first place.

Mary walked over to Reggie's office. "Will you be needing me any further, Mr. Donaldson?" she asked as she stood in the doorway.

Claire heard him mumble something, as usual, it was hard to interpret his monotone voice, but it must have been a dismissal for Mary soon headed for the coat rack, reaching for her coat and cloche hat. She stood at the office doorway.

"Good night, Claire," she said brightly, as though a breath of fresh air overcame her. She buttoned up her coat and placed her cloche hat firmly on her head. "I'll see you Monday morning."

She turned to leave, closing the office door behind her. As usual, Claire heaved a sigh of relief but then realized she was not alone. The banker's lamp was still on in Reggie's office. What was he doing here so late, she thought rather irritably? Of course, he wasn't due in court until Monday afternoon. She collected her pocketbook from her desk, securely locked each drawer, and was about to go for her coat and hat when Reggie suddenly called out to her. She hesitated, totally unprepared for an after-hours talk with him. She left her pocketbook on top of her desk and then entered his office.

Reggie was busy reading a report. He took off his glasses, blew smoke from a cigarette, rubbed tired eyes, and beckoned Claire to sit in the chair before his desk. He had never spoken to her after hours and she felt rather uncomfortable sitting before him because she didn't know what to expect. She waited for him to speak.

"Claire, you've been with me for many years now."

"Yes, and I enjoy my work here very much."

"And we've been on good terms, right?"

"Yes, we've been on good terms. What's the point?"

"The point is that I don't like when a member of my team talks about me behind my back. What I do outside of this office is my business, do you understand?"

Claire looked at his hard eyes. "What are you getting at?"

"Don't play dumb, Claire. You're not good at it. You know about my business with bootleggers and I'm sure you know how profitable it's been, too. I'm not stupid, Claire, although you may think that of me. I could tell by the subtle hints you'd throw the last couple of months. You'd stab me in the back if you had the chance and you know it. I assume you found that out from your many friends at the speakeasies and dance halls. Word gets around a city like this." He paused. "You need extra money, do you? Blackmail is a serious offense, and it could lead to dangerous and perhaps even deadly consequences."

"Well, I never meant anything, of course." She paused, almost shaking from nerves. "I may listen to what I hear at the dance halls, but that doesn't mean I believe everything."

"Oh, I think you do. You entertained thoughts of blackmail. No one else knows about my bootlegging activities, not even Laura. So, it's a little secret between us, isn't it, Claire?"

"You're going to fire me, aren't you?" She had never seen this side of Reggie Donaldson and wasn't sure what to make of it.

Reggie smiled, but it wasn't a nice smile. "No, Claire, I don't plan to fire you. You know too much about my business practices. You'll continue working here as usual."

Claire bit her lip. She knew there was something more. "What do you have in mind?"

Reggie opened his desk drawer and took out a small notebook, one that had been well used and was almost in shreds. He watched Claire closely and her expression alone was enough to make him realize he needn't worry about Claire and her anticipated blackmailing schemes any further.

"Yes, Claire, that's right. Look familiar? It's how you made your living in Elmira so many years ago. And you were married at the time, too?"

"Where did you get that? That's my business. That was years ago!"

Reggie looked at her dubiously and almost laughed. "Don't you know I always investigate my employees before I hire them?"

"You've had that all this time? You can't tell anyone about my former life in Elmira. I was poor and my husband hardly made any money."

Reggie nodded, lit another cigarette, and addressed her again. "We have secrets, Claire. But you're a clever woman. As I said, blackmail can have bad consequences. I could easily do the same with you. But why don't we call a truce? It'd be better for you that way."

Claire was at a loss for words. "Of course," she stumbled, shakily. She clutched the pearls around her neck nervously. "What do you want from me? You could destroy my name in this city. And I'd have nothing, nothing at all."

"I don't plan to do that, Claire," Reggie said, rather honestly although Claire didn't trust him. "But you won't plan on telling anyone about my side business deals, either. Because if you do—and I will know if you do—I will expose your past life in Elmira and your name will be smeared in mud. And in a city like Albany, it's hard to start over."

Claire was mesmerized into shocked silence. "Yes, it's hard to start over," she mumbled as though in a trance. She stared at Reggie, who simply looked at her as though a business deal had been closed and was now over.

"That's all till Monday, Claire," he said, closing a file and about to open another. He took a few puffs at his cigarette. "Why don't you go and enjoy the weekend."

It was a dismissal. She thought of asking him to return the notebook, but she knew he wouldn't. Claire returned to her desk, snatched her purse, rather wildly grabbed her coat from the rack, almost causing it to tilt and fall, and then abruptly left the office.

CHAPTER NINE

Monday morning brought more harsh winds to Albany. There was a hint of snow in the air and pedestrians scurried about, dodging snowflakes, sleet, and freezing rain. Predications for a cold winter were already broadcast and hardware stores kept up a supply of snow shovels and rock salt, preparing for the onslaught of customers.

In their comfortable brownstone house on Dove Street, Mary Olson sat at the kitchen table, sipping her coffee, and reading the morning newspaper. She glanced at her husband James, who sat across from her, absently putting sugar into his coffee, and stirring it continuously.

"Is something wrong, dear?" she asked, looking up from the paper. She could tell by his downcast eyes that something was troubling him. She glanced at the wall clock and noticed it was just seven-thirty, so they had plenty of time to dress and get ready for the workday. They took the same trolley from the corner of Washington Avenue and Dove Street which brought them downtown to the Douw Building and to the D & H Railroad Building in no time.

"I keep thinking of the Drakes," James finally said, taking a bite of toast. "First, their nephew is murdered and then they discover a body at the Port of Albany." He paused, uncertainly.

"I have to work Wednesday, but fortunately Mr. Donaldson is closing the office the day after Thanksgiving." She paused. "I'll call Sophie this evening. We should invite them here for dessert on Thanksgiving or perhaps during the weekend." She glanced down at the newspaper again. "James, how about we have Thanksgiving dinner at the Capital Club this year?"

James Olson frowned. "The Capital Club? Well, I never thought of having the holiday there. Are they open for Thanksgiving?"

Mary folded back the paper to show her husband the advertisement in the *Albany Times Union*, detailing the sumptuous Thanksgiving feast being held this Thursday at the Capital Club. Although the club was open to members, the public was invited to enjoy the holiday this year for the first time. The advertisement listed the food offerings, with turkey being the main choice, along with fish, meat, and several potatoes, vegetable dishes, and delectable desserts.

James looked closely at the advertisement, reading it several times as though trying to memorize it. He then looked up into the pretty face of his wife, who smiled at him and without words convinced him the Capital Club was the place for them at Thanksgiving.

"Go ahead, dear," he said, smiling wanly and handing her back the paper. "Make the reservation for Thursday before they're sold out."

Mary finished her coffee, cut the advertisement, and put it in her pocketbook, which lay on the kitchen table so that she wouldn't forget to make the reservation later in the day.

Henry and Marjorie were also at the breakfast table, although it was still early for them. Henry had mentioned the Capital Club after meeting Arthur there last week, but he didn't pursue it. Now, with the holiday only three days off, he mentioned it again.

"Marjorie, what do you think of the Capital Club for Thanksgiving?"

"I don't know, dear. I'm too preoccupied with Thomas's murder and with Sophie and Arthur finding that dead body last Sunday." She hesitated, buttered a slice of toast but did not eat it. "And what about Sheila? She's in Jamestown." She poured more coffee for herself and her husband and shook her head.

"We already decided we wouldn't go there this year," Henry said. "Sheila will understand. I think it'll do us good to eat out for the holiday. And you won't have to cook or clean up."

"Well, I don't know. I'll speak to Sophie later this morning. She didn't mention Thanksgiving when we spoke yesterday."

"Arthur was interested in the Capital Club dinner when I saw him there last week."

Marjorie shook her head. "Sophie didn't mention it when I spoke to her yesterday."

"I'll make a reservation and if we decide not to go, we can always cancel."

"I did buy a turkey. It's in the icebox."

Henry managed a smile. "It won't go to waste. I'll make the reservation this morning."

Marjorie reached out her hand to his and held it tenderly. "I'll look forward to it, dear."

In the spacious brownstone house on Chestnut Street, Laura Dupont sat across from her stepfather in the kitchen, having just prepared scrambled eggs and bacon. She grimaced slightly as she was not one for cooking much less cleaning up afterward. A diehard feminist, Laura was repulsed by traditional female roles, and she considered cooking diminished the female intellect.

Reggie merely smoked in silence while glancing through the morning paper. As usual, he made small talk with Laura, but nothing of any great importance. He butted his cigarette and was about to light another when Laura asked him what he wanted to do for Thanksgiving.

Always the businessman, Reggie hardly gave a second thought to the holiday. With his law practice prospering like never before and his illegal bootlegging activities bringing in extra money, he was more concerned with hard cash than eating turkey. He folded the paper and placed it on the kitchen table.

"I haven't given it much thought, Laura," he admitted truthfully. "We could eat here as we've done before. Unless you have some suggestions."

"I saw an ad for the Capital Club," Laura said. "They're having Thanksgiving dinner and it's open to the public." She grabbed the newspaper, turned the page, and pointed to an advertisement for the Capital Club sponsoring a Thanksgiving dinner. Reggie looked at the paper and frowned.

"The Capital Club? I haven't been there in years."

"It's better than cooking, Daddy," Laura said. "And I hate to clean afterward. A woman's place is not in the kitchen, you know."

"I know, Laura," Reggie said firmly, cutting her off before she started a tirade on women's rights. Reggie looked at his stepdaughter, smug and brusque as always, and didn't quite understand what the suffragettes wanted. With the right to vote just eight years ago, he'd have thought they would've been satisfied. Drawing heavily on his cigarette, he realized times had indeed changed.

"When I get to the office," he told her, "I'll call the Capital Club to see if they're still open for reservations."

"Why don't we invite Mrs. Palmer?"

Reggie almost gagged on his cigarette. Was she serious? Invite Claire to spend Thanksgiving with them at the Capital Club? He knew his stepdaughter had outrageous ideas, but this was to the extreme.

"I don't know, Laura. I'm sure she has other plans."

"It doesn't hurt to ask unless you'd like me to ask her for you."

Reggie said that wouldn't be necessary, but Laura insisted.

"Fine, Laura, although I must admit I don't understand why you want to ask her in the first place. You don't know her."

"Well, she doesn't have family here in Albany, so perhaps she'd appreciate it." She paused. "If I stop by the office later today, I'll ask her. Are you in court this afternoon as usual?"

Reggie mentioned he'd be in court in the afternoon but if he wasn't tied up, he'd return before the afternoon was over.

Laura then went upstairs to dress for work, while Reggie remained at the kitchen table, smoking incessantly, his mind turning over various impressions; Claire and her machinations of blackmail, his self-centered, egocentric stepdaughter and the Drakes, old Sophie and even older Arthur who looked like they were already on their death beds. Then there was pathetic George; rather quiet, observant, questioning, the type Reggie didn't trust. And his doleful sister, Susan, who was pretty enough but so naïve, at least it seemed to him. Why would they be content to live with their elderly aunt and uncle?

But there had to be secrets somewhere, Reggie thought, besides what he knew of Claire. The Drakes must have skeletons, too and even the Olsons and the Olmsteads. The good-natured appearances they gave in public must conceal something. If he knew for sure, he might resort to blackmail too.

"Well, pretty soon the lion will come out of its den," he laughed to himself.

With sleep still in his eyes, George opened the front door and collected the morning paper and the milk bottles left in the box near the front steps. He buttoned the top of his fleece sweater, wincing from the harsh wind and quickly closed the door. What sleepiness he may have had vanished as the cold wind woke him up abruptly. He shivered slightly and walked down the hallway to the kitchen where his uncle, aunt, and sister were already having breakfast. He deposited the paper on the table and the milk bottles on the counter.

"Eggs, George? Or cereal?" Sophie said standing near the counter.

"Corn flakes, I think," he mumbled and then sat at the table.

Sophie began to crack eggs in a bowl and slice a loaf of wheat bread when Sue interrupted her. She got up, stood by her elderly aunt, and placed her hands on her shoulders affectionately.

"Why don't you sit down, and I'll fix breakfast?" she said tenderly.

Sophie smiled tiredly, thanked her niece, and then joined Arthur and George at the kitchen table. Arthur was already crunching on toast and George poured milk for his corn flakes. He finished his coffee and lit a cigarette.

"What about the Capital Club for Thanksgiving dinner?" Arthur asked his wife and niece, and nephew. He looked at the advertisement in the paper and showed it to Sophie. "Henry and I discussed it last week. It'll do us good to get out of the house and enjoy a nice meal. Henry told me he'd mention it to Marjorie. We can join them."

George could tell his aunt wasn't too fond of the idea. He wasn't either, but then Uncle Arthur had a point. Why shouldn't they have a nice meal out and try to forget the horror of the last two weeks?

Sue joined them at the table, with a plate full of scrambled eggs and bacon. George and Arthur ate little, and Sophie just picked at the eggs on her plate. Sue also ate little and wondered why she made so much in the first place.

George looked at his aunt, uncle, and sister, trying to figure out what they were feeling. His aunt looked worn out and George was surprised she had the strength to carry on. Uncle Arthur looked rejuvenated somehow; perhaps the idea of Thanksgiving dinner out gave him something to look forward to. His sister appeared sullen and withdrawn, but then George had seen her like that many times before, so it was nothing new.

Quite suddenly the telephone from in the hallway rang, sharply, practically startling everyone at the kitchen table. Early morning calls were not the norm at the Drake house. Arthur and Sophie looked at each wondering if it was more unpleasant news.

"Who'd call so early?" George asked as Sophie rose to answer it.

From the kitchen, they heard Sophie talking, quite calmly and pleasantly. The conversation lasted at least five minutes before she returned to the kitchen table. She managed a weak smile, poured herself another cup of coffee, stifled a yawn, and looked at her husband, niece, and nephew as though she had something to tell them but hesitated.

"That was Marjorie," Sophie told them. "She and Henry plan to have Thanksgiving dinner at the Capital Club." She paused. "So, there's no need for us to go to the market today." She made it seem like skipping the market for groceries was a catastrophe. "I guess we will have our Thanksgiving there, too."

Arthur smiled and even Sue seemed pleased. George was somewhat hesitant at first, but then relented and joined his family in welcoming the idea. Sue then gulped her coffee and with George hurried upstairs to get ready for work. Sophie cleared the table and told Arthur she'd make the reservation this morning. Arthur smiled and helped to clean up the breakfast dishes.

"It'll do us good, Sophie," he reassured her. "It'll be an event we'll never forget."

It was close to one thirty. Claire returned from lunch to find Reggie and Mary out of the office. Reggie had several court cases this afternoon and most likely would not return for the rest of the day. And that included annoying Mary Olson, too, Claire was pleased to note.

She lit a cigarette and sat back in her desk chair. She hadn't forgotten the after-hours conversation she had had with Reggie. So, he knows about my past life, she thought. She had already searched his office, hoping to find her notebook, but most likely he kept it hidden, locked safely away in a desk drawer.

How did he get hold of it, she wondered? So, we called it even, she thought rather angrily. She'd never mention his bootlegging activities and he'd never mention her past life in Elmira. Was it that simple? She shook her head. She didn't trust him. Or his infuriating stepdaughter.

As though on cue, Laura Dupont suddenly and unexpectedly entered the office, closing the door with a bang. She looked at Claire innocently and batted her eyelashes.

"Hi, Mrs. Palmer," Laura said pleasantly.

"Hello, Miss Dupont," Claire answered, wondering what this vixen was up to.

Laura looked at Claire curiously. "Isn't Daddy back yet?" She didn't wait for Claire to answer. "You must like your work for Daddy. You dress very nicely, Mrs. Palmer."

Claire thanked her and added nothing more. She wondered when she'd get to the point.

"You must be a great help to Daddy," Laura said and sat at a chair against the wall. "When's Daddy returning? I thought I'd take the trolley with him. I left the hotel a little early today."

"He's in court, as he usually is in the afternoon," Claire said abruptly. "Why didn't you call to see if he was available?"

"Well, it was rather at the last minute, you know. Besides, I don't like to plan. I like to do things impulsively." She looked around. "Where's Mrs. Olson?"

"Mrs. Olson is with your father, in court."

"Oh well, I guess I'll have to catch up with him later." She paused. "Do you always go to the dance halls, Mrs. Palmer?"

"Miss Dupont, I believe you should leave," Claire said, pleasantly but firmly. "I have work to do. So, if you'll excuse me." She opened a folder and absorbed herself in her work.

Laura, on the other hand, wasn't easily rebuffed. "Daddy and I plan to have Thanksgiving dinner at the Capital Club on Thursday." She hesitated. "Would you like to join us?"

Claire looked up from a report she had been reading. She was about to start typing but froze before inserting paper into the typewriter. Did she hear her correctly? Why would this hideous, selfish, self-centered young woman want her to have Thanksgiving with them?

"Do you have plans for Thursday, Mrs. Palmer?"

Claire paused, her fingers still frozen on the keyboard. No, she didn't have plans, she thought, she'd be alone as usual. She had never made much of the holidays. She had dated a man who frequented the Capital Club but that was years ago. Thanksgiving dinner with Reggie and his stepdaughter? Well, why not, she thought suddenly.

"That's very kind of you, Laura." She switched to her first name. "I'd be delighted to have Thanksgiving dinner at the Capital Club with you and Reggie."

Laura smiled, took from her pocketbook a small notebook, and wrote down the details. She thanked Laura again for her kindness and watched as she disappeared out the office door.

Claire leaned back on her chair. Why would she want to sit at the same table with Reggie, anyway? But then why would Laura ask her to join them in the first place? A random act of kindness? Maybe she was trying to change. A strange young woman, indeed. Claire shook her head dubiously but then thought light of it.

Well, what was wrong with spending the holiday with them? It was just a harmless Thanksgiving dinner and at a nice place, too. She needn't worry. What could possibly go wrong?

She inserted a fresh sheet of paper into her typewriter and returned to work.

CHAPTER TEN

George finished what he hoped was the last transaction of the day, a new savings account opened for a young man starting college. He had attended to different requests today. Many clients commented on the stability of the stock market, seeing the fruits of their investments and cashing checks, with money to enjoy the holidays and opening new accounts, too.

It was Wednesday, the day before the holiday, and the morning was unexpectedly busy at the Home Savings Bank. He didn't think he'd have as many clients to attend to today.

His thoughts then returned like a tidal wave to the murders. The police had not found who was responsible and apparently had no leads to follow up. Thomas was wild, irresponsible, reckless. Most likely he had gotten in with a bad group and paid the consequences.

But what were the consequences of murder? More deaths, he thought grimly. Such as the murder of Szymon Bartosz. George could not figure out who the man was, what he was doing at the Port of Albany, and who wanted to kill him. Two unsolved murders in less than a week? And was the second murder somehow connected to the first?

As the five o'clock hour approached, George crushed his cigarette in the ashtray on his desk, preparing to leave for the day. The candlestick phone on his desk started to ring. He promptly and professionally answered and was surprised to hear his sister at the other end.

"George, you won't believe this," Sue said, keeping her voice rather low as she was still in her office at the Ten Eyck Hotel. "Laura just left and told me she, Mr. Donaldson, and Mrs. Palmer are planning to have Thanksgiving at the Capital Club! Of all the rotten luck!"

Momentarily speechless, George cleared his throat. "You think she was just making it up?"

"No, I know Laura pretty well. When she says something, she means it. Hopefully, our table will be further away from where they'll be sitting."

George couldn't help but laugh slightly to himself. He understood where his sister was coming from. Laura Dupont was a tough shell to crack, a definite character, an outlandish flapper who had little regard for other people.

"I'll meet you in front of the hotel in about ten minutes," Sue told her brother. "I just need to finish some things here and I'll be down."

George replaced the receiver on the candlestick phone and reflected on what his sister just told him. Well, Laura and her stepfather will be at the Capital Club tomorrow. And the secretary, too, Mrs. Palmer. George remembered he had met her just once a long time ago. Strange that she'd join Mr. Donaldson and Laura for Thanksgiving, unless, of course, they were on good terms, although he couldn't imagine anyone being on good terms enough to share a holiday dinner with Laura and Mr. Donaldson.

George put on his plaid Mackinaw jacket and his cap said goodbye to colleagues, and left the bank, on his way to the other side of North Pearl Street to wait for his sister. His mind was churning over and over about the murder, always Thomas and his murder, now two weeks ago.

He was so preoccupied with thoughts of the murders that he didn't notice Laura Dupont on the other side of North Pearl Street, watching him leave the building, a fixed, hard look to her face.

Thanksgiving morning and the cold remained in place. A sprinkle of snow blanketed the city, covering tree branches, cars, and trollies with a fine layer of white powder. A light fog swirled here and there, finally burning off, allowing an uncertain sun to poke through the mist, with hopeful and intermittent rays of sunshine.

By early afternoon, the weather showed signs of improvement. After listening to the forecast on the radio and glancing out the living room windows, Sophie decided they would walk to the Capital Club as it was only a short distance. The snow, she commented, was light and powdery and would not be difficult to walk in. Arthur agreed as parking would be a nuisance.

Bundled in her winter coat, Sophie ushered her niece and nephew out the front door, with Arthur securely locking it behind him, before joining the others on the sidewalk. Rather cheerfully, they walked down Lancaster, Arthur commenting how handsome George looked with his three-piece suit and Sue pretty as ever in her new dress of olive green, taking a left onto Dove Street before finally reaching the corner of Dove and Washington Avenue. Several trollies passed before they crossed and proceeded on Dove Street to the Capital Club.

Upon arrival, George noticed it was already busy with waiters rushing back and forth, customers enjoying appetizers and drinks, which he assumed included liquor. Upon leaving their coats at the coat check,

Sophie looked toward the two large dining rooms and commented on the lovely décor. The club host welcomed them and showed them to a reserved table, in the main dining room.

A waiter, a pleasant middle-aged man dressed as all the wait staff in black slacks and white shirt, soon approached and presented them with cards, explaining the choices for Thanksgiving dinner. Arthur told the waiter they'd have the traditional turkey. It was agreed upon that stuffing, gravy, and green beans would accompany the main course along with au gratin potatoes.

He looked around and fortunately did not see anyone he knew. He hoped it'd stay that way, although he knew somewhere in the club Laura and her stepfather would make a showing. He glanced to his left and noticed the Olsons two tables over, ordering and speaking it seemed rather animatedly to the waiter. After he left, Mary nodded to George and then caught Sophie's attention who waved to her and smiled. Arthur also waved to James who smiled and seemed pleased to see them. Everything happening normally, George thought.

The waiter had just returned with their drinks, including ginger ale and coffee for all, when George suddenly heard a loud and rather obnoxious voice calling his sister's name.

"Hey Sue, what a kick to see you here! If this isn't the cat's meow! Hey Daddy, look it's Sue and her aunt and uncle and George, too! How's everyone doing?"

It was Laura, dressed to perfection in true flapper style, with an abundance of make-up, perfume, and jewelry. George thought she looked pretty but her demeanor and personality would be enough to turn anyone's stomach.

Without waiting for the host, Laura entered the dining room and approached the Drake's table. Reggie and Claire followed and greeted Sophie, Arthur, Sue, and George cordially.

"Your table is here, sir," said the host, an elderly man with distinguished business acumen. He held chairs for Laura and Claire then called over a waiter to explain the dinner choices.

The table next to ours, George lamented to himself and almost gagged on his glass of ginger ale. Even Sophie felt a knot in her stomach. George glanced at Reggie, Laura, and Claire and thought of all the bad luck, just what his sister didn't want, to see Laura much less be seated near her. Fortunately, Sue's back was to them so although she could hear them, she didn't see them. She cast a quick glance at her brother, rolled her eyes heavenward, and gave a dry smile.

Sophie looked up and saw Marjorie and Henry making their way across the dining room. Marjorie wore a dress of navy blue, with pearls accentuating her pretty white hair. She wore little make-up but looked charming. Henry, dressed conservatively in a three-piece brown suit, smiled at seeing Sophie, Arthur, George, and Sue.

"Our table is near yours, Sophie," Marjorie said. "We'll talk after the meal."

"Hello, Mrs. Olmstead," Laura said a little too loudly.

Marjorie turned and was surprised to see Laura, Reggie, and Claire sitting together. She greeted them cordially, wished them a happy Thanksgiving, and quickly made her escape with Henry to the table in back of the Drakes.

From his viewpoint, George looked at the people around him; Mrs. Palmer looked especially attractive; a long, slim black dress, with a gold necklace and flashy rings. She conversed amicably with Mr. Donaldson and Laura while looking at the dinner choices. Mr. Donaldson was dressed, like Uncle Arthur and Mr. Olmstead, rather conservatively in a business suit but nothing to distinguish him from the other gentlemen in the dining room. He looked past them to see the Olsons, sipping coffee and chatting between themselves. Mrs. Olson was pretty too, he thought, but rather plain. Her dress was simple but nothing outstanding. Mr. Olson too was dressed straightforwardly in a vest, shirt, and tie, his jacket flung against an empty chair.

George thought the food would never arrive. It was busy, as he anticipated, and the waiters catered to many tables, some full of families of ten or more. There was much laughter and lively conversation amongst the diners, a piano player provided soft music in the background.

The turkey and stuffing were excellent, and Sophie, Arthur, George, and Sue enjoyed their meal. They relaxed and chatted about the possibility of George and Sue pursuing graduate school. The recent murders seemed far from their minds, at least for the moment.

It was as the waiters were busy clearing the tables, presenting the dessert choices, and serving coffee when, as George later described it, all hell broke loose.

"Enjoying yourself, dear?" Sophie asked her husband, sipping her coffee.

Arthur looked at Sophie and smiled. Her proud head was held high, her gray hair tastefully arranged, her dress and pearl necklace were becoming and pleasant.

"Yes, and also happy that we came."

"I'm glad too, Uncle Arthur," Sue said, finishing her coffee. "The dessert choices look incredible! Chocolate layer cake, pumpkin pie, blueberry pie, apple pie! I don't know which to choose! But I always enjoy pumpkin pie on Thanksgiving."

George agreed. "It wouldn't be Thanksgiving without pumpkin pie."

He looked around and admired the piano player, softly playing favorite tunes, creating an inviting and relaxing atmosphere in the elegant dining room. The fireplace warmed the room comfortably. George felt at peace, with his wonderful family, enjoying their company, the tranquil surroundings, the delicious meal, and the soothing piano music. He sighed contentedly.

Arthur attempted to get the attention of the waiter, who was busy with customers at another table when suddenly a high-pitched scream erupted from the dining room entrance. It was a loud, piercing scream, which caused nearly everyone to turn and see what had happened.

George also turned, not knowing what to expect. He saw a rather heavy-set, middle-aged woman, wearing a waitress uniform of black skirt and white blouse, come rushing into the dining room, screaming at the top of her lungs, wielding a large carving knife. At first, George didn't know what to make of it, thinking it was just a server, but then realized it was hardly that.

The woman ran halfway across the dining room and flung herself onto Laura, who, taken off guard, screamed in terror and fought like a wild cat to grab the deadly knife from the woman. With her youth and vigor, she managed to shake her off, but the woman then lunged for Reggie, who had risen and tried to help his stepdaughter. He also was taken off balance by the large woman. They swayed back and forth, the woman screaming in an unknown language while Reggie attempted to wrestle the knife from her.

The other diners were shocked into silence and paralysis, not believing the scene before them, until James Olson called for someone to ring the police. The host sprang into action and by this time other patrons had approached to assist Reggie, who was still struggling for the knife with the unknown woman. As the club manager arrived in the dining room, demanding to know what was happening, it soon ended. The woman froze, looked at Reggie with wide, startled eyes, clung to him momentarily, and then collapsed heavily onto the floor, the carving knife sticking out from her chest, blood oozing from the wound and onto the floor.

Screams of shock and disbelief from patrons not expecting murder at their Thanksgiving dinner, in addition to exclamations of shock, panic, horror and disbelief. A woman burst into tears and two women fainted.

Sophie, who had risen with everyone else, slowly sank back onto her chair, clutching her hand to her chest. Marjorie and Henry were too aghast to even speak. They remained in their chairs as though the shock of the scene made them incapable of movement. Mary and James had risen but returned to their seats, unsure what to do to alleviate the chaos. Several men in the dining room, including the host, tried to control the situation, while several patrons from the other dining room entered, wondering what had happened.

Reggie collapsed onto his chair, confused, shaken, clearly disturbed from the experience he just endured, his jacket and shirt saturated in blood, the dead woman practically lying at his feet. The tablecloth was pulled halfway off, knocking over plates, silverware, and coffee cups. Claire, who had also risen during the mayhem, approached Laura, and attempted to comfort her. Laura, understandably, was shaken and crying from the horrendous ordeal.

The club manager, along with several waiters, approached Reggie, still gasping for breath. Another waiter took a tablecloth and placed it over the dead woman, while another waiter ushered the patrons into the other dining room. The club manager apologized profusely to whoever could hear him that this sort of mayhem did not occur at the Capital Club and beckoned them to stay and enjoy their dinners in the other dining room.

George looked at the overturned chairs, the spilled coffee, the plates, utensils, and food scattered on the floor and then looked up at Laura and Reggie, still overcome with shock. He looked toward the windows overlooking Washington Avenue and saw a flashing red light. In no time, an ambulance pulled up in front of the Capital Club and three men entered the chaotic dining room, to remove the body. At almost the same time, police officers arrived, clearly disturbed by the scene before them. There was a police photographer who took pictures of the crime scene, including the body before the ambulance men were permitted to remove it.

Excluding Reggie, Laura, Claire, and the Drakes, the other patrons were moved to the other dining room. George wasn't sure why he, his sister and aunt and uncle needed to remain, until an officer told them that since they were the closest to the table where the incident took place, they wanted to speak with them, after questioning Reggie, Laura, and Claire.

Sophie and Arthur were still in shock at the graphic scene of violence they witnessed and were clearly overcome by the tragedy. Sue was afraid the undue stress would get the best of them at their age, and so she rose and went over to them, calming them the best she could.

George stayed in his seat, closer to Reggie's table and could hear the police officers speaking to Reggie, Laura, and Claire. It was clear that the woman wanted to inflict harm on either Reggie or Laura, or both, and Reggie, still clearly shaken, acted in self-defense. George tried to listen while the policemen spoke first to Laura and then Claire. Both denied knowing the dead woman. Laura was still quite affected by the attack.

"Did you know the woman, sir?" the young policeman turned to Reggie, notebook in hand.

"Yes, I recognized her," Reggie said weakly, surprising Laura.

"Her name, sir, if you please," the policeman continued.

By this time, the club manager returned, clearly perturbed at the events having occurred in his club. He looked at Reggie, Laura, and Claire and then his gaze went to George, Sue, Sophie, and Arthur. He again apologized for what transpired and offered to drive them home if they wished.

"Her name, sir," the policeman repeated, somewhat impatiently.

"I don't remember her name, but it was a foreign name."

"And how did you know her?"

"She was a client. It was over a year ago. She tried to become a citizen but there were problems with her paperwork. She was a refugee, from Poland, I think."

"So, she wanted to inflict harm to you or your stepdaughter because of that?"

Reggie shrugged weakly. "I couldn't say. People hold grudges. I didn't know she worked here. I had no contact with her at all."

The club manager cleared his throat and intervened. "Yes, Sofia worked here only a short time, but I can't say I knew her." He admitted he didn't know her last name, as most of the wait staff were temporary or paid under the table, something he did not like admitting to the police.

"I do remember she was a client last year," Claire spoke, supporting Reggie's statement. "But something went wrong with her paperwork, and we never heard back from her."

George frowned in consternation. He glanced at his sister, aunt and uncle who were speaking to a policeman before he in turn was questioned by another officer. They commented that they didn't know the dead woman and explained what they saw exactly as it happened. The policemen thanked them for their information, wrote down their names, address and phone number and told them they were free to leave.

The club manager tried to encourage Sophie to remain at the club, to finish dinner in the other dining room, but she politely declined. She said goodbye to Reggie, Laura, and Claire, who remained at their table, speaking to the police, while Sue went for their coats. Arthur told Reggie and Laura, they could call them at home later if they needed them.

Some Thanksgiving dinner, George thought ruefully, following his aunt, uncle, and sister as they exited the club and along Dove Street, crossing at Washington Avenue and continuing to Lancaster Street. They walked in silence as they were still too much in shock to speak.

Walking up Lancaster Street, he reflected on the murder he had just witnessed. Who'd believe the Thanksgiving holiday would turn so tragic? He shook his head. But then he wondered; was there a connection between the first murder, the murdered man found at the port and this woman who attacked Mr. Donaldson and Laura? Unless somehow, they knew each other or crossed paths somewhere?

And, George thought, hadn't he heard something about refugees before?

CHAPTER ELEVEN

Albany Times Union
November 23, 1928

A horrific scene at the Capital Club yesterday while patrons enjoyed Thanksgiving. An employee of the club, whose name has not been released, attacked diners with a carving knife, apparently with intent to inflict harm. The intended victims were Miss Laura Dupont and her stepfather, Mr. Reginald Donaldson, residents of Albany. Miss Dupont and Mr. Donaldson attempted to wrestle the knife from the perpetrator. In the struggle that ensued the perpetrator died at the scene. Stunned patrons were ushered into another dining room, while Miss Dupont and Mr. Donaldson, along with Mr. Donaldson's secretary, Mrs. Claire Palmer, were questioned extensively by police. Further investigation is continuing into this bizarre attack.

George read the article several times, before handing the newspaper to his sister. Sue took it from him, sleep still in her eyes. They were seated at the kitchen table, with Sophie and Arthur, having breakfast. Or at least attempting breakfast, George thought, as he had little appetite and was surprised, he was able to sleep last night.

It was the day after Thanksgiving and most businesses were closed for the day. Sue was on the phone with the hotel, relating to her manager the incident from yesterday. She told him she was too discombobulated to work today. The manager told her not to worry, he had read about it in the paper and heard it on the radio. Laura also had spoken with him as she was still quite distressed from her ordeal. George had already called the manager at the bank and relayed to him what had happened yesterday. The manager suggested a day off and George concurred with his idea.

Sue replaced the receiver on the candlestick phone and returned to the kitchen, where Sophie poured more coffee and placed a plate of muffins on the table. Arthur took one and buttered it, but found, like George, he had little appetite. They sat in silence for quite a while, not wishing to discuss the tragedy, yet it remained at the forefront of their minds, an unspoken nightmare they hoped would go away.

"That woman had to be insane," Sue said at last. "She attacked Laura and Mr. Donaldson. She could've attacked us, too, since our table was next to theirs!" She gave a slight shudder.

Sophie laid her hand on her arm reassuringly. "We don't know why that woman attacked Miss Dupont and Mr. Donaldson. I'm sure the police will discover the truth."

"She looked foreign," George commented. "Her screams weren't in English, either."

Arthur sipped his coffee. "I noticed that, too."

"So now there have been three murders in less than two weeks in this part of the city," George continued. "I wonder if this is a pattern. Maybe there's a mass murderer around."

"George, please," his sister said, almost pleadingly. "I don't think I want to walk around anywhere at night. It just isn't safe anymore!"

Sophie looked at Sue, unsure what to say to comfort her. She then glanced at Arthur who cleared his throat and addressed his niece and nephew.

"Most likely they'll be an inquest. And we may be called to relate what we saw."

"Mr. Donaldson said the woman was a former client," Sophie said. "Something to do with her paperwork to become a citizen. Perhaps her mind snapped upon seeing him and Miss Dupont."

Arthur agreed. "She could've been a refugee."

George sat up, rather as though a cold wave had struck him. There was that word again. Refugee. He had heard that word about someone else, too. At the moment he couldn't remember.

The doorbell rang just then. Sophie went to the hallway and upon opening the front door was glad to see Marjorie. The two friends hugged and then Sophie stepped back to allow her to enter. Taking off her coat and hat and leaving them on a hallway chair, Marjorie followed Sophie down the hall to the kitchen where she sat at an empty chair next to George.

"I wanted to stop by to see how everyone was after yesterday," she said, almost tearfully. "It was just awful! I had nightmares about it, too."

Sophie had poured coffee and placed the cup and saucer in front of her, along with the sugar bowl and the jug of cream. She declined a muffin and looked first at Sophie, then Arthur, Sue, and George. She wanted to say more but found she couldn't, as though the events from yesterday robbed her of speech.

"How is Henry taking it?" Arthur asked, breaking the silence.

"I think he's taking it better than me," Marjorie said, finding her voice. "He was listening to the news when I left to come here." She paused. "There was so much blood! Of course, as a nurse, I've seen death before."

"And practically on our doorstep," Sue put in.

George agreed. "That woman could've attacked anyone."

"Poor Mr. Donaldson," Marjorie added. "He could've been killed and Miss Dupont, too."

Everyone murmured an appropriate comment, but the conversation lapsed, and an uneasy silence pervaded the kitchen. Sue then announced she had laundry to do while Arthur commented he'd start a fire and clean the living room. Sophie and Marjorie did likewise in the kitchen, washing the breakfast dishes and cups and talking amongst themselves.

George sat alone at the kitchen table, lighting a cigarette. He reached in his robe pocket and found only two Lucky Strikes left in a rather crushed cigarette pack. He should have the fifteen cents for a new pack in his wallet. He finished his coffee and went upstairs to his room.

With the door closed, he was able to think. He removed his slippers, finished his cigarette, and butted it in the ashtray on his desk. He then lit another cigarette, rather nervously and then paced back and forth, gesticulating with the cigarette as though to emphasize his thoughts.

Two unsolved murders and now another homicide, all in less than two weeks! His thoughts returned to Thomas. And again, the incredulity concerning his younger brother and even the murder he witnessed yesterday of that foreign-looking woman. There was something wrong with the whole picture, he thought, drawing heavily on his cigarette, and pausing near the window overlooking Lancaster Street. He was deep in troubled thought.

He was closest to Mr. Donaldson's table and had a good view of what happened. He realized he had the best vantage point, as Sue's back was to their table and Aunt Sophie and Uncle Arthur were further against the wall. Sitting sideways to Mr. Donaldson's and Laura's table, he had a clear view of what transpired and what was said, too.

He turned and looked in the mirror above his dresser. He combed his rather short brown hair and felt the stubble on his face. He was about to collect his shaving things when he felt a quick chill run up his spine, seeing the picture more clearly, startling him momentarily.

His reverie was broken by an abrupt knock on the door. Sue stood in the doorway and asked if he'd like to go downtown to shop. Still barefoot and in his robe, cigarette in hand, George looked at his sister as though he had never seen her before.

"Of course, Sue," he told her, collecting himself. "Give me some time to get dressed."

Sue smiled, closing the door behind her. George then proceeded to prepare for the day. While shaving, dressing in his usual pleated slacks, comfortable shirt, and vest, he did his best to wipe away the incredulous thoughts that were penetrating his mind every minute.

When the snow first arrived, with winter over a month away, it was simply a seasonal nuisance, the inconvenience of slippery sidewalks and slushy pavements. Residents endured two weeks of colder than usual temperatures, with freezing pipes and icy drafts. The children of the city enjoyed making snowmen, throwing snowballs and frolicking in Washington Park.

In her brownstone on Dove Street, Mary Olson paid little attention to the snow. Too preoccupied with the memories of the horrendous scene at the Capital Club she and her husband witnessed yesterday, she prepared breakfast for James but afterward told him she planned to shop downtown.

"In this weather, dear?" he asked, at the kitchen table, sipping coffee.

Mary nodded, also at the table. "I need to get out of the house, James. Yesterday was hardly a happy occasion. I've never witnessed a murder before."

"Mary, what's wrong? I know you too well. Something's bothering you."

"Of course, something's bothering me. Isn't it bothering you, too? I'm talking about the murder yesterday. And all that blood. It was just terrible!"

James nodded but then hesitated. Although he was also clearly disturbed by yesterday's events, he didn't quite understand why his wife was taking it to the extreme, or at least it seemed that way to him.

"Who was that poor woman?" Mary pondered. "The paper didn't release her name."

"You think Mr. Donaldson stabbed her purposely?"

Mary was abhorred by the thought. "Of course not." She paused. "That's why I want to go shopping today, just to get out of the house."

James nodded. "If you wait, I'll go with you. I'd like to get out, too."

Mary smiled. It was agreed upon that they would shop at Whitney's and Myer's and have lunch at Keelers afterward. James's heavy wool sweater, along with corduroy slacks, helped him brave the harsh weather. Mary decided a warm dress, with her usual chain of pearls, lipstick and rouge were best for her. Not one for excessive make-up, she thought it might help to cheer her up.

In no time, they locked the front door, walked over to Lark Street to catch the trolley and were soon downtown at the corner of State Street and South Pearl Street. They crossed at the light and walked up North Pearl Street until they came to Whitney's Department Store. They were almost in front of the store, pedestrians brushing past them when Mary suddenly stopped in her tracks. Realizing his wife was not with him, James turned and saw her standing practically in the middle of the sidewalk, apparently deep in thought, blocking the way of egress of shoppers, who walked around her rather than colliding with her.

"Mary let's go in," James said, coming up to her. "It's freezing outside here." He paused. "Don't you want to do some shopping? Looks like there are some great sales today."

Mary looked up at her husband, as though she had no cognizance of where she was or who was speaking to her. After a moment, she blinked and smiled wanly at James. Bundling the fur collar of her coat tighter around her neck and pulling her cloche hat lower on her head, she walked the short distance to Whitney's and joined James in entering the large department store.

As she looked around at the festive holiday decorations and the throng of shoppers, Mary's mind was still disturbed over images from yesterday, as though in conflict over what she saw and what she believed actually occurred.

The inquest on the dead woman was held the following Wednesday. The Thanksgiving weekend was now over, children were back in school, and people returned to work. Life went on as normal.

Little normality, however, was occurring in the lives of Reginald Donaldson and Laura Dupont. In the days since the bizarre attack, there had been a thorough investigation by the police, who identified the woman as Sofia Bartosz, a Polish refugee. Reggie and Laura had been brought to police headquarters and questioned extensively but not charged and were released, pending further investigation.

When this information was recorded by the press, in the newspaper and on the radio, it mentioned the homicide victim at the Port of Albany, just a week and a half earlier, by the name of Szymon Bartosz. While no other relatives of either victim were located in Albany or the surrounding area, it was speculated that Sofia Bartosz was the mother of Szymon Bartosz, also a refugee, although further verification of this conjecture was continuing.

Reggie sat in the living room, listening to the updates on the murder on the radio, a cold cup of coffee beside him on the end table. The curtains were drawn and although the sun was out, little of that light made its way into the room. Laura also was there, sipping coffee, reading the morning paper, and listening to the news. Claire had called and mentioned she was contacted to give testimony at the inquest as she was seated at their table and a witness. Reggie soothed her as best he could over the phone as he could tell Claire, like Laura, was still quite shaken from the tragedy. He told her he and Laura would see her at the medical examiner's office soon.

Reggie had canceled all appointments and left Mary in charge of the office for the week. Laura had also called the Ten Eyck Hotel and spoke with Sue. She told her she was to give evidence at the inquest and was still too disturbed by the events from Thanksgiving to work.

Sue told her she'd relay the message to their manager and wished her well. Reggie and Laura soon were on their way by taxi to the coroner's office to attend the inquest.

At the Albany County Medical Examiner's office, the inquest was solemn and dignified. The newspapers did not magnify it to sound improper or startling, much to Reggie's relief.

Reggie and Laura settled into chairs, and both felt as though they were in a court of law and about to receive a sentence. Reggie took a quick look around and thankfully did not see anyone he knew. He straightened in his chair and looked at the man who was about to speak.

The inquest began with the appropriate identification of the body by a Mr. Lewis, who had worked with refugee families in Albany for many years. He was a tired appearing middle-aged man whose age was probably late forties but who looked more of sixty.

Sofia Bartosz, he told the coroner and the inquest committee had come to the United States from Poland with her son, seeking a better life. She settled in Utica, where she lived for several years with her younger sister and worked odd jobs. From her own admission, she also was mistreated while in Utica and after so many years, came to Albany to make a new start. The woman, in his opinion, had emotional difficulties and mental disturbances.

Mr. Lewis added that Sofia Bartosz was a difficult refugee and did not appreciate anything that was done to assist her and her son. Her knowledge of English had improved but she had much hardship while adapting to her new life in Albany. She had been employed as wait staff and dishwasher at the Capital Club just three months ago. He also stated that he believed the man whose body was discovered on November eleventh was her son.

The coroner mentioned that conjecture by a witness was not admissible during the proceeding but stated that further investigation was ongoing regarding the murder of Szymon Bartosz, the man found at the Port of Albany.

Mr. Rinehart, the general manager of the Capital Club, was called next. He was a tall, thin middle-aged man with a curt manner, who was clearly perturbed at having to give evidence at an inquest. He commented that Sofia Bartosz had been in his employ for less than three months. He had had little contact with her, but she seemed suspicious and not very trustworthy. While a decent worker, he considered dismissing her but with the Thanksgiving holiday, the club would be full, so he decided to keep her on staff to assist that day. He offered nothing further to help in the proceeding.

Reggie was soon called to testify. Upon taking the stand, he looked so drawn and ashen that Laura thought he would faint. She listened carefully to the testimony he was about to give.

"It was just so terrible, and it happened so fast. She ran into the dining room, although I didn't see her as I was seated with my back to the entrance. My stepdaughter, Laura, saw her wielding a knife and when she realized she wanted to attack her, she managed to fight her off. But then, the woman attacked me. I tried to wrestle the knife from her, but it struck her in the chest during the struggle." He paused. "I thought this woman was going to kill us." He seemed hesitant to continue.

The coroner, a patient man in his mid-fifties with thinning hair and a rather serious manner, asked Reggie if he deliberately stabbed the woman.

"No, of course not."

"Did you know the victim, Mr. Donaldson?"

Reggie reluctantly admitted that Sofia Bartosz was a former client. "She wanted to become an American citizen, but there were problems with her paperwork. Her limited English was also a hindrance. While in my office, she cursed repeatedly in Polish and told me and my staff she'd get revenge on me and all Americans. I believe her sentiments were anti-American to the extreme."

The coroner thanked Reggie and then called Laura to the stand. Upon leaving the bench and walking back to his seat, his eyes met Laura's. His look made her uneasy, as though the apprehension he felt was somehow contributing to her own inner turmoil and trepidation. Laura, looking pretty as always in her pristine black dress with white pearls, smiled shortly and turned to the coroner.

The coroner asked her if she had ever seen the victim before or had any contact with her, like her step-fathered admitted.

"No, not at all. I never saw her before in my life. I don't have any contact with refugees or people like that." Her tone implied that refugees were people without status or class.

In answering more questions put by the coroner, Laura explained how she and her stepfather looked forward to Thanksgiving dinner at the Capital Club and in no way perceived any trouble. "It was quite relaxing," she said tearfully, "until that woman came rushing in with the knife. She tried to kill us right there in the dining room!"

"You feel certain that the victim was intending on harming you and your stepfather?'

Laura was adamant. "Yes, I do indeed. Daddy couldn't see her enter, but I did, and she looked crazy. Her face was contorted and full of rage. She tried first to kill me than Daddy. I don't understand Polish, but she was screaming at the top of her lungs."

The coroner thanked Laura and dismissed her. After reaching the chair next to Reggie, Laura almost collapsed from weariness and put her head on his left shoulder. Reggie attempted to comfort her when the coroner suddenly called another name to the stand.

"Mrs. Claire Palmer, please."

Reggie and Laura both turned to see Claire make her way to take the chair in front. She nodded briefly to Reggie and Laura and fixed her eyes firmly on the coroner. He noted her fine appearance, her appealing bobbed hair, pretty brown eyes, and comfortable beige dress, but then coughed slightly and began the questioning.

"Do you concur as to what Miss Dupont and Mr. Donaldson have told us, Mrs. Palmer? Have you anything to add to help in this investigation?"

"I do agree with Miss Dupont and Mr. Donaldson as I was seated at their table and a witness to what happened. The woman rushed into the dining room, with a large carving knife, with the intent to inflict harm. She appeared distraught and enraged."

"Were you acquainted with her?"

"She was a client once of Mr. Donaldson's, last year I believe, but she never paid her bill and there was some trouble with her paperwork. She was a most difficult client."

"Were you acquainted with the young man who was found at the Port of Albany on November eleventh?"

"No, I didn't know him."

"What did you do when the woman attacked Miss Dupont?'

"I didn't realize what happened until Miss Dupont started to scream. I was shocked, of course. It all happened so fast."

The coroner nodded. "Did you see the knife enter the victim, Mrs. Palmer?"

Claire squirmed a little in the chair. "Well, yes, I did, and it was a horrific scene."

"Would you explain what you saw, please?"

Claire hesitated. "Well, after Miss Dupont wrestled her away from her, the woman flung herself at Mr. Donaldson, with the carving knife raised, in an attempt to kill him."

"And had she tried to kill Miss Dupont also?"

"Yes, but Miss Dupont fought hard and tried to retrieve the knife. She then turned to Mr. Donaldson, who had risen to help his step-daughter when she flung herself at him."

"And how did the knife enter her body, Mrs. Palmer?"

"It struck the woman in the chest. She clung to it and was attempting to stab Mr. Donaldson. They struggled and it struck her instead."

"Did you think possibly that she intended to harm someone else, other than Mr. Donaldson or Miss Dupont? That she mistook them for her real targets?"

Claire looked at him carefully. "I really don't know. She may have mistaken Mr. Donaldson and Miss Dupont for people she may have had a grudge against."

"Do you remember when Sofia Bartosz was in Mr. Donaldson's office, threatening him?"

"Yes, I remember quite well. It was only a year or so ago. She was outraged because her citizenship would take much longer than she anticipated. She blamed Mr. Donaldson and threatened him. I do believe she meant what she said."

"Thank you, Mrs. Palmer. That will be all."

Claire left the stand and sat in the back, near the wall and away from Reggie and Laura. There was little more evidence to give. The coroner administered that Sofia Bartosz died as a result of a struggle with a knife and that Mr. Donaldson acted in clear self-defense, and as such was exonerated from all blame. Other than perceptions from Reggie, Laura and Claire, there was no more evidence to show what could have been the state of the dead woman's mind. She might have also borne a grudge against Mr. Donaldson, although the exact motive could not be determined except for the victim being of a deranged mind. Quite possibly she may have mistaken Mr. Donaldson and Miss Dupont for others she wished to harm, although so far, the police in their questioning of people present had not identified anyone at the club who was acquainted with the woman. According to her own story as verified by Mr. Lewis, the woman suffered great bereavement in her own country which might have affected her deeply. The murder of her supposed son at the port also could have added to her unbalanced nature.

The members of the committee concurred with the coroner. Mr. Reginald Donaldson and Miss Laura Dupont were exonerated from all blame in the death of Mrs. Sofia Bartosz.

The next day, Thursday, George was busy at the bank as usual. He had plans to meet Sue for lunch at the hotel but called her to cancel. He didn't feel much going out today, he'd grab a sandwich later at a deli nearby on North Pearl Street. He glanced at the tall windows, saw intermittent snowflakes, and felt the icy air when customers entered through the revolving doors. It had turned sharply colder than the previous day and the temperatures hovered near freezing and were expected to drop into the teens overnight.

The weather was the least of George's concerns at the moment. Although he concentrated on his work in assisting customers, he was too confused and troubled over the three murders that occurred over the last several weeks to really concentrate. As he finished helping a woman with a new savings account, he saw James Olson in the lobby. James also saw him and walked over to him.

THE CONSEQUENCES OF MURDER

"George, it's good to see you," James said pleasantly, shaking hands with George as he rose to greet him. James looked professional, wearing a business suit underneath his stylish Oxford coat.

"Same here, Mr. Olson," George replied and smiled. "Can I help with anything?"

"No, I'm here to make a withdrawal. I forgot that you worked here. You've got quite a position." His tone was sincere, and George was rather flattered by his remarks.

"Well, I worked my way up. How's everything at the D & H company?"

James commented that the railroad business was busy as usual, with more people taking trains like never before. He mentioned how the car industry was booming too and eventually may overtake the railroads, but he highly doubted it.

"The train is the way of the future," he said, rather awkwardly, wondering where this conversation was heading.

"Mr. Olson, what do you think happened at the Capital Club last Thursday?"

James hesitated. He looked at George carefully and couldn't help feeling rather sorry for the young man. With his brother's murder, his aunt and uncle discovering the murdered man at the port, and now the murder at the Capital Club, it had to be overwhelming for him and, he imagined, his sister. James pulled the collar of his Oxford coat closer, and his Fedora hat a little lower on his head, to stall for time in answering.

"Well, I really don't know, George. Mr. Donaldson and Miss Dupont were attacked by that woman, who had to be insane. She could've attacked anyone in the dining room. We couldn't see much from our table, but the woman collapsed and died."

George wasn't easily put off, however kindly the recommendation. "I know, Mr. Olson, but I saw it too and am still confused by it. It seemed like Laura or Mr. Donaldson wanted to stab her instead of the other way around!"

James looked at him in shocked silence. "What do you mean?"

George lit a cigarette, exhaled a fine ray of smoke, and continued. "In the struggle with Mr. Donaldson, that woman died. Of course, it was a wild struggle, but first, it seemed like Laura wanted to stab her and then Mr. Donaldson actually did stab her!"

"Not purposely, George," James told him, rather aghast at the idea.

"But from my viewpoint, it seemed like it. I realized he was only protecting himself and Laura, of course." He hesitated. "The police haven't any new clues about Thomas."

"Murder investigations take time," James said, trying to console him. "They'll let you know once they have more information." He paused. "I should go now, George. it was good to see you again and please tell your aunt and uncle that Mrs. Olson and I will stop by some time soon."

George rose from his desk chair and shook hands again with James and watched him leave the bank, rather curiously, as though Mr. Olson knew something he was reluctant to mention.

After eating a quick lunch at a nearby deli, George had no sooner returned and sat at his desk, as multiple new clients requested his assistance in conducting diverse transactions, many of which were quite long in completing. The four o'clock hour was almost upon them, much to his relief, when he looked up from his work and noticed Mary Olson waiting in line for a teller. Nothing unusual with that, as the Olsons had accounts here and he'd seen her before. Upon completing her business, she noticed George and smiled.

"Hello, George," she said pleasantly, looking every bit the flapper with her stylish cloche hat. Looking at her carefully, George didn't think Mrs. Olson the flapper type but then realized so many women of all ages were flappers. And they looked great, too, George noted with approval.

"Hello, Mrs. Olson. It's funny seeing you here. Your husband was in the bank a few hours ago. It was nice to chat with him. I hadn't seen him in a while."

Mary's face turned a sudden red, as though she had been afflicted with extremely disturbing thoughts. She was looking at him with a startled expression.

"My husband was here, in the bank?" She made it seem like his going to a bank was something he'd never done before. "Of course, we have accounts here and he did mention he needed extra cash for the holidays." She tried to brush it off. "How are you doing, George? My deepest sympathy on the death of Thomas."

George thanked her and then mentioned he was managing well as was his sister. Small talk ensued for the next few moments until Mary mentioned that he, Sue and his aunt and uncle should stop over some evening before the holidays. Perhaps for coffee and cake, she suggested.

"I think we all need a little respite," Mary lamented. "With last Thursday's unpleasantness at the Capital Club…" She stopped talking and let her sentence hang in mid-air. She looked at George as though she wanted to tell him something. George, on the other hand, asked what she thought of the ordeal from last week.

"We spoke with the police earlier this week. All I saw was the woman falling to the ground. But then, your table was closer than ours. You must have seen more."

"I saw the whole thing," George admitted. "Almost as though…"

At that moment, the bank guard announced the bank was soon closing. Mary gave a last smile and wished George well. She drew the fur collar on her coat closer and her fashionable cloche hat lower on her head, to brace herself for the hostile weather. She scurried off to the entrance along with several other customers, just as the guard was ready to lock the revolving door.

As the assistant manager, George, like most of his associates, worked until the five o'clock hour, completing business. When the time came for his departure, he put on his plaid Mackinaw jacket, along with his cap, bid goodbye to a few coworkers and made his way to the lobby. Once there, he was jostled by office workers erupting out of the elevators on their way out. Before leaving, he stopped to look at the building directory, posted on the wall behind a frame of glass, between the two elevators.

Albany's newest office building for 1927, the Home Savings Bank had many tenants, lawyers, bank offices, stockbrokers. He looked at the various names and firms and then at the titles with the letter S. He nodded in satisfaction. He found the listing he was looking for.

CHAPTER TWELVE

S loane Sheppard paused in front of the mirror in the hallway of his apartment on Madison Avenue, tying the knot on his tie, adjusting it several times as he was never really good at that sort of thing. Satisfied with a less than perfect knot, he put on his vest and jacket, slicked back his black hair, and after putting on his trench coat and hat, headed for the door and to the sidewalk to wait for the trolley. He took the morning paper as he never had enough time to read it until he got to his office.

A harsh wind greeted Sloane as he walked out of the apartment building. Fortunately, a trolley soon approached and Sloane eagerly boarded. It wasn't long before it arrived downtown. He exited on State Street and made his way in the cold amongst the crowds to the Home Savings Bank building where his office was located on the tenth floor.

"Good morning, Mr. Sheppard," said Andrew, the elevator attendant, an amiable man in his seventies. "Glad it's Friday, aren't you?" He didn't need to ask Sloane what floor he wanted. Several other people joined the elevator before Andrew closed the gate and the lift shot upward.

It finally arrived at the tenth floor and Sloane was the only person to get off. Andrew opened the gate and Sloane exited. Upon arriving at his office, the key in the lock, the door open, he turned on the lights, including the banker's lamp on his desk, hung his coat and hat on the rack behind the door and then settled himself at his desk to start his workday. As was his custom, he unfolded the *Albany Times Union*, noting that it was the last day of November, while reviewing his calendar, to verify his appointments scheduled for today.

Sloane Sheppard was a well-known and well-respected private investigator who had worked in Albany for over ten years. His cases varied greatly: divorces, murders, robberies, kidnappings. In such a short time in the profession, Sloane had seen much criminal activity and helped city police in tracking down numerous criminals and gang activity. He also worked with individuals for more personal matters, usually involving family members.

A knock came on his door and without looking up, Sloane knew it was Lois, the secretary from the law firm down the hall, bringing him a cup of coffee and today a fresh bagel.

"Good morning, Mr. Sheppard," she said pleasantly, depositing the coffee and bagel on his desk. Lois was an efficient secretary in her mid-thirties with pretty blue eyes and an appealing smile. She cared for the tenants on the tenth floor as though she was a den mother and Sloane admitted to himself that he didn't mind it at all.

"I still say you need a secretary, Mr. Sheppard," Lois continued

"Well, thank you, Lois, that's kind of you," Sloane said gratefully, sipping the coffee. "But I run a one-man operation, so I do it all myself. Besides, this office isn't big enough for two people."

Lois gave a sardonic smile to the handsome man seated at the desk. If she wasn't married with two kids, she'd consider him fair game. She admired his strong features, slicked black hair, his penetrating brown eyes. Always well-groomed, with a fine dress shirt, vest, and tie, his clothes were impeccable. She figured he stood about six feet tall, maybe taller. Lois wondered how many women looked at him more than once.

She knew she certainly did. And how old was he anyway? Couldn't be older than thirty-eight or so, just a few years older than herself.

"Looks like an early winter," she commented, gazing out the window behind Sloane that gave out onto North Pearl Street. "Tomorrow's December first already! It'll be Christmas soon."

"Let's not rush the season, Lois," Sloane said with a smile.

Lois smiled, closed his office door, and returned to the law firm where she worked, leaving Sloane to begin his daily routine.

He opened a few files, wrote notes on cases he recently completed, made calls to his contacts at the Albany Police and noted an appointment he had at Albany City Hall for later in the day. He spoke at length with several clients on the telephone; a woman seeking grounds to divorce her third husband and another woman whose son was arrested for shoplifting. Amid this activity, he stopped to drink his coffee, grimacing slightly as it had gotten cold. Noticing it was almost noontime, he finally had the chance to unfold the newspaper and read the latest headlines, when someone knocked on the door.

"It's open," he called, putting the newspaper aside and waiting for whoever was at the other side to enter. When no one came in, he got up from his desk chair and opened the door himself.

"Oh, hello, Mr. Sheppard?"

A young man, no more than twenty-five, stood in the doorway. Sloane figured he was a salesman, as he looked respectable enough, rather dapper in a shirt, tie, vest, and pleated pants. He wasn't tall but had a commanding presence. He referred to Sloane by name, so he had no other choice but to acknowledge his greeting.

"Can I help you with something?"

"My name is George Latimer." He anxiously twisted his cap and clutched his plaid jacket. "I realize I don't have an appointment, but I would like to speak to you." He paused. "It's really important."

"Well, it's almost noontime," Sloane told him. "Why don't you call me tomorrow morning and make an appointment? I'm free tomorrow afternoon."

"No, it can't wait," George said, his voice rising. "I must speak to you before it's too late."

Sloane looked at him carefully. This young man was disturbed about something. Of course, from long practice, Sloane knew it could be just about anything but usually something not worth his time. But he decided to stand aside to allow George to enter his office. He motioned him to a metal chair in front of his desk.

"How can I help you, Mr. Latimer?" Sloane asked as he sat at his desk chair. He moved the newspaper and a few files aside to give his attention to George.

"I know you're a private investigator. I read about the Cary murder case earlier this year."

Sloane nodded and asked him to continue.

"It's about my brother, Thomas. You may have read about his murder in the paper or heard it on the radio."

"Yes, I've read about it in the paper," Sloane commented.

"I'd like you to investigate, Mr. Sheppard." He hesitated, unsure how to continue. "My brother was murdered, followed by another man at the port that my aunt and uncle discovered and then a strange woman tried to kill Mr. Donaldson and Laura at the Capital Club on Thanksgiving! It's been too much for us. I'm concerned for Aunt Sophie, Uncle Arthur and my younger sister, Sue."

Sloane coughed slightly and asked George to start at the beginning. He realized he was upset and found it difficult to formulate words to convey what exactly happened.

George told Sloane about his brother Thomas, his lifestyle, his multiple arrests and then his murder three weeks ago, stabbed outside a speakeasy on South Pearl Street. He mentioned how his aunt and uncle discovered the body of a man at the Port of Albany, whose name was Szymon Bartosz. And he ended his narrative with the events of Thanksgiving Day at the Capital Club, the murder he, his sister, aunt, and uncle, as well as a dining room full of people, witnessed. He added Sofia Bartosz may have been Szymon Bartosz's mother, but the news didn't confirm that information yet.

George sighed and took a breath, somewhat relieved he had gotten it all out in the open. He looked at Sloane with wide eyes, wondering what he was thinking or if he could help in any way.

Sloane moved the candlestick phone on his desk to the right, picked up a paperweight and placed it on top of a pile of papers and shifted slightly in his chair. It would be hard not to believe him, he thought, looking up at George and noticing again the anxious expression, the eagerness to see justice done.

Sloane offered George a cigarette. He lit his and then one for himself leaned back on his chair and asked George about himself. Where did he work, his home life, did he frequent dance halls and speakeasies?

George mentioned that his Aunt Sophie was their only living relative, his father's sister, so he, his sister and brother came to Albany to live with her and their Uncle Arthur after their parents died. He mentioned how their father died in the war and their mother died during the flu pandemic ten years ago, while still in Utica.

He told Sloane he worked in this building, at the Home Savings Bank as an assistant manager. He mentioned he was a graduate of Union College and how he and his younger sister, Susan, also a Union College graduate, lived with their aunt and uncle on Lancaster Street in a comfortable home, convenient to downtown and to work. He told Sloane his sister worked across the street at the Ten Eyck Hotel, and they would usually take the same trolley in the morning and in the evening, too.

"Aunt Sophie and Uncle Arthur don't like us to travel alone," he added. "With so much crime and the gangsters in this city, it's kind of dangerous." He paused. "I don't go to dance halls and speakeasies. I've been to dances, with my sister and we've gotten to know people there. And I stay connected with friends from college, including girlfriends."

"I don't see what you want me to do," Sloane said, rather bluntly. "The police are investigating the three murders." He paused, trying to find the right words to continue. "I've read about them in the paper. The police are competent and will get at the truth soon."

"But you don't understand," George pleaded, drawing heavily on his cigarette. "You've got to help me, Mr. Sheppard." His voice verged on slight hysteria. Before Sloane could say anything, George took out from his jacket pocket several photos. He handed them to Sloane across the desk.

"Nice looking family," Sloane commented, looking at each photo. Photos of George, Sue, Sophie, and Arthur, having dinner, enjoying a picnic in Washington Park and shopping downtown. Another photo was of the family shoveling snow in front of their house. And still another was taken in the living room before the fireplace, dated Christmas 1927, just one year ago.

"I'm still not clear what you want me to do," he finally said, returning the photos to him. "And may I call you George?"

George smiled wanly. "Yes, that's fine. And I'd prefer to call you Mr. Sheppard."

Sloane finished his cigarette. "Of course." He thought that spoke well of George Latimer. A good upbringing, respectful, courteous, polite. Unlike so many of the young people today, who frequented speakeasies and lived a decadent lifestyle. "But please answer my question. What can I do for you?"

George swallowed hard. "I don't believe my brother is dead."

As a private investigator, Sloane was used to the whims and fancies of clients. He was not prepared for George to relate to him his suspicions about his brother's death. Sloane looked at him rather dubiously and waited for him to continue.

"I don't believe Thomas is dead. And I believe there's more to it than that."

"What proof do you have? Records are kept and can easily be verified."

"I just showed you the proof," George said, rather irritably. "Look at the pictures again." He handed them back to Sloane who glanced at them again, not sure what he was looking for. "Do you see the differences?"

"Differences?" Sloane asked.

George leaned closer to Sloane's desk. "Look at this picture. Don't brother and sisters have similar traits? Sue and I are practically twins! We look so much alike. But look at Thomas."

Sloane looked carefully at the pictures and saw for himself the differences, now that his attention was focused more closely on the young man in question. George and his sister were fairer skinned, with lighter features, including eyes and hair color. Sloane noted their smiles and facial features, and expressions were quite similar. The other young man in the picture was of a somewhat darker complexion, with no apparent distinguishable traits to those of George and Sue. His hair was darker, almost black and his eyes were a dark brown. Sloane looked closely at the photos, noting resemblances between George, his sister and even their aunt, but not seeing much of a likeness in the other young man.

"So, what you are saying, George?" Sloane handed him back the pictures and looked him squarely in the eyes. "Have you discussed this with your sister and aunt and uncle?"

George shook his head. "I haven't discussed anything with them because I don't think they'd believe me. I don't think that he was our brother. I think he was an impostor."

Sloane looked at him wondering what he could do for this young man. He had resolved impostor cases before, many occurred before the war and a few during the conflict. Impersonation could be difficult to prove. He looked at George and gave him his best advice.

"I think it best to speak to your aunt and uncle first," he told him. "Wouldn't they know more about your younger brother?"

George told Sloane how he and his brother and sister were born and raised in Utica and spent their childhood there, before moving to Albany to live with their aunt and uncle ten years ago.

"So, you and your brother and sister have been living with your aunt and uncle since that time?" Sloane asked him. "And you've just noticed differences in your younger brother?"

George shook his head. "No, it was as a teenager that I started looking at Thomas differently and realizing we had none of the same characteristics. I never said anything to Sue or Aunt Sophie or Uncle Arthur."

"Why don't you speak to them this evening? That's my best recommendation."

"Mr. Sheppard, would *you* please speak to them?" His voice was almost pleading. "If they hear it from you, they'll take it seriously." He hesitated. "If it's a question of money, I have enough to pay you for your services."

Sloane paused, lit another cigarette, and shuffled a few papers. The candlestick phone rang suddenly. He picked up the receiver, spoke briefly to a client, made a few notes on a pad, and ended the call, not wishing to divulge information in front of George for purposes of confidentiality. He then looked at his desk calendar and noted his appointment at city hall this afternoon. He looked up at George and asked him their address on Lancaster Street.

"Is about six-thirty a good time, George?"

"That's fine, Mr. Sheppard. I'll tell Aunt Sophie and Uncle Arthur to expect you." He smiled gratefully, got up and shook hands with Sloane. "Thank you, Mr. Sheppard. I really do appreciate it."

Sloane thanked him for stopping by then opened the office door and watched George walk to the elevators, a highly intelligent and determined young man. He realized George Latimer was firm, resolute, and determined to uncover the mystery, if indeed one existed, about the identity of Thomas Latimer.

How George managed to get through the rest of the day he never knew. His concentration at work was minimal and he found himself looking at his watch, impatiently waiting for the five o'clock hour. When it finally came, he grabbed his jacket and cap and hastily left the bank. He joined the crowds on the sidewalk and crossed at the light to wait for Sue.

Sue came out of the hotel on time, looking rather cheerful but that cheerfulness disappeared upon seeing her brother. George was uncommunicative, deep in thought, his mind turning over things he discussed with Mr. Sheppard earlier in the day. Dodging the usual crowds on North Pearl Street, they walked to the trolley stop and waited.

As they sat in the trolley, with a sizeable crowd, Sue noticed the anxious state apparent in her brother. Usually, he asked her about her day, but George remained tight-lipped and morose.

Given the time of day, the trolley was slowly snaking along Washington Avenue, gaining more passengers in front of city hall, the state capital, the state library, and Harmanus Bleecker Hall. As it turned left onto Lark Street, Sue turned to George and asked him what was on his mind.

They got off at the corner of Lark and Lancaster and waited for traffic to pass, George still sullen and incommunicative. Walking amidst snow showers, George finally answered her question.

"I spoke to a private investigator today," he said, seeing his breath in the chilly air. "He's coming to see us this evening."

Sue fumbled for words. "A private investigator? Are you serious?" She sighed deeply, exhaling a rather long frosty breath. Without giving George time to answer, she continued. "Have you mentioned this to Aunt Sophie and Uncle Arthur? What will they think? And what about *Amos n' Andy*? We always listen to *Amos n' Andy* on Friday nights. It's your favorite program! Aunt Sophie and Uncle Arthur enjoy it, too."

They finally arrived at the Lancaster Street house. George turned to face his sister.

"We can miss *Amos n' Andy* tonight. I'll explain it to Aunt Sophie and Uncle Arthur."

He put his key in the lock and was soon greeted with the pleasant aroma of Sophie's cooking and Arthur meeting them in the hallway, smiling and pleased to see them. He took their jackets and ushered them into the living room, where the fireplace blazed brilliantly. Arthur went to the radio console and lowered it, as he had a jazz station turned up rather loudly, creating an upbeat atmosphere.

"You like Duke Ellington, Ethel Waters and Bessie Smith," George said to his uncle, sitting on the couch and stretching his legs. "They're the bee's knees to be sure."

Arthur smiled, looking every bit his eighty years, but feeling rejuvenated in the company of his young nephew and niece. "I love the jazz music of today."

George agreed. "Maybe there's another dance soon at Harmanus Bleecker Hall. I'll stop there this weekend to take a look."

"Looking forward to *Amos n' Andy* tonight?" Arthur asked his nephew.

George cast a quick glance at his sister, as she sat in the chair opposite from the couch. He was about to tell his uncle of Sloane's visit when Sophie entered at that moment.

"Hello, dears," she smiled at her nephew and niece. "I've made meatloaf and sweet potatoes and for dessert, chocolate cake." She paused, noticing a certain tension she couldn't quite determine. "You like my chocolate cake, George. You always have seconds."

"Thank you, Aunt Sophie," George said with a tired smile.

"Your meatloaf is the best," Sue added.

"Thank you, dear. I've invited the Olmsteads and the Olsons for coffee and cake later. And we can all listen to *Amos n' Andy*, too."

"Aunt Sophie, you should know…," George started but then was deterred from finishing by the sharp ringing of the phone. Sophie quickly went to the hallway to answer it.

"Why don't we sit at the table and get ready for dinner?" Arthur suggested.

Mechanically, as though rehearsing a stage play, George, Sue, and Arthur gathered in the kitchen, taking their respective places at the table. Sophie returned, beaming that it was Marjorie who called. She promised to bring homemade muffins and sugar cookies this evening.

While serving the delicious dinner, Sophie again noticed some sort of undercurrent between the two young people, although she could not determine what it was about. Arthur also noticed the same slight tension. Toward the meal's conclusion and to George's chagrin, Sue turned to her aunt and after finishing her last piece of meatloaf, told her that George had spoken to a private investigator today and that he was coming to the house this evening.

If looks could kill, George thought his sister would be dead at once. Why didn't she wait for him to mention it at the right moment? Certainly not at the dinner table. At times, his sister infuriated him. And he wanted to tell them himself since he initiated it.

"A private investigator, George?" Arthur said, looking at his nephew quite intently. "The police are already investigating Thomas's death."

Sophie agreed. "Why didn't you consult with us first?"

"I didn't think you'd want to hear it," George replied, rather meekly. "His name is Mr. Sloane Sheppard. He works in the Home Savings Bank building, where I work."

"Personally, I think it's a waste," Sue said, helping to clear the dishes and set the dessert plates. "What could he possibly ask us that the police haven't already?"

Before George could respond, the doorbell rang. He noticed it wasn't six-thirty yet unless Mr. Sheppard was in the habit of arriving early to appointments. Arthur got up from the table and went to the hallway. From the kitchen, George, Sue, and Sophie could hear him chatting amicably with the Olmsteads, who arrived at the same time as the Olsons. They heard him welcoming their guests inside and down the hallway to the kitchen.

"Hello everyone," Marjorie said pleasantly, carrying a basket. She deposited the contents of it on the kitchen table, homemade muffins, and sugar cookies. She smiled at Sophie, George, and Sue.

"Thank you, Marjorie," Sophie said sincerely. She motioned for her to sit, while Mary also joined them at the kitchen table. Sophie, George, and Sue greeted the Olsons and Mr. Olmstead with a warm greeting, then Arthur ushered James and Henry into the living room, leaving Mary and Marjorie with Sophie, George, and Sue.

"What a charming home," Mary said, looking around at the cozy kitchen. "And you're such a good cook, Sophie! I should take lessons from you."

"Thank you, Mary dear," Sophie said and smiled wanly.

Mary also smiled but could tell there was something wrong. Of course, with the murder at the Capital Club and the two other murders, she was impressed Sophie was taking it all so well, wondering how she could carry on, especially at her age.

George and Sue continued sitting at the table, silently drinking coffee, and eating the chocolate cake. Sophie got up and poured coffee for Marjorie and Mary and then returned to her seat at the head of the table.

"I spoke to a private investigator today," George said, looking at Mary and Marjorie.

He knew Mrs. Olmstead better than he did Mrs. Olson, but they were both pleasant enough. Mrs. Olson was in a long blue dress with pearls, looking as she did when George saw her at the bank, rather like a flapper but without much make-up. Mrs. Olmstead was like a grandmother to him and Sue; very motherly, nurturing and looking well for her age, in a gray dress with white lace at the neckline. He thought she was somewhere in her mid-seventies, close to Aunt Sophie's age.

"A private investigator?" Mary asked, sipping her coffee while biting into a sugar cookie.

George nodded. "He should be here soon. His name is Mr. Sloane Sheppard."

"Mr. Sheppard," Marjorie mused, stirring her coffee. "I've read about him in the papers."

George nodded. "He's solved a lot of cases here in Albany."

"I didn't know about this," Sophie said, casting a quick glance at her nephew. "So, I'm afraid you and your husbands will be here when he arrives." She looked at Mary and Marjorie, feeling rather embarrassed that they would not especially relish meeting much less listening to a private detective.

Arthur stood in the doorway and told his wife that Henry and James would like coffee. She started to rise but he had already entered the kitchen, poured two cups of coffee, placed them on a tray, along with the sugar bowl and a jug of cream. He also added a few muffins and sugar cookies on a plate.

"I told them about Mr. Sheppard coming here this evening," he mentioned as he was about to leave the kitchen and rejoin them in the living room.

"Marjorie and Mary know also," his wife commented, making it sound as though it was the worst scenario possible for their invited guests.

"Don't worry, dear," Marjorie told her. She smiled, looking at George and Sue. "You did the right thing, George. The police don't have more leads yet. Of course, that woman who went berserk at the Capital Club…" She let her sentence hang in mid-air as her smiling face turned into a deep frown.

"Marjorie is right, George," Mary said encouragingly. "He may uncover leads the police haven't been able to find." She paused, putting the coffee cup to her lips. She looked around the table at Marjorie, Sophie, George, and Sue and hesitated before speaking again. "Do you think, George, the murder we witnessed at the Capital Club is related to the death of Thomas?"

George also had his coffee cup to his lips. Setting it down on the table, he looked at Mary Olson with interest. "I don't really know, Mrs. Olson. There've been three murders in such a short period." He paused. "Somebody has to find out what's happening. The police just drag their feet and get nowhere."

At that moment, the doorbell rang. George looked at the wall clock and saw it was exactly six-thirty. Right on time, he thought, rising to answer the door. Sophie started to get up, but George told her it'd be better if he answered it, since he had already met Mr. Sheppard.

By this time, the gentlemen in the living room were also interested but skeptical of George's decision to inquire into a private investigator. Like Arthur, they were anticipating his arrival and decided to join George in the hallway.

Upon his opening the front door, they saw a well-dressed man, no older than the late thirties, in an Oxford coat and wearing a Fedora hat, very professional-looking, with a rather rugged but handsome face. George welcomed him and was surprised that his uncle, Mr. Olson, and Mr. Olmstead were there as he hadn't heard them enter the hallway. He introduced Mr. Sloane Sheppard to his uncle Arthur, and to Mr. James Olson and Mr. Henry Olmstead, then took his hat and coat.

"Please come in, Mr. Sheppard," Arthur said, inviting him into the living room.

Sloane followed Arthur and George down the hall and to the living room on the right. He looked around favorably; it was a most comfortable place, with deep armchairs, a fashionable sofa and a fireplace that helped to take the chill out of the air. A rather large radio console between the two front windows was on playing jazz music in the background. Arthur went over to it and turned it off, then introduced Sloane to James and Henry, who shook hands with them. George sat on the couch, alongside Sloane.

"Would you care for coffee, Mr. Sheppard?" Arthur asked him.

Sloane shook his head. "No, thank you. I'm here to speak with you and your wife and George's sister regarding the death of his younger brother." He paused, looking at the faces before him. Arthur was perplexed, not knowing what to expect. Henry was more immobile, with a slight look of suspicion to his face. James, like George, was more entuned to what Sloane was saying and leaned forward on the armchair as though he was afraid, he'd miss something he said.

Sophie, Marjorie, and Sue entered at that moment, making for a rather crowded living room. George collected a few chairs from the kitchen while Arthur introduced his wife, niece, and Marjorie Olmstead to Sloane. He stood and shook hands with the women, then sat down again on the sofa.

Sloane was offered an ashtray and he lit a cigarette, as though stalling for time to begin speaking to the family. After disposing of the match, he looked again at the faces before him and wasn't sure who these people were, except for the Drakes, relatives of George.

"We didn't know you were coming this evening, Mr. Sheppard," Sophie said with a slight smile and quick glance at her nephew. "George only told us at dinner. These are our friends, the Olsons and the Olmsteads, who I invited over for coffee and dessert."

"Aunt Sophie's chocolate cake is the best," Sue put in.

Obviously, this was George's sister and Sloane could see the resemblance between the two even greater now that they were in front of him, rather than by mere photographs.

"What can we tell you, Mr. Sheppard?" Arthur began. "We've spoken to the police, but they haven't been able to find who killed Thomas. We had nothing to do with the body at the port."

"Except that we discovered it," Sophie added dryly.

Sloane cast a quick glance at George, who merely nodded as though telling him to proceed.

"George came to see me today with great concerns about the death of his younger brother. Or the person he thought was his brother."

This comment brought a crescendo of remarks, ranging from serious to absurd. Everyone seemed to look at George as though he had lost his mind.

"George showed me photographs of his family. He pointed out the similarities between himself and his younger sister. I can see for myself that they do share similar traits."

"What does that have to do with Thomas?" Marjorie asked before Sophie or Arthur could talk. She looked at them and thought they were too numb to even attempt to speak.

"George thinks—and has thought for a great many years, according to him—that Thomas was not really his brother, that he was an impostor."

This time Sophie spoke up, firm and to the point. "George, this is ridiculous! Are you saying Thomas wasn't our nephew or your brother? For the past ten years, we've had a stranger living here?"

"Yes, I think that is the case," George finally spoke, looking first at his aunt, than everyone else. "He was different while we lived in Utica. I could tell the differences, but I was too young to say anything."

"Did you tell your parents your concerns?" James asked him.

George shook his head. "I didn't have the chance to speak to them about it."

"George, dear," Sophie said, "if there was something different about Thomas, wouldn't your parents have told us before you and your sister moved here to live with us?"

"Not necessarily," George said, rather defiantly. "Mother was too sick to get out of bed. And Father was off in Europe. We never saw him again until the funeral."

"Mrs. Drake, is there anything you can tell me about your nephew?" Sloane asked.

Sophie hesitated, looking at Arthur and then Marjorie, Henry, Mary, and James. She cleared her throat and began. She told Sloane how her brother and sister-in-law, while living and working in Utica, had three children, George, Susan, and Thomas. They were a happy family and lived comfortably. The children attended school there. Lydia Latimer, Sophie's sister-in-law was employed as a telephone operator and Max, her brother, worked in a paper factory. But Max was called up in the draft and was soon sent abroad and at almost the same time, Lydia came down with that terrible flu and was quite sick, requiring hospitalization. Sophie promised her sister-in-law she'd care for her children if anything happened. Max was killed in the war and Lydia died shortly after.

"And that's the story of how the children came here to live with us," Sophie ended her narration. She sighed in relief, knowing that her story was finished. Or almost finished, as Sophie soon realized Sloane was not quite satisfied with everything he heard.

"And you and your husband are their legal guardians?"

Sophie nodded. "Yes, until age twenty-one, of course. George is twenty-five, Susan is twenty-three and Thomas was twenty."

"Do you have records about their childhood?"

"Reports cards from schools, health records and birth certificates. Others may have gotten misplaced when they moved in with us. Honestly, I don't remember Lydia giving us any documents about the children."

"You would have needed them to be their legal guardians."

"If I remember correctly," Sophie continued, thinking back ten years ago. "The birth certificates were provided by the county. The guardianship was established quite easily."

Sloane nodded. He could tell the Drakes were role models for their niece and nephew and provided a warm and nurturing home for them.

"How can you tell if the Thomas we knew was an impostor?" Sue asked.

Sloane turned to her, butting his cigarette in the ashtray. "Well, the easiest way would be to exhume the body."

Both Sophie and Arthur were vehement in their denial of this suggestion.

"That will not take place," Arthur spoke before his wife had the chance. Even Henry and James agreed. "We will not have our nephew exhumed for any reason."

"Unless a court order permits it," Sloane pointed out. "But I don't think it'd come to that, Mr. Drake. There are other ways to prove identity, of course."

"What is the point of all this," Sophie said, clearly perturbed and at the same time rather angered by George, who instigated this ridiculous charade. "Thomas was not an impostor! How could he be? Wouldn't Max and Lydia have known something was wrong?"

"Do you have family still in Utica?"

Sophie hesitated, then looked at Arthur as though for reassurance. "No, I don't think we have relatives there anymore. Max and Lydia lived there after they were first married. George, Susan, and Thomas were born in Utica, but came here in 1918."

"I can see you've raised two fine young people," Sloane said looking appreciatively at George and then at Sue.

"Thank you, Mr. Sheppard," Sophie said gratefully.

"How can you prove someone is an impostor?" Mary asked, from the chair next to her husband. "What other ways are there to prove identity?"

"There are many ways," Henry spoke up. "Fingerprints, blood samples, even hair samples."

"Do you have a fingerprint card of Thomas when he was a baby, Mrs. Drake?" Sloane asked.

Sophie frowned, lost in thought. "No, I don't think so, Mr. Sheppard. My sister-in-law may have had a fingerprint card for each of her children, but after her death, many things were thrown out or lost."

There remained an uncomfortable silence, as though everyone was trying to figure out what was being presented to them by Sloane Sheppard and were not reaching a satisfactory conclusion.

"Do you think Thomas is still alive?" Marjorie asked him.

"I couldn't say," Sloane said honestly. "I'd need more information."

"Such as?" Arthur said.

"Fingerprints are the next surest way to prove identity."

"Where would you get Thomas's fingerprints?" Sue asked, rather confused. "And what would you compare them to?"

"That's a good question," Sloane said and looked at her with a slight smile. "As I mentioned, I'm just beginning my investigation. It may be that the young man you knew as Thomas was indeed Thomas. On the other hand, as George pointed out by the numerous photographs he showed me, he may have been an impostor." He paused. "I'm basing that on the differences between George, his sister, and his younger brother. From what I could see in the photographs, George and Susan bear a resemblance, but Thomas does not look like either one."

Sophie agreed, although reluctantly. "That doesn't mean anything, Mr. Sheppard. Many brothers and sisters don't look alike and are related."

Marjorie cleared her throat. "If you don't mind Sophie and Arthur, I noticed myself that Thomas was rather different. In his looks and certainly his temperament."

Henry agreed with his wife. "Perhaps there was a switch at the hospital that his parents never realized. Strange things have happened, you know. Before the war, too."

144

Sophie was clearly flustered. "Oh, please, stop this, all of you!" She was upset and her voice trembled somewhat as she spoke. "I don't want to hear any more of this nonsense! Thomas is dead and buried and we must honor his life, not question it!"

"I'm sorry, dear," Marjorie said, consolingly. "I'm as concerned as you."

"Thanks, Marjorie," Sophie said, tearfully. "I used to notice differences with Thomas, but not to the extent that he was someone else."

"What more can we tell you?" Sue asked Sloane.

"Do you think your brother's murder is related to the murder of the man found at the port and the woman who attacked Mr. Donaldson and Miss Dupont on Thanksgiving?"

Sue was appalled. "No, of course not. Thomas didn't know that man."

"We don't know that," George spoke up. "Thomas knew a lot of people, gangsters, bootleggers. There could be a pattern we don't know about."

"The police also may have more information on Thomas," Sloane said.

He glanced at his watch, thanked them for their time and rose to leave. He said goodnight to the Olsons and the Olmsteads, who remained seated, as though they were too stunned from the information they heard to get up.

"Thank you, Mr. Sheppard," Sophie said, as she gathered his coat and hat from the hallway. "I wish I knew what to say to help you, but I don't think there is any mystery about Thomas."

Sue agreed, standing next to her aunt and uncle as though for support. "Thomas was different, but he was indeed Thomas!"

Sloane said goodnight to Sophie, Sue, and Arthur. He joined George near the front door and noticed Sophie and Sue had retreated to the kitchen, while Arthur had already gone back to his guests in the living room.

"I'll be in touch, George," he promised him.

George shook hands with Sloane and watched as he walked on Lancaster Street, heading north toward Lark to catch the trolley. From in the living room, he heard the Olsons and the Olmsteads talk about playing bridge and on the radio the end of *Amos n' Andy*. He closed the front door and stood with his hand on the knob, deep in thought. He wondered what else his aunt and uncle would say to him about his contacting a private investigator. They didn't seem so happy about it. He paused before returning to the living room.

George joined them in the bridge game. Any further discussion of an impostor or Thomas or murders in their midst was not mentioned. But it remained in their minds, like a dead weight, a heavy and oppressive burden.

CHAPTER THIRTEEN

Monday, December third dawned cold and wintery with scattered snow showers and few breaks of sun. It was the first Monday of the month and downtown Albany was busy with Christmas shoppers beguiled by early sales and businessmen rushing to their offices before the nine o'clock hour.

Claire looked down at Broadway from the windows in Reggie's office in the Douw building on Broadway and State Street, observing the usual morning rush. She looked up State Street hill toward the capitol, a view she always admired. Turning from the windows to return to her desk, she hardly thought it was back to the same routine. How could it be with that horrid murder they witnessed on Thanksgiving? In her fifty-five years, Claire had seen much turmoil and suffered personal anguish, but never before had she been involved with murder.

She opened her desk drawer and took out her compact. Applying fresh lipstick, she was rather pleased with her appearance. Her new dress, bought over the weekend at Whitney's, was low-waisted and rather sleek, fitting her fine figure and accentuating the curves she worked hard to maintain. She brushed her bobbed hair, put the compact back in her desk drawer, and looking around the empty office, sighed deeply. She didn't trust Reggie Donaldson now that her past life was open to him. But on the other hand, with the Thanksgiving murder, perhaps he forgot about it? Unlikely, as Reggie wouldn't forget something in which he knew he had the upper hand. But didn't it bother him that she knew he was involved with bootleggers? Well, they called a truce of sorts, she thought miserably if she wanted to call it that. She didn't trust him or irritating Mary Olson either.

She glanced at the wall clock and noticed it was ten minutes after nine. Reggie had called and mentioned he'd be in court for part of the morning. He didn't ask about Mary and Claire didn't volunteer any information. Busy with typing a few reports, the ever-efficient Claire was totally absorbed in her work that she didn't notice Mary enter, later than usual, flustered and out of breath.

"Good morning, Claire. I was running late this morning. The weather is nasty, too! The trollies were packed, and I had to stand the whole way! Not that it's really far, of course."

Claire glanced up and had hoped she'd be in court with Reggie but apparently not today. As though reading her mind, Mary explained.

"Reggie called me at home and mentioned he didn't need me in court today. He only has one case and should be here soon."

With that, Mary settled herself at her desk, busy with writing court reports, affidavits, calling clients and arranging appointments. Glancing at her quickly, Claire was glad she decided to absorb herself in her work rather than make small talk, something Claire hated. It had been over a week since the murder at the Capital Club and Mary mentioned it whenever she felt the need to, which Claire found inappropriate since her work was late in getting done.

It was close to eleven o'clock when the office door opened and Reggie walked in, looking as though he hadn't slept, his glasses halfway down his nose, his grayish-brown hair more ruffled than usual. He left his briefcase on the table near the door and greeted his office workers cordially albeit tiredly. He appeared preoccupied and Claire knew he hadn't yet gotten over the murder at the Capital Club. But then, she thought, how could he? Looking at him carefully, she was surprised he didn't have a nervous breakdown.

"Mrs. Norris canceled her appointment for today," Mary told him. "She rescheduled for Wednesday morning."

"Foolish woman," he grumbled. "She'll never get her will straight."

Mary agreed. "Did you know the Drakes are having Thomas's murder investigated?"

Reggie, on his way to his office, turned to look at Mary. Claire couldn't determine if he was stunned, bewildered, or irritated by what Mary just told him. She too didn't understand it, but she certainly wasn't going to ask her to explain. She assumed Thomas Latimer's murder was under investigation by the Albany City Police as well as the murder of the man found at the port and the murder of the woman at the Capital Club. So, what did annoying Mary mean? She continued typing and figured she'd rattle on and on once she knew she had an audience.

"Investigated?" Reggie said, looking first at Mary and then at Claire. "Of course, the police are investigating, Mary."

"No, I mean a private investigator!" She paused, looking at two questioning faces, as though marveling that she held their attention with new information. "James and I visited the Drakes on Friday evening for coffee and while we were there, we met a private investigator. I think George hired him, but I'm not sure. I can't remember his name, but he was genuinely nice."

Reggie looked at her, clearly astonished. Claire paused in her typing and tried to conceal her surprise. Mary continued, relishing the spotlight as though she were on stage performing.

"The Olmsteads were there, too. George said he thought that Thomas wasn't Thomas, that he might have been an impostor or something like that. Sophie and Arthur didn't know what to make of it. Personally, James and I didn't, either. How could Thomas have been an impostor? Wouldn't they have known or suspected years ago?"

"I find that information most disturbing, Mary," Reggie said. "This must be devastating to Sophie and Arthur."

Claire offered to make a cup of tea for Reggie, which he gratefully accepted. She went to the kitchenette, a small room in the back of the office, containing a stovetop and sink. She lit the gas stove and put the kettle on for tea. She regretted missing what more stupid Mary said but, in time, the water began to boil. Quickly she filled the cup and dashed out to the main office, where Reggie sat in a chair reserved for clients and Mary was still talking about George, the Drakes, and this private investigator.

"So that's all I know," she concluded. She looked first at Claire and then again at Reggie, who was clearly disturbed and bewildered by the news.

Claire thought it was a combination of everything that had happened, not simply hearing about a private investigator from someone who didn't have the facts straight.

"Did he say that he was investigating Thomas's murder and the other two murders?" Claire asked, as she too was curious but rather stunned at the same time.

"He didn't say," Mary said. "But I assume it was just Thomas, as George was intent that his brother was an impostor or something like that. Personally, I think it's ridiculous."

"What was this private investigator's name?" Claire asked.

"Well, as I said, I don't really remember." She paused, deep in thought and then as though a light bulb suddenly went on in her mind, she nodded. "Of course, it was a Mr. Sheppard. I found his last name kind of funny. Sheppard, as though a shepherd watches his flock!" She giggled slightly then stopped as neither Reggie nor Claire found humor in her remark.

"I've dealt with private investigators in this city before," Reggie said thoughtfully. "Maybe I know him, but it doesn't sound familiar." He paused. "I'll go tend to reports on my desk." He looked at Claire intently. "I'll speak with you later, Claire." He carried the cup of tea and then closed his office door with firmness.

"Well, that must've upset him," Mary remarked, busy at her desk.

"It was upsetting," Claire agreed. "Sometimes things are best left alone."

Mary turned to look at her, surprised by her remark. "What do you mean, Claire?"

Claire had gotten up, with reports in hand, on her way to see Martha Neale on the lower floor. "If I were you, I wouldn't keep talking about Thomas Latimer." She paused, looking at Mary. "The consequences of murder can be harsh. Just don't mention it anymore."

Hardly one to tolerate a rebuff, Mary tossed her hair, ignored Claire, and continued with her work. As soon as Claire left, however, she looked up at the windows with snow falling now in earnest, and at Reggie's office door, closed as though shutting himself off from the world.

She felt a chill run up her spine, uncomfortably. She wondered what Claire Palmer, someone she never trusted or even liked, meant by that crude, rather threatening remark.

In his office on the tenth floor of the Home Savings Bank building, Sloane Sheppard picked up the candlestick phone on his desk and waited for the operator. He read the newspaper article on Sofia Bartosz, the murdered man at the port now identified as her son and the murder of Thomas Latimer. He was reluctant to pursue the impostor theory put forth by George, although he agreed to take on his case.

Finally, the operator came on. He asked her to ring the Albany City Police. In no time, he was connected with Inspector Harris.

"Hello, Mr. Sheppard," the Inspector said cordially. Usually when Sloane Sheppard called there was a case pending or something afoot. He waited to hear what the private investigator was about to tell him.

"Hello, Inspector," Sloane said also cordially. "I need some information."

The inspector grimaced but refrained from voicing his displeasure. He had worked with Sloane Sheppard on numerous crimes in the past. He knew Mr. Sheppard as a meticulous private investigator who worked endlessly until he resolved the most arduous of cases. He cleared his throat before speaking.

"Certainly. What can I help you with?"

"The murder of Thomas Latimer," Sloane answered, referring to the notes he wrote when he spoke with George. "And I'd like to know more about Sofia Bartosz."

Inspector Harris coughed. "We know now that Szymon Bartosz was Sofia Bartosz's son. We were able to make an identification, using fingerprints and blood samples."

Sloane explained how George Latimer came to see him last week and that he agreed to look into the murder of his brother, or the young man he thought was not his brother. Inspector Harris asked Sloane to explain further.

"Mr. Latimer believes the young man murdered on South Pearl Street was an impostor."

"Are you saying Thomas Latimer is still alive?"

Sloane lit a cigarette, blew smoke, and hesitated before answering. "I don't know. That's why I need more information about him. And Szymon Bartosz."

"We have little information on Mr. Bartosz or his mother. They were refugees from Poland who settled in Utica before moving to Albany. Szymon Bartosz had a criminal record. His mother spoke little English and couldn't hold down a job. She worked at the Capital Club, in the kitchen, helping to prepare food and set the dining room." He paused. "But your guess is as good as mine as to why she went berserk there on Thanksgiving."

"She attacked Mr. Donaldson and Miss Dupont," Sloane said, consulting his notes and looking at the newspaper article on the attack. "Isn't he a lawyer in the city? That name sounds familiar."

"Yes, a well-respected attorney. His stepdaughter works at the Ten Eyck Hotel. We questioned them extensively and haven't produced anything to connect them with Sofia Bartosz or her son."

Sloane held onto the candlestick phone, almost clutching it, while trying to figure out a pattern, if a pattern existed, with the three untimely deaths. He was silent for so long Inspector Harris asked if he was still on the line.

"Yes, sorry about that," Sloane said, finishing his cigarette. "I need to find out more about Thomas Latimer. He had a police record. So, there must exist fingerprints."

"Of course," the inspector told him. "We can look them up for you."

"And the Bartosz woman lived in Utica? The Latimers lived there, too, for several years. Mr. Latimer mentioned he and his brother and sister were born there."

"You've cracked difficult cases before. What do you think happened?"

"With Thomas Latimer, I haven't been able to determine anything about an impostor like his brother claims. Sofia Bartosz's son was murdered, his body found at the port by the Drakes, as I read in the paper. I don't know yet if his murder is connected to the Latimer murder. Then the Bartosz woman attacked Mr. Donaldson and Miss Dupont. I don't know if the three murders are connected."

"She caused quite a commotion at the Capital Club," the inspector said.

"You mentioned Mr. Donaldson and Miss Dupont had no contact with her," Sloane said thoughtfully. "I'd like to speak to them about Thomas Latimer." He noted on his pad to contact the law office of Mr. Donaldson and the Ten Eyck Hotel to speak with Miss Dupont.

Sloane then mentioned to Inspector Harris how he had questioned Sophie and Arthur and their friends, James and Mary Olson and Henry and Marjorie Olmstead at the Drake's home, all of whom were present at the Capital Club on Thanksgiving Day and witnessed the attack.

"You questioned them all at once?" the inspector asked incredulously.

"They were invited by Mrs. Drake for coffee. I had the chance to speak to George, his sister, Mr. and Mrs. Drake and the others."

There was another slight pause. Inspector Harris wondered if they were disconnected.

"No, I'm still here," Sloane said thoughtfully. "Just thinking about Sofia Bartosz. I wonder if she attacked the wrong people. And that her intended target could have been someone else."

Laura strolled through the aisles of Whitney's Department Store on her lunch hour, more from boredom than anything else. She ate a sandwich at the lunch counter on the first floor and then proceeded to the hat department on the second. She wasn't in the mood for shopping, but it was better than returning early to the Ten Eyck Hotel and her desk. Although there were plenty of guys to flirt with at the hotel, even that became tedious after a while.

She loved hats, especially the stylish cloche hats and it wasn't long before Laura was trying on several, finally deciding on a cloche hat with lace trim, very chic and sophisticated. As she approached the clerk to make her purchase, she almost collided with Marjorie and Henry, who were also looking at hats and scarves. Laura expressed surprise at seeing them.

"Mr. and Mrs. Olmstead, what a surprise! I didn't know you shopped at Whitney's."

Henry looked at Laura and thought that was a stupid remark. Since they lived downtown, like she and her stepfather, where else did she think they shopped? North Pearl Street was the shopping district for city residents, wouldn't she know that? But then he thought better of it, given the shock Laura and Reggie went through on Thanksgiving Day.

Marjorie smiled. "Yes, we like to shop on weekdays when the stores aren't so crowded. Of course, with Christmas coming, they'll be more people crowding in here!"

Laura agreed and smiled. "Do you like this hat?"

Marjorie commented that it was indeed lovely and very modern, too. Even Henry said it was pretty, although he knew next to nothing about women's hats.

"How are you holding up, Miss DuPont?" Henry asked her.

"Thank you for asking, Mr. Olmstead," Laura answered. She looked pretty as ever, very made up, her fur coat fitting her shapely figure, but there was something different now about Laura Dupont. Both Henry and Marjorie could tell. Perhaps, Henry thought, a change for the better.

"It was quite a shock," Marjorie added, making way for a rather large woman and her two children to pass. "I haven't gotten over it."

"We heard on the radio the man murdered at the port was the son of the woman who attacked you and your step-father," Henry said. "Strange coincidence."

"I'm sure Laura isn't interested in hearing that," Marjorie said, casting a disapproving eye at her husband.

She looked at the Christmas decorations around the store, the Santa Claus figures scattered here and there. Garland was draped over display cases and small Christmas trees were set up in different locations. Certainly, Whitney's wasted no time in preparing for the holiday. Laura too glanced around but the holiday décor meant little to her. She avoided Henry's eyes and did not comment about the man murdered at the port, the son of Sofia Bartosz. In fact, she appeared agitated, not the reaction Henry was expecting.

Marjorie nodded. "Henry and I felt so bad for you and your step-father. Let us know if there is anything we can do for you."

"Well, the inquest was quite an ordeal," Laura admitted, surprising herself. She didn't really know the Olmsteads. She knew they were friends with the Drakes and the last thing she thought she should do was to confide in them, fearing they'd relate everything back to Mr. and Mrs. Drake, along with George and Sue. But then Mrs. Olmstead didn't give Laura the impression she was a gossiper.

"I'm sure it was difficult for you," Henry said sympathetically. "How is Reggie holding up?"

"We're supporting each other," Laura said. "But we could've been killed that day. You both saw it, didn't you?"

Henry and Marjorie looked at each other wondering why she'd ask. Of course, they were there, Laura must know that. And quite close to their table, too. Henry thought she spoke nervously, as though she didn't really want to speak with them, perhaps out of fear or something else.

"Do you think the recent murders are related somehow?" Henry asked her.

She looked at Henry, aghast at such a suggestion. Her glance then went to Marjorie; kind, caring, compassionate, even nurturing. Certainly, the motherly type.

"I really don't know," was Laura's response. "I haven't given it much thought." She paused, looking at the elderly couple before her. Glancing at her watch, she noticed the time. "I should be getting back to the hotel, Mr. and Mrs. Olmstead. It's been great seeing you." And with that, almost as though she couldn't wait to leave them, Laura walked to the staircase to the ground floor.

Marjorie and Henry then strolled through the aisles. Marjorie looked at scarves but didn't find one she really liked. She suggested they go for coffee at the lunch counter. Descending the stairs, she chatted with her husband about their Christmas plans.

Henry listened and smiled but couldn't help but wonder why the revelation of the murdered man's identity was so disturbing to Laura. And if she knew more than she was willing to admit.

At the Home Savings Bank, George was pleased that the noon hour was approaching, and it was time for lunch, although he admitted to himself that he wasn't particularly hungry. He had spoken with Sue earlier, who called him to say she wasn't in the mood for lunch today.

"You have to eat something, Sue," her brother told him. "You have to keep up your strength, you know. Especially for Aunt Sophie and Uncle Arthur."

"I guess a salad wouldn't hurt," Sue said. "What about the diner on South Pearl Street?"

George told her he'd meet her in front of the hotel so they could walk to the restaurant together. He had just finished with a customer, a young woman opening her first checking account when he saw an associate approach his desk.

"Hello, Alek," George greeted him pleasantly.

"Say, George, how about a bite to eat?"

A young man of George's age, Alek Wojcik worked in the loan department upstairs. He and George started at the bank at around the same time, almost four years ago. He was of medium height, with a fair complexion and expressive blue eyes.

"Sue and I plan to eat at the diner on South Pearl. Want to join us?"

Alek carried his jacket and cap and put them on. "Of course, I'd like that, George. I haven't seen Sue for a while and the food at the diner is the best!"

George also put on his jacket and cap and the two young men left the building, crossed at the light, and arrived at the front of the Ten Eyck Hotel. Amidst swirling snow showers and brief periods of sleet, George and Alek waited for Sue who exited the revolving door and came up to them.

"Hi George, hey Alek! Long time, no see! Are you joining us?"

"Yes, George invited me."

"Well, let's get out of this snow and find a booth at the diner," George said.

Sue agreed and after crossing at State Street, they arrived at the diner and were pleased it wasn't too crowded yet. They settled themselves at a table, took off their coats and hats and left them on the rack near their booth. They took menus the waitress brought over, ordered coffee and lit cigarettes.

"You don't smoke, Sue?" Alek asked her, depositing the match in an ashtray.

Sue shook her head. "No, but George smokes like a chimney."

Looking at his sister through a haze of smoke, George grinned. "Well, I could have worse habits, you know. Besides, there's nothing wrong with a good cigarette!"

Alek laughed and the three young people were soon talking animatedly, making plans for Christmas and New Year, and discussing the latest hit songs on the radio and movies playing locally.

"I have to see Mary Pickford's new film," Sue said, sipping her coffee. "I just adore her!"

While they ordered sandwiches and Sue ordered a salad, conversation ensued until Alek mentioned the three murders. George and Sue lapsed into an uneasy silence, which didn't go unnoticed by Alek. He looked at the faces of his friends and apologized.

"Don't worry, Alek," George said, blowing smoke from his cigarette. "It's been a long three weeks and we're still getting over it."

Sue agreed. "Three murders in such a short period."

The waitress soon arrived with their orders. She refilled their coffee cups and departed.

"I read in the newspaper that the guy found at the port was the son of the woman who attacked Mr. Donaldson and Miss Dupont," Alek said, amidst a mouthful of French fries

"Aunt Sophie and Uncle Arthur have been devastated," Sue said.

"Sue, try not to think about it," her brother consoled her.

"When I read in the newspaper about Sofia Bartosz," Alek said, "it mentioned she was from Utica or settled there before coming to Albany. Weren't you from Utica, George?"

George finished his sandwich and sipped his coffee. "Yes, we were born there, and father and mother worked in Utica until he was sent overseas during the war. And then mother caught the flu ten years ago." He broke off, not wanting to continue.

"Well, you know what's funny," Alek said. "My parents and grandparents immigrated to this country from Poland. They settled in Utica, before moving to Albany. I was born in Utica, too."

"Sue, Thomas and I went to school in Utica before moving to Albany," George said.

"It's kind of strange," Alek said. "That woman and the guy found at the port were related."

Neither George nor Sue said anything. George lit another cigarette and Sue asked for more coffee from the waitress. Alek finished his sandwich and also lit another cigarette.

"The last name was Bartosz?" Sue asked her brother and Alek.

Alek nodded. "I wasn't acquainted with him, although it sounds Polish."

"I wish mother and father were here for us to ask them, too," Sue lamented.

"I don't remember much about Utica," George admitted. "Seems so long ago."

"Another lifetime," Sue added. "I don't remember any kids with that name when we were in school there."

George agreed. "Aunt Sophie and Uncle Arthur didn't recognize the Bartosz name."

He then asked for the check from the waitress, who brought it over and offered them dessert which they declined. Sue noted the time and mentioned they had to return to work. After paying at the cashier and then bundling themselves in their jackets, George and Alek put on their caps while Sue placed her cloche hat delicately on her small head.

Wind seized them upon leaving the diner. Crossing at the light, Sue said goodbye and scurried off to the hotel, while George and Alek waited at the light to cross to the other side of North Pearl Street.

"Thanks for lunch, George," Alek said as they entered the bank.

George smiled and told his friend they needed to get together more often. Alek agreed and then made his way to the staircase in the corner to the loan department one flight above. George then returned to his desk, removed his jacket and cap, deep in troublesome thoughts.

The afternoon began with George attending to numerous bank customers. He opened the ledger book on his desk, attentive to the requests of his clients. But while completing transactions, he couldn't stop thinking of the recent murders and especially the murder of his brother, or the person they thought was Thomas. That was just foolishness on his part, of course.

Suddenly, he knew he should give Mr. Sheppard a call, to tell him he wasn't needed in this half-witted investigation. Thomas was Thomas, he told himself repeatedly. What proof did he have, really, other than the pictures? And the pictures were hardly proof of an impostor.

The woman who went berserk at the Capital Club was from Utica, so he assumed correctly her son was from there, too. He drummed his fingers on his desk. Why should that bother him? Why would he even think of it? There was no connection between his parents and this Bartosz woman. Utica was a big city and the likelihood of his parents knowing her was nil. He didn't remember them mentioning people with that name. And even if they did know her, what difference did it make?

He closed the ledger book with finality. Well, that's the end of it. Nothing more to think about. Thomas was Thomas, he told himself again and that was that. He was just being foolish and stubborn. Case closed. Or was it?

CHAPTER FOURTEEN

Mary stepped off the trolley at the corner of Washington Avenue and Dove Street, shielding herself as best she could from the harsh wind. In front of her stood the Albany Institute of History and Art. She and James were regular patrons of the arts, and they spent many enjoyable evenings attending exhibits. She thought of entering, more to escape the cold than anything else, but decided against it.

It soon started to rain, frozen pellets that hit her face stingingly. She gathered her scarf from under her fur coat and wrapped it around her face, up to her nose, creating a barrier between her skin and the icy rain. She then crossed at the light and made her way along Dove Street, finding temporary shelter in the Harmanus Bleecker Library. While inside, she glanced at the current books on display and sat for a while, to catch her breath before having to bear the elements outside again.

It was just before five o'clock and as Mary was preparing to leave the office for the day, her husband had called to tell her he needed to work a bit later and would not be catching the same trolley with her as usual. Claire had already left and Reggie, who was still in court, had called to tell her she was free to leave early if she wished.

Mary smiled to herself wistfully, wishing her husband could get home earlier. She wanted to plan a pleasant evening meal since she had more time to cook. Realizing the library was soon closing, she got up, bundled herself in her fur coat and walked toward the exit, dreading the weather conditions she knew were awaiting her.

The stormy downpour sent pedestrians scurrying into the warm comforts of their homes along Dove and State Streets. Mary steadily made her way until she came to her well-kept brownstone, on the corner of Dove and Hudson Avenue.

Once inside, it was warm and pleasant. She turned on the lights, hanging her fur coat in the hallway closet, then proceeded to the kitchen, where she immediately planned to cook the pot roast, she prepared the evening before. With the gas stove lit, the meat in the oven, she lit a burner to boil broccoli and then set the kitchen table for herself and James.

While the roast cooked in the oven, Mary walked over to the living room, casually turned on the radio to a jazz station, kicked off her high heels and did a little dance. She was feeling exuberant and had much to think about. She was cleverer than anyone, except perhaps her husband, realized. Just then the phone in the hallway rang, startling her. She was glad to hear Marjorie's voice on the other end.

"Hello, Mary, dear. Sorry to be calling during dinner, but I am so concerned for Sophie. She's taking everything so badly, you know. With this private investigator and George's idea that Thomas wasn't really Thomas, I'm surprised she hasn't collapsed!"

Mary commented that she also was concerned for the Drakes and then asked Marjorie if she had heard the news on the radio about the identity of the man murdered at the port.

"I did hear about it. He was the son of the woman who attacked poor Reggie and Laura."

"I know, it's strange, isn't it?" She paused. "I'd like to invite you and Henry and Sophie and Arthur for the holidays."

"That'd be nice, Mary. And I'll bake a cake for us, too."

Mary and Marjorie then discussed the weather, the holidays, and other trivial matters of little importance. Marjorie told her she'd call her again on Wednesday and then hung up. Mary then returned to the kitchen, to check on the roast, when the phone suddenly rang. She quickly went back to the hallway and upon answering, was happy to hear the voice of her husband.

"I'll be home soon, dear," James said. "I'm just finishing a report and I'll be on my way."

Mary smiled. "We're having pot roast and baked potatoes, your favorite!"

James laughed and they hung up, Mary feeling content, more from her future plans than cooking dinner for her husband.

Many people, including brainless Reggie and obnoxious Claire, had taken her for a dim-witted fool, someone who didn't know anything. Unbeknownst to them, she learned things easily enough and now was the time to make use of that cleverness. She figured someday it would come in useful. During her time alone in the office, she had free rein to look around, in desk drawers, cabinets and bookshelves, too. And she found plenty to interest her; Claire's diary with the names and phone numbers of high-ranking gentlemen she'd entertain while in Elmira and Reggie's bootlegging side business. And if he wanted to secure secret information, wouldn't dear Reggie keep his desk drawers locked? How stupid they were, she thought, as though I were the dumb one.

Thanksgiving at the Capital Club was horrific, but Mary could see it all. That crazy woman attacking first Laura, taking her totally by surprise and then turning on Reggie, almost killing him. She thought long and hard over what she had witnessed. And then her thoughts turned to the young men murdered recently. Who would kill them and why?

As she returned to the living room, settling herself comfortably on the sofa with a magazine, the news came on the radio. The opening report made her sit up and listen carefully.

> The murdered man at the port of Albany on November 11th has been identified as the son of the murdered woman who attacked two people at the Capital Club on Thanksgiving Day. The victim's identity was confirmed by police. Police are looking further into the murders of Sofia Bartosz and her son, Szymon. Anyone with information is asked to contact Albany Police.

She had heard it this morning, so of course, they'd repeat it again. Was there a connection there, between the two? And now George, who believes his brother wasn't his real brother. Maybe he murdered his own brother and is trying to cover it up? And Sue couldn't stand her younger brother, either. Of course, she couldn't imagine Sophie killing anyone, but Arthur, who had a temper, could get angry enough to do harm. That could be said for Henry Olmstead, too. Like Sophie, Marjorie seemed harmless. She had known them all for so long, but underneath, there was always a different person, it seemed, someone you didn't really know.

That Bartosz woman could have intended to kill someone else and mistook Laura and Reggie for her intended target. She looked so insane, wielding that carving knife like a lunatic! Mary shuddered. She felt frightened then and frightened now. She slowly realized who was responsible for the two murders and who was the intended victim of the Thanksgiving attack.

Her reverie was broken by the opening of the front door. Her husband called from the doorway that he was home. Mary hurried to greet him, her machinations momentarily forgotten and put to rest.

It was a somber atmosphere in the Drake house on Lancaster Street. It was close to seven o'clock and George and Sue along with their aunt and uncle had finished dinner and were relaxing in the living room, listening to a radio program on the upcoming Herbert Hoover administration. Sophie commented it was a shame their governor, Al Smith, did not win the presidency. Arthur mumbled something about 1929 being a better year with new leadership.

Trivial talk, George noted, perhaps in place of the thoughts actually permeating their minds. His uncle had the *Albany Evening Journal* open on his lap, but he wasn't reading it. His aunt was knitting a sweater for George, but she kept missing a stitch and finally gave up, her mind too preoccupied. George sat in the armchair near the fireplace, reading *Sense and Sensibility*, his favorite Jane Austen novel and smoking incessantly, his mind also preoccupied and full of contradictions. Sue sat next to Sophie on the couch and was flipping the pages of the latest issue of *True Story* magazine while also attuned to the radio program, attempting to block distorted thoughts from clouding her mind

Arthur looked at his nephew. "George, why didn't you tell us you consulted a private investigator? Furthermore, what's this about Thomas not being Thomas? You should've spoken with us first." His tone held strict disapproval.

"I didn't know if you'd believe me. I wondered about Thomas for a long time. He was always so different, even in his appearance."

"Other than the pictures, what proof do you have, George?" Sue asked her brother.

"Well, I don't, actually," he said, feeling uncomfortable.

"I agree that Thomas was different," Sophie said. "But if there was something else, your mother would've told us. Besides, why would your parents have an impostor living with them?"

George stubbed out his cigarette. "Maybe they didn't know he was an impostor. A lot of unanswered questions. That's why I thought Mr. Sheppard would help to clarify this mess."

"You think it ties in with the guy murdered at the port," Sue said, more of a statement than a question.

"Again, I don't know," George replied irritably. "I meant to call Mr. Sheppard to tell him his services weren't needed any further." He hesitated as he realized they were looking at him intently. "But I didn't have the time today."

"George, if it makes you feel better then let him continue with his investigations," Sophie said, much to his surprise. "Of course, it's your expense. In the end, you will find it a waste of money."

"Suppose Thomas's murder does tie in with the guy at the port," Sue said. "That would prove whoever killed Thomas, killed the other guy, too."

"Sue has a point," Arthur mentioned. He reflected for a moment, glancing down at the paper on his lap and then again at his nephew. "It's okay for this Mr. Sheppard to continue, George."

George felt relieved upon hearing his uncle's support. "The police haven't come up with anything regarding Thomas's murder."

The radio program on the Hoover administration ended and the evening news began with the daily headlines. As the announcer spoke, they waited to hear any possible updates on the three murders. After a lengthy discourse on the local government news and the weather report, they looked at the radio in silence.

> As previously announced, the murdered man at the port of Albany on November 11ᵗʰ has been identified as Szymon Bartosz, the son of the murdered woman who attacked two people at the Capital Club on Thanksgiving Day. The victim's identity was confirmed by the police. Police are looking further into the murders of Sofia Bartosz and her son, Szymon, as well as the murder of Thomas Latimer. Anyone with information is asked to contact Albany Police.

Arthur looked at his wife, niece, and nephew in dismay, wondering what more could happen to confuse them. Sue put *True Story* on the coffee table and went to the kitchen as though she couldn't handle any more of the distressing news. Even George, usually more collected than his sister, lit another cigarette and stared blankly ahead of him. Only Sophie found the courage to speak. She paused, in some frustration as though she wished she could take control of the situation but couldn't. "I agree with you, George, there may be a connection."

Sue reentered with a cup of tea. "But that doesn't have anything to do with Thomas."

George looked at his sister. "It just might, Sue."

"Have you spoken with Mr. Sheppard since last week?" his sister asked him.

He shook his head. "Do you have records of us when we were younger, Aunt Sophie?"

"There were few records, George," she told him. "I believe school immunizations began in 1922. You, Susan, and Thomas, received the smallpox vaccine at that time."

George nodded, his mind going back ten years ago, in 1918 when their mother died, and they left Utica to live with their aunt and uncle in Albany. It was a difficult time, with the war ending, their father already dead and buried and now the loss of their mother, due to the flu pandemic. He wondered how he and his sister were able to get through it. He then looked up at his aunt and then at his uncle and saw the reason. He smiled at them, knowing their love and support carried them through that arduous year, making a new life for them, starting school in a new city, and adjusting to life without their parents

"George, who don't *you* tell us what you think is going on," Arthur said.

George swallowed and slowly nodded. "Well, I think Thomas was not really Thomas."

"Didn't Henry say something about a switch at birth," Arthur said, trying to remember what his friend said on Friday evening. "I suppose he has a point. During the war and afterward, hospitals were a shambles and poorly staffed. Marjorie told us that then."

"Yes, she'd know that since she was a nurse," George said.

Sue sipped the tea and addressed George. "If Thomas's murder and the Bartosz murder are related, how does his mother fit into it?"

George was deep in thought. "I don't know, Sue, but I intend to find out." He got up suddenly, impatiently. "I don't understand why our brother, or who I thought was our brother, would be murdered and the police haven't found his killer. And I believe his death is related to both Bartosz's murders."

Sue looked at her brother, practically with her mouth open. "Are you saying that woman attacked Laura and Mr. Donaldson purposely? That they were responsible for her son's death?"

"No, I'm not saying that," George said. "But there may be a connection somehow."

Sophie nodded. "We all feel the burden of not knowing what happened to Thomas."

"You still think there's a connection between these deaths?" Sue asked him.

"You don't have proof, George," his aunt reminded him kindly.

"There's got to be a link somewhere," he told them, his eyes almost bulging, his face practically contorted in a strange mixture of anger and helplessness. He stubbed out his cigarette in an ashtray on the coffee table and turned to his aunt, uncle, and sister. "Something fishy is happening right under our very noses and I intend to get to the bottom of it."

And with that, George hastily walked out of the living room and ran upstairs to his room, leaving Sophie, Arthur, and Sue staring after him.

Sitting on a trolley bound for upper Madison Avenue, Claire thought back to the wonderful evening she had just spent with a politician from Rochester. She had dinner earlier in the evening with him at the new DeWitt Clinton Hotel and enjoyed his company, the sumptuous meal, and the fine wine, camouflaged as sparkling water. It certainly pays to have a wallet full of cash, she mused, as she saw her dinner date slip the waiter a fifty-dollar bill and in return, a nice well-hidden bottle of New York State's finest white wine was soon brought to their table. It also gave her the chance to see what the new hotel was like, and it was well worth her time. Politicians and businessmen proliferated the lobby and she marveled that she had found a new place to socialize with distinguished gentlemen.

She accompanied her companion to Union Station, where he boarded a train heading west. She left the train station, feeling buoyant and boarded a trolley to bring her to her apartment on Madison Avenue.

Arriving home, she picked up the evening paper left on her doorstep. Upon entering the spacious apartment, she hung her fur coat in the hallway closet, went to the kitchen to make a cup of tea and then entered the living room, settling herself comfortably on the sofa. She unfolded the evening paper and looked at the front page closely. She read about Sofia Bartosz, her murder and the identity of the man found at the port last month. She lit a cigarette and shook her head. Three murders in Albany in less than three weeks? Who killed Thomas Latimer?

Well, the possibilities were endless, she thought, turning a page of the paper. His brother or sister could have killed him, knowing full well his devious lifestyle and having had enough of him, decided to do him in. But then Claire thought otherwise. She couldn't picture Sue Latimer plunging a knife into her brother's stomach. But she could very well picture George doing so. There was something about George Latimer that irked her terribly, a know-it-all, superiority. Even at the Capital Club, from her vantage point at the table with Reggie and Laura, she could tell as he sat with his family, he exuded an air of, what was it, something more than confidence?

That Bartosz woman must have mistaken Reggie and Laura for someone else, she thought. She remembered when Sofia Bartosz came to their office, threatening Reggie because her immigrant paperwork had been delayed. She was a large, heavy-set woman, who looked like she'd kill if she had the chance. That day in the office she wanted to call the operator to summon the police, but Reggie managed to coax her out the door, down the elevator and out the building. Looking back on that incident, she thought if that wasn't proof the woman was insane, she didn't know what was.

Claire leaned back on the sofa and suddenly thought of Laura Dupont. Poor, pitiful Laura. She saw her in a different light now, as a young woman, scared, rather shy and insecure, putting on a front like so many women do, acting tough and flamboyant but underneath was a totally different person. Perhaps the attack on her life changed her. She could still see the struggle for the carving knife, how Laura managed to push the bigger woman away and then how she lunged for Reggie. But why did she attack them in the first place?

She couldn't see the Olsons from where she sat, but she was sure nosy Mary took it all in. And she'd mention the private investigator George Latimer hired to look into his brother's death. Well, that was his business, after all, and none of busybody Mary's.

Claire grimaced just thinking of Mary Olson. She set her straight with her rather threatening remark, about not mentioning the murders any further. But then, what else did stupid Mary have in her life? Except butting into other people's lives. Hadn't she seen her snooping through Reggie's desk drawers more than once? That was enough for him to fire her, she thought. But then, Reggie wouldn't do that. He loved the attention she bestowed on him, he craved it. She wondered if Mary discovered her notebook that somehow Reggie found, which he'd use to blackmail her if it came to that. Claire suddenly sat upright. Suppose Mary *did* find that notebook? That might explain her coyness around her, her subtle hints, even her phony niceness. She thought back to the conversation she had with her earlier in the day. What had she told her? Oh yes, she remembered, the consequences of murder were harsh. She didn't remember Mary expressing any genuine grief over the murder of Thomas Latimer. On the other hand, neither did Reggie. When he told her he attended the wake, she was surprised.

Mary attended because she didn't want to miss anything. She thought bitterly how hard she had worked over thirty years, pinching pennies, saving every nickel and dime just to survive. And then Mary, whose husband had an excellent position with the railroad, who must have a good salary, for them to afford their nice brownstone on Dove Street. Why would she even work if she didn't have to?

Maybe she should finish it off and somehow get rid of nosy, meddlesome, ostentatiously virtuous Mary Olson. And who'd care about the consequences?

Claire sat in her living room, meditatively, smoking a final cigarette.

George lay still and listened to the howling wind and the sleet battering his bedroom window. It was close to midnight and the family had retired over an hour ago. The lights were out downstairs, and the house was quiet. But George could not sleep. He tried reading Jane Austen, but even her wonderful prose didn't help him to relax. His mind was still turning over images and unresolved conflicts from the last three weeks.

Now, as he heard the grandfather's clock in the downstairs hallway chime the midnight hour, he irritably sat up, wide awake, switched on the bedside light and reached for his cigarettes. He lit one, deposited the match in the nearby ashtray and sat up in bed, fuming, too anxious to sleep.

Although he tried to dispel the intense thoughts swirling round and round in his mind, he could not banish what was at the forefront. It could've been anyone that woman attacked, even Aunt Sophie and

Uncle Arthur. From his seat, he could clearly see the hateful, hideous expression on the woman's face. And the fear in both Laura and her stepfather. He cursed himself for not rising and assisting Laura and her stepfather. Laura managed to wrestle her off but then she turned toward Mr. Donaldson and the knife slipped and plunged into her chest. George blew smoke, his mind replaying the scene over and over.

Of course, Mr. Donaldson wasn't a murderer. Why would he do something like that in front of so many people? So, the woman had been a difficult client or something like that. That was no reason to kill her.

George finished his cigarette and immediately had another out of the pack and to his lips. Before striking a match, he swung himself out of bed, walked across the floor in his pajamas and bare feet, running his fingers through his short brown hair. Haphazardly he lit the cigarette and as was his custom when agitated, began to pace back and forth with the cigarette in his hand, trying to figure out what he saw and what actually occurred. He dropped the match in the ashtray on the bedside table, deep in thought.

There had to be something else, something that took place right in front of a dining room full of people and no one could see what actually happened. Except me, George thought. He stopped pacing, looked at *Sense and Sensibility* on the bedside table. He then went to his desk for paper and a pen and then sat upright in bed, making a careful list.

On the first list, he wrote the names of everyone he knew that attended the Thanksgiving dinner at the Capital Club. The next list, the names of people who knew Thomas, who could have had an ax to grind with his younger brother. The third list was empty as nobody that he knew was acquainted with Szymon Bartosz, the son of Sofia Bartosz.

George looked at his lists and realized he had accomplished nothing. He wondered if what he saw, so close to the actual attack, was what

175

others witnessed. The tables were scattered around the large dining room, so viewpoints varied, but on reflection, he realized he had the best vantage point. Sue's back was to their table, so she only saw the attack after Laura wrestled the woman off of her. Mr. Donaldson's back was to her, too, so Sue never saw the fatal thrust that killed Sofia Bartosz. Aunt Sophie and Uncle Arthur also could not see it, as they sat further against the wall.

Who else could have seen what he saw? The Olmsteads were further away from their table. Mrs. Palmer could have seen something, but didn't he notice her head down as she was still eating? Mrs. Palmer had witnessed the struggle, but not the moment when the knife plunged into the woman's chest, as Mr. Donaldson's back was to her, too. But George saw everything.

He shuddered as he drew the blanket over his legs. Should he express his concerns to Aunt Sophie, Uncle Arthur and to Sue? No, they didn't believe his assumptions about Thomas. He didn't believe Laura or Mr. Donaldson were murderers. Aunt Sophie and Uncle Arthur had known Mr. Donaldson for years. Sofia Bartosz may have meant to attack someone else in the dining room that day. But who and why?

The Olsons seemed to have a good view. He remembered how Mr. Olson got up from the table, stunned and almost incapable of speech, calling for the staff to contact a doctor. Mrs. Olson stood with her hands over her mouth, as though she were going to vomit. He could see her eyes wide open, startled, even frightened. He realized the Olsons had a good perspective of the attack, better than Sue, Aunt Sophie, and Uncle Arthur and the Olmsteads.

He wondered if Mr. Sheppard had found anything on Thomas. Or the phony Thomas, he told himself irritably. There must be a pattern in all this mess. Sofia Bartosz was murdered, as the knife plunged into her chest by Mr. Donaldson, in an attempt to wrestle it away from her. Her son, Szymon was murdered at the port, possibly because he was involved in underhanded business or had seen something he shouldn't have. George irascibly blew smoke and listened to the wind rattle his windowpane.

Then why had his brother or the person he didn't believe was his brother been killed?

CHAPTER FIFTEEN

The next morning, the harsh weather from last evening had improved and the sun showed in spots. The sleet and harsh winds had subsided, although it remained cold and blustery.

A typical December day in Albany, Sloane Sheppard thought, stepping off the trolley at the corner of State Street and North Pearl Street. He waited with a rather large crowd of office workers and Christmas shoppers and finally crossed the busy street. Arriving at the Home Savings Bank building, Sloane entered an elevator, greeted Andrew the attendant, and got off on the tenth floor. He unlocked his office door and entered, switching on the ceiling light.

Taking off his coat, jacket, and Fedora hat, he left them on an empty chair and then sat down at his desk. He looked at his calendar and noticed three appointments for the morning, leaving the afternoon open for research. He was about to review the files of this morning's clients when his phone suddenly rang.

"Hello, Mr. Sheppard," said a young male voice. "This is George Latimer. I'm calling from the bank here. I'd like to know if you've produced anything on my brother's murder."

"Not yet, George," Sloane told him. "I'm planning to go to city hall today, to search for a birth certificate."

"I still don't believe he was my brother," George said, rather stubbornly.

"After that, I'll go to the police station," Sloane said, ignoring George's last remark. "I want to get fingerprints when he was arrested."

George said that was a good idea. "God knows he was arrested often enough. But what will you compare them to?"

Sloane hesitated. "That's what I need to find out. I'll let you know soon enough, George."

He replaced the receiver on the candlestick phone and then sat back thoughtfully. George Latimer was a clever young man. Indeed, what would he compare them to? Establishing identity could be challenging, as Sloane readily knew, but with fingerprints and a birth certificate, he hoped this particular identity case could be handled easily enough.

The morning continued with his appointments arriving on time and business went on as usual. As the noon hour approached, Sloane grabbed his jacket and coat from the chair, along with his Fedora hat, locked his office door and headed for the elevator. Once outside, he crossed at the light, ate a quick lunch of sandwich and coffee at a diner on North Pearl Street then caught the trolley heading up State Street.

He got off in front of Albany City Hall. As he entered and walked up the stairs to the Office of Vital Records, he wondered what information, if any, he'd find. He waited several moments while a few people were ahead of him. Mrs. Endicott, the office manager, recognized Sloane from previous visits and gave him a welcoming smile.

"Good afternoon, Mr. Sheppard," she said, coming up to the counter where transactions were conducted. She was an older woman with a head of white hair, vivid green eyes, a pleasant smile, and a helpful disposition. "It's good to see you. I'll be retiring soon, so you'll have to get used to my replacement."

"Retiring, so soon?" Sloane said and grinned. "You're a young woman yet."

Mrs. Endicott smiled "Thank you, Mr. Sheppard. That's truly kind of you. How can I help you today?"

"I need a birth certificate of the brother of a client of mine." Sloane filled out a form for the requested information and handed it to Mrs. Endicott.

She looked at it carefully. "Mr. Thomas Latimer?" Without waiting for him to answer, she said, "Do you mean the Thomas Latimer who was murdered recently? I read about it in the paper."

Sloane nodded. "I'm investigating his murder. I need a copy of his birth certificate. He was twenty years old, and he was born in Utica."

Mrs. Endicott made a few notes on the form. "Twenty years old? So, he was born in 1908. And in Utica." She finished writing, told Sloane she'd be with him momentarily and welcomed him to the chairs in the waiting area, while she disappeared into the stacks of archival material that looked to Sloane as though you'd need a compass to find your way out. Rows upon rows of folders, portfolios and binders containing documents of vital records from across the state, going back decades. As a private detective and librarian, Sloane was used to researching but didn't think obtaining data from a plethora of documents was a job he'd ever want for himself.

After a wait of about twenty minutes, Mrs. Endicott returned, holding a folder containing several papers. Sloane joined her at the counter.

"This is the Thomas Latimer you're looking for," she said, extracting a birth certificate.

Sloane looked at the document. It was indeed a birth certificate. It listed Thomas Latimer, born April 21, 1908, in Utica, New York, son of Max and Lydia Latimer also of Utica. Other details such as St.

Elizabeth's Hospital where the birth took place, the time of birth, hair and eye color and dimensions were also noted. Sloane took out from his jacket pocket a small notebook and copied down the details.

"I have the information I need," he told her gratefully. "Thank you, Mrs. Endicott, for your help. And I hope you change your mind about retiring."

Mrs. Endicott smiled. "Thank you again, Mr. Sheppard."

Once outside, Sloane crossed the street and despite the chilly air sat on a bench in Lafayette Park. Neither the pristine row houses on Elk Street, nor the imposing State Capitol held his interest, as they usually did. He took the notebook from his jacket pocket and read again the information on Thomas Latimer. Of course, he'd reveal his findings to George and to the family. Didn't Mrs. Drake say she didn't remember a birth certificate for Thomas Perhaps in the children's relocating to Albany, it got lost. And with the burden of their mother's death ten years ago, a birth certificate could have been overlooked. She mentioned they were provided by the county at the time of establishing guardianship, so at least he knew the birth certificates for George, Susan and Thomas did exist. And now he had the information from Thomas's birth certificate for himself.

Sloane thought back to what George told him about Thomas and the pictures he saw of the young man. It was hard to determine anything based on those findings. He shoved the notebook back in his jacket pocket and walked over to Washington Avenue, where he caught the trolley uptown before finally arriving at Albany City Police headquarters on the corner of Central Avenue and Quail Street. He walked in and asked the policeman at the front desk for Inspector Harris. Within a few moments, he was ushered into a small office in the back of the building, where both Inspector Harris and Lieutenant Taylor were sitting, busy with papers on their desks.

"Hello, Mr. Sheppard." The inspector stood and shook hands with Sloane. "Please sit down."

Lieutenant Taylor acknowledged Sloane with a brief nod and then returned his attention to the papers on his desk. Sloane gave him a brief nod and then turned to Inspector Harris.

"You mentioned you'd find the fingerprints of Thomas Latimer."

The inspector nodded. "Just a moment, please."

He disappeared out of the small office and into another room, where cards and files of warrants and fingerprints were kept. It wasn't long before he returned, holding out a fingerprint card.

"Thomas Latimer's fingerprints," he told him, returning to his desk. "We arrested him for burglary a few times. He was involved with the liquor trade here in Albany, too."

Sloane looked at the fingerprint card. It was dated November 10, 1927, his last arrest, just a little over a year ago. He hesitated, his mind turning over possibilities, then handed the card back to the inspector. "I may need to take a trip to Utica."

"Utica? Didn't the family live there?"

Sloane nodded. "The children were born there. The father was called up to serve in the war and was killed overseas. The mother died ten years ago during the pandemic. That's when the children came to Albany to live with their aunt and uncle."

"You think he had an arrest record in Utica?" he asked curiously. "He would've been a child then since he must've been ten when he came here."

"Utica must have a juvenile division as we do in Albany." He stood and thanked the inspector. "I'll be in touch, Inspector Harris."

Sloane made his way out of the police station and out onto Central Avenue. It had started to snow lightly and the sun that promised at least a blue sky disappeared behind low and thickening gray clouds.

He walked down Central Avenue, missing several trollies, his mind deep in thought.

As he waited at the corner of Central and North Lake Street, he crossed at the light. Hopping on the first trolley, he got off at the corner of Washington Avenue and Dove Street. His next stop was the Harmanus Bleecker Library.

Shaking fresh snow from his coat, he entered the library where it was quite busy, with patrons checking out books and children already out of school for the day, occupying the children's room, engaged in homework and others selecting books. Sloane went up to the reference desk and spoke to Mrs. Sawyer, a reference librarian he knew from previous visits.

"Hello, Mr. Sheppard," she said pleasantly, having just assisted a businessman with information on a local company. She was a friendly middle-aged woman, with brown hair worn in a fashionable bob. She had worked at the new library since it opened four years ago. "How can I help you?"

"I'd like to look at the city directory for Utica."

"State-wide directories are on the far wall, to the left."

Sloane thanked her and proceeded to the area where the directories for various cities in the state were shelved. He noticed Buffalo, Ithaca, Rochester, Syracuse and then spotted the city directory for Utica. Fortunately, both the 1927 and 1928 Utica city directories were available. He took the 1928 volume off the shelf and sat at a table.

He had visited Utica only once, several years ago, while working on a case. He didn't know the city, so the street names were not familiar to him. He came to the L listings and looked for the Latimer name. There was a Latimer Plumbing Company and a Latimer Upholstery. Sloane knew George's parents were not from Utica, so it was unlikely those businesses had anything to do with them. He told him his Aunt Sophie was his only living relative and that she had always lived in Albany, where she and her brother Max as well as her sister-in-law Lydia were born and raised. So, the likelihood of Latimers related to Max and Lydia Latimer in Utica was unlikely. As Sloane continued scanning the L listings, there were no people with the last name of Latimer in the city directory. He then realized what he needed to search for. Of course, the B section!

Several listings for businesses, many last names beginning with B; he saw a listing for Bartosz, a Lena Bartosz. He copied the address and number in his notebook, wondering if she was related to the woman who tried to kill Mr. Donaldson and his stepdaughter at the Capital Club and the man found at the port last month. Hadn't they immigrated to Utica from Poland? He had read about it in the paper and heard it on the radio, so possibly there was a relative still there. Of course, there were many immigrant families in cities across the state. There was a large Polish community in Albany, so perhaps Utica had one, too. But he knew it was a slim chance. He'd need more information. And the only way to get it would be to talk to this Lena Bartosz.

Having completed his research, and feeling more satisfied than when he first arrived, Sloane got up from the table, replaced the city directory on the shelf, nodded goodbye to Mrs. Sawyer, and walked out of the library. He made his way to Washington Avenue, where he caught the trolley downtown. He reviewed what he knew so far in this case.

Thomas Latimer had last been seen at a speakeasy on South Pearl Street. He knew the police had already been there, but Sloane decided to investigate it himself.

It was quite busy with Christmas shoppers rushing about. Sloane descended the trolley at South Pearl Street, passing several businesses: shoe stores, a dress shop, a fur store, and a jewelry store. It was in the back of the jewelry store that he decided to head, turning left onto Maiden Lane, one of several back streets, near the seedier part of the city. As he expected, there were theaters and cafes, but one door, in particular, was partially hidden, down a small flight of stairs, wedged between a theater and a coffee shop. He climbed down the stairs and knocked on the door. When a peephole opened, the man asked Sloane for the passcode, to which Sloane told him he didn't have a passcode but wanted information. The man was about to close the peephole when Sloane told him it was a murder investigation. The door then opened slowly, only an inch, allowing Sloane to see a rather rough-looking older man, with a deep frown, wondering who he was looking at and what he wanted.

"The murder of Thomas Latimer," Sloane said. "And Szymon Bartosz, who was murdered at the port. Do you have information? Latimer may have come out of this speakeasy and was stabbed on South Pearl Street." Sloane paused. "Over a month ago, in early November."

"Yeah, I remember," the man said, unpleasantly. "Look, mister, I don't give information out to just nobody. Who are you and what do you want?"

"I'm a private investigator," Sloane told him, handing him his business card. "I'm investigating these murders."

The man returned the card and was about to close the door when Sloane stopped him. "If you have information that can help in this investigation…"

"We've already spoken to the police," the man said abruptly. "Several times. Latimer was here that night. He was wild, drunk, loud, and obnoxious. He was arrested for bootlegging." He paused. "We run a decent place and we don't want no bootleggers here."

"A bootlegger?" Sloane said, trying to hide his astonishment.

"Yeah, that's right, mister. On lower Broadway, there's an old house, that's where they get the liquor from boats on the river, coming up from the city. That's one place I know of. Probably lots of others." The man paused, haughtily. "Now, don't go telling the police. They probably know about it anyway, but they can't keep up with it."

Sloane thanked the man and climbed the stairs to the sidewalk. On Maiden Lane, he looked around for other clandestine establishments but found the rest of the area respectable enough if not as alluring as State and North Pearl Streets. He continued to South Pearl Street, where he stopped at a diner for lunch.

While finishing his sandwich, coffee, and several cigarettes, he wondered if George, with his inquisitive nature, had surmised the truth. And if by surmising the truth, he was putting his life at risk.

It was a busy day in the business office at the Ten Eyck Hotel, but the atmosphere had hardly returned to normal, at least not for Sue and Laura. While occupied with letters, memos, and renovation reports which all needed typing, they barely concentrated on the tasks at hand, their minds too disturbed over recent events. Managers streamed in and out of the office, seemingly oblivious to their state of mind, demanding this and that and other sundry duties.

Sue filed a few letters and reports and then closed the file cabinet firmly. Laura looked up from her work and watched as she returned moodily to her desk, an anxious look on her face.

"I understand George is having a private investigator look into things," Laura remarked, as she inserted a fresh sheet of paper into her typewriter. "Daddy mentioned it to me. What does he hope to accomplish?"

"I really don't know," Sue said, not taking her eyes off of her work. "The police haven't found anything about Thomas, so maybe a private investigator can get to the bottom of it."

"Well, I think Thomas was involved with something he shouldn't have been," Laura said, uncaringly. "And that insane woman who tried to kill me and Daddy. Did you see it, Sue?"

Sue now looked up from her work. "No, my back was to your table."

"Oh yes, that's right. George had a clear view of it all."

A strange silence permeated the room. The phone rang several times and managers came in and out of the office. It wasn't until almost five o'clock when Laura asked Sue what she thought happened to Thomas. And why that Bartosz woman attacked her and her stepfather.

"I really don't know, Laura," Sue said, putting the plastic cover on her typewriter and closing her desk drawer. "Thomas and I weren't especially close. He was always different."

"When we dated, I could tell he was different," Laura commented. "I didn't really like him, to tell you the truth. I'm glad I broke up with him."

"How's Mr. Donaldson?"

"Daddy? He's doing better. He should be getting out of work soon, too." She glanced at the wall clock. "Well, it's five, Sue. Care to join me in the elevator?"

Sue relented with a weak smile. As much as she couldn't stand Laura, there was some degree of civility in her that was apparent every so often.

Bundled in their coats, scarves and cloche hats, the young women left the office, waited for the elevator to arrive, told the attendant to bring them to the ground floor and once the gates were closed, waited patiently while other passengers from lower floors also entered. Finally reaching the lower floor, Sue and Laura walked through the lobby and out the revolving doors.

"Good night, Sue," Laura told her. "I'm meeting Daddy at his office. See you tomorrow."

"See you tomorrow," Sue said. She watched as Laura blended into the after-work crowd, heading toward lower State Street, where her stepfather worked.

Although cold and snowy, with a gusty wind, it was busy on North Pearl Street. Holiday shoppers and theatergoers blended with the after-work crowd, creating busy and rather congested sidewalks. Trollies were practically standing room only and cars snarled in heavy traffic.

As she stood on the corner of State and North Pearl Streets, waiting for George, Sue shivered slightly. She looked to her right and noticed Mr. Olson, walking surreptitiously, down State Street, heading toward the Douw Building, where Mrs. Olson worked. That's where Laura was headed too, Sue thought. Strange how in a large crowd she'd recognize someone. Strange, too, that Mr. Olson was headed *toward* the Douw Building from State Street instead of from Broadway, where he worked. He was making his way steadily, as though late for a meeting, jostling with others on the sidewalk.

She gave it no more thought as she waited for George to catch the trolley home.

Amidst snow showers and increasing wind, Sophie walked along State Street, avoiding the slushy pavement as best she could, on her way to see Marjorie. She wore her heavy winter coat and wrapped her scarf firmly around her neck. As she finished preparing dinner, she told Arthur she needed to get out for a while. She rang Marjorie, who invited her for a cup of tea. She told Arthur to light the gas stove again by five o'clock when she'd return.

The Olsmteads lived in a charming brownstone on lower State Street, diagonal to the state capitol. It was within walking distance of the shopping and theater districts, convenient to the trolley and everything else downtown Albany offered.

Shaking snow from her shoes, Sophie climbed the front steps and rang the bell. Almost immediately, as though she was waiting behind the door, Marjorie opened it abruptly.

"Sophie, dear, please come in. I told Henry we'll have an early winter for sure."

Sophie crossed the threshold, took off her coat, hat, and scarf, left them on the hallway chair and then followed Marjorie to the kitchen.

Certainly, a warm and pleasant room, Sophie thought, sitting at the round kitchen table, while Marjorie poured tea and set a plate of freshly baked corn muffins on the table. She had been busy cooking lamb and getting potatoes ready for the oven. The aroma of cooking and the coffee was extremely pleasing, and Sophie sighed, rather contentedly, knowing she was with her good friend, who had been with her throughout the years. Marjorie sat across from her, putting sugar in her teacup.

"Any news, Sophie? Anything on Thomas?"

"Nothing on Thomas, except that George thinks he's an impostor."

"Well, what do *you* think, Sophie?"

Sophie hesitated, the teacup to her lips. "I don't know what to think," she said, putting the cup down and tasting the corn muffin. Realizing it was quite tasty, she finished it and found the sugar gave her some much-needed energy.

"That Mr. Sheppard certainly seemed capable," Marjorie commented. "And George is determined to get to the truth."

"That's what bothers us," Sophie told her friend. "Just what is the truth? That Max and Lydia's son wasn't their son? That he was really someone else?"

"Seems hard to believe," Marjorie agreed. Changing the subject, she asked Sophie if she and the family had plans for Christmas.

"I haven't even thought of the holiday," she admitted. "I've been too preoccupied. Mr. Sheppard could learn something. He's a private investigator, after all. They have all kinds of ways to find things out." She paused. "The woman who attacked Mr. Donaldson and Miss Dupont at the Capital Club is the mother of the man Arthur and I found dead at the port. Of course, that doesn't relate to Thomas's murder."

An uncomfortable silence fell on the elderly women, each thinking that perhaps it did tie in with Thomas's murder, but neither wanted to admit it. Marjorie wished she could find the right words to comfort her friend. At that moment, the front door opened, startling Marjorie and Sophie.

"Hello dear, I'm home," Henry said from the hallway. "What a cold day it's been! It's snowing steadily now, too." He entered the kitchen, his face red from the cold, his gray hair ruffled from the wind. He was pleased to see Sophie. "Oh, Sophie! It's good to see you!" From the uneasy silence, he could tell something was not quite right. "Am I interrupting something?"

Marjorie smiled at her husband. "Would you like some tea before dinner, dear? We're having lamb and baked potatoes."

Henry sat at the kitchen table with his wife and Sophie. Knowing his wife and Sophie too well, he asked them what was troubling them.

"George still believes Thomas was a phony," Sophie said. "Arthur and I have been upset since that Mr. Sheppard first came to the house."

"Have you heard from him again?" Henry asked.

Sophie shook her head. "Although George is adamant about this whole mess." She paused. "And what does that woman who attacked Mr. Donaldson and Miss Dupont have to do with Thomas?"

"There've been three murders in this city recently," Henry said. He hesitated. "Maybe this Mr. Sheppard could resolve it, Sophie." He hoped his words were comforting but Sophie merely lifted her head from the teacup and gave a tired smile.

Marjorie invited her to join them for dinner, but Sophie declined. She mentioned she must go, as George and Sue would soon be home and she wanted to have dinner ready for them. Without waiting for either Marjorie or Henry, Sophie got up and went for her coat, hat, and scarf in the hallway.

"You're sure you'll be all right, Sophie?" Henry asked, joining his wife in the hallway.

Sophie wrapped her scarf around her neck and her cloche hat firmly on her head. She managed a smile and told them she'd be fine. She hugged them, said goodbye and as Marjorie held open the door, told them not to worry about her.

"I'll call you tomorrow," Marjorie promised her. "We'll go to Whitney's to shop."

"Thanks, Marjorie, that sounds like a good idea."

She waved to them as they stood at the front door and then turned and began walking up State Street. Finding it much darker now, Sophie, unused to nighttime activities, quickened her pace, as though afraid of walking in the dark. There were plenty of people about and as she came to the corner of State and Dove, noticed Mary coming out of the Harmanus Bleecker Library. She spotted Sophie and went up to her.

"Sophie, what a cold night for you to be out! What brings you here at this time?"

"I was visiting Marjorie and Henry," Sophie said, her teeth practically chattering from the cold. "I see you have a library book."

Mary nodded. "Did you know there are a lot of bootleggers here in Albany, Sophie?"

Sophie looked at Mary and didn't understand why she'd make that comment. "Yes, of course, Arthur and I hear it on the radio. And we read about it in the papers, too."

"Maybe it has something to do with Thomas," Mary said, stepping aside as a mother and her two children came out of the library. "Wasn't he involved with those kinds of people?"

As much as Sophie liked chatting with Mary Olson, she was not in the mood for idle small talk, especially in the cold weather. Yet, as she listened to her ramble on and on, she couldn't help feeling that there was more to what she said, that she was hiding information, that she knew something she didn't mention.

"…that Mr. Sheppard may learn the truth," Mary was saying, as though she was gifted with a sixth sense. "And the truth will come out, Sophie. I have an idea about things, you know."

"Well, it's been nice seeing you, Mary dear," Sophie said, eager to end the conversation. "I'd walk with you, but I need to stop at the market on Lark Street." Which was a lie, Sophie knew, but she had to say something to get away from her. Strange, she thought, listening to her talking, she had never felt that way about her before. "Please stop over some evening with James for coffee."

Mary smiled, returned the invitation, and then crossed Dove Street, hurrying in the snow to reach home. Sophie momentarily stared after her, wondering what she knew or surmised. She continued walking north on State Street, rather quickly. She stopped as she realized she should have followed Mary down Dove Street and over to Lancaster. She had momentarily lost her way, distracted by Mary's flippant demeanor. She no sooner turned to walk back in that direction, when she almost collided with a woman, who was walking north on State Street.

"Oh, Mrs. Palmer," Sophie caught her breath.

"Hello Mrs. Drake," Claire said, startled. "I'm just on my way to the library."

Sophie smiled. "A good book is perfect on a night like this."

Claire agreed. "What brings you out this evening?"

"Just visiting the Olmsteads," Sophie answered.

"Soon it'll be Christmas," Claire said, almost shivering from the cold.

"Yes, it comes so quickly," Sophie commented, wishing to end the conversation.

"Well, it's been nice seeing you, Mrs. Drake," Claire said, rather nervously.

Sophie wished her good evening and then scurried off in the direction of Dove Street, confident that Mary had already reached home and that she wouldn't bump into her. Sophie turned briefly and noticed Claire going in the opposite direction of the library toward Washington Avenue, furtively, as though she was involved with something clandestine.

Upon reaching Lancaster Street, Sophie wondered if Claire Palmer had seen Mary. A sharp thought crossed her mind. Claire Palmer was walking north on State Street. The library was on the corner of State and Dove, and she had already passed it. Certainly odd. And there was something odd about Mary just now, too.

Well, it's none of my business, Sophie thought, shaking snow off her shoes. Still, she shivered, more from apprehension than the cold. She inserted the key in the front door and, greeting Arthur in the hallway, eagerly and anxiously, as though she had been away for eons, entered the house and the welcoming arms of her husband.

CHAPTER SIXTEEN

S loane Sheppard was at his desk early the next morning, reviewing his notes on the Thomas Latimer case. He looked through them, in frustration, as he tried sorting them out.

Upon arriving at his office, he accepted a cup of coffee from Lois. Thank goodness for Lois, Sloane thought, taking off his suit jacket. Glancing at his calendar, there were three appointments this morning: one about a false arrest and two divorce investigations. So far, the afternoon was clear, leaving him time for research. He then opened the top drawer of his desk and removed a file, containing notes on the Latimer case. He lit a cigarette and began to ruffle through his notes.

First, the murder of Thomas Latimer, with no witnesses or suspects. Ditto that for Boris Bartosz, found at the Port of Albany, by the Drakes. As though that wasn't enough, a Polish refugee, and an employee at the Capital Club, Sofia Bartosz, with no previous criminal record, went berserk and inexplicably attacked Mr. Donaldson and his stepdaughter, Miss Dupont at the club on Thanksgiving. Sloane shook his head. Was she confused and mistook them for someone else? Then who was the intended target? And what was the connection, if one existed, between Thomas Latimer and the Bartosz murders?

The first two murders had no known witnesses. The third had a dining room full of witnesses, who clearly saw the woman struggle with Miss Dupont and then Mr. Donaldson when the knife slipped, and she was stabbed and bled to death.

Sloane looked at the birth certificate information on Thomas Latimer, and the address and phone number of Lena Bartosz in Utica. Was Thomas Latimer an impostor, as George so adamantly claimed? His aunt and uncle steadfastly refused to believe the boy they knew was an impostor. Sloane admitted to himself, it was difficult to accept. Although he knew, from his work before and during the war, impersonations were common, and he had solved several such cases.

Sloane crushed his cigarette in the ashtray on his desk and glanced toward the window, overlooking North Pearl Street. Few snow showers, gray clouds, a weak sun trying to break through. He sighed, rather irritably as he realized the investigation was going nowhere. As was his custom, he ran his fingers through his wavy black hair, lit another cigarette, got up from his desk and paced the floor. In service to his client, George Latimer (and a persistent client at that), he intended to pursue the Thomas Latimer case to the end. He'd call George at the bank with news on the case but at the moment he had no news to give him.

He then picked up the candlestick phone on his desk and upon hearing the operator, asked her to put through a call to Utica. He gave her the number and waited patiently, momentarily putting his cigarette in the ashtray.

"All circuits are busy, sir. Would you care to try back?"

Sloane gripped the phone, rather impatiently. "Yes, thank you." He hung up, resumed smoking, and sat brooding for a few moments. At times he hated using the phone, waiting for an operator to put the call through, such a nuisance. Recently he read in the paper about direct dialing where people could place calls themselves, something the phone company hoped for the future. He then picked up the phone again and asked the operator to dial the number of Mr. Reginald Donaldson, Attorney-at-Law in the Douw Building. In no time, he was connected, and the call was answered promptly by Claire Palmer. He introduced himself and asked if he could stop by to speak to Mr. Donaldson today if he was available. The always efficient Claire looked at Reggie's agenda.

"He'll be here this afternoon," she told him. "Is one o'clock good for you, Mr. Sheppard?"

"Yes, that's fine. I'd also like to speak to you and Mrs. Olson."

Claire hesitated. "Of course, Mr. Sheppard. We'll be here then. Thank you."

Sloane sensed the anxiety in her voice. He thanked her for the appointment and hung up. He had just finished the call when his first appointment, an overwrought middle-aged mother with her teenage son, arrived. Sloane was soon busy at his desk, writing notes, making a few additional calls to the Albany City Police, and clarifying data on his client's previous arrest. The last client, another middle-aged woman seeking grounds to divorce her second husband, left the office, rather haughtily, as though she would see justice done by obtaining a bill of divorcement. Sloane was finally able to lean back on his desk chair, light a fresh cigarette, finish the coffee Lois brought him which had grown cold hours ago and relax, a least for a while.

Despite being busy with his morning caseload, his thoughts returned to Thomas Latimer and the Bartosz murders. He got up rather fitfully and opened the office door. He stood in the doorway pensively, his cigarette between his lips, his hands in his pockets, when one of the two elevators on the tenth-floor lobby suddenly opened and out stepped George.

"Mr. Sheppard," he said, smiling slightly, coming up to him. He had on his jacket and carried his cap in his hand. "I'm on my way to have lunch with my sister, but I wanted to come here first." Sloane smiled at the young man in front of him. "By all means, George, come in." He stepped aside for George to enter. He sat down at the chair in front of the desk while Sloane returned to his chair and offered his visitor a cigarette.

"What progress have you made concerning Thomas? We haven't heard from the police!"

Sloane nodded. "I'm speaking with Mr. Donaldson this afternoon, along with Mrs. Palmer and Mrs. Olson." He paused. "I'd also like to speak with Miss Dupont."

"I'll tell Sue to let Laura know," George said, exhaling a cloud of smoke and then hesitated. "There must be more that can be done. The person who I thought was my brother was not my brother! He was an impostor!"

"I understand your frustration," Sloane said. "But I need proof and to collect evidence."

"Do you think Thomas's murder is connected with the Bartosz murders?"

Sloane hesitated. "Well, I found some interesting information recently." He related to George his discoveries at the Office of Vital Records, the birth certificate information, the fingerprint card dated November 1927 and the name and phone number of a Lena Bartosz in Utica. George's face lit up and he could hardly contain his emotion.

"That's terrific, Mr. Sheppard! We're making headway!"

Sloane nodded. "Right now, George, I have a few matters to take care of before I go to see Mr. Donaldson. Why don't you go and enjoy lunch and then I'll be in touch soon?"

He came back from around his desk and shook hands with George.

"Do you think this woman in Utica could be of some help?" He finished his cigarette and butted it in the ashtray on Sloane's desk.

Sloane told him he wasn't sure. "I don't know what she can tell me, if I can reach her."

He joined George in front of the elevators, assuring him he would continue to learn as much as he could about his brother. As an elevator just arrived, George thanked Sloane again, waited for the attendant to open the gates and then stepped in. Once the gates and the door closed, Sloane returned to his office and walked over to the window overlooking North Pearl Street. His thoughts returned to Lena Bartosz, in Utica. He went toward his phone but impulsively decided on another course of action.

He glanced at his watch and realized he had time before his appointment with Mr. Donaldson. He donned his suit jacket and overcoat, locked his office door, waited for the elevator and once in the lobby on the ground floor, made his way outside. It was cold and blustery with intermittent snow showers blanketing the streets and sidewalks. As it was the lunch hour, he brushed past office workers and shoppers, enjoying the festive store window displays and packing the assorted fine eating establishments lining North Pearl Street.

Sloane walked to the Western Union office on State Street, with a determined, hard look on his face. He entered, completed the necessary form, and paid the fee to the attendant, who put the telegram through.

TO: MISS LENA BARTOSZ, UTICA, NEW YORK.

MR. SLOANE SHEPPARD, PRIVATE INVESTIGATOR ALBANY STOP WISHES TO SPEAK TO YOU STOP WILLING TO COME TO UTICA STOP PLEASE RSVP ALBANY NO. PEARL 3016. STOP.

At the office of Mr. Reginald Donaldson, Attorney-at-Law, Claire looked up at the wall clock and noticed it was not quite one o'clock. She had told Reggie and Mary about Mr. Sheppard's visit. Reggie scowled and almost gave her hell for making the appointment, then relented and realized he had nothing to lose by seeing him. Mary commented that she'd spoken to him once before at the Drake's house but of course, she'd do whatever she could to help.

Of course, dear Mary would help, Claire thought bitterly.

It was at one o'clock when the office door opened, and Sloane Sheppard entered. He greeted the women pleasantly, introduced himself, recognized Mary from his visit to the Drakes and said he was there to meet with Mr. Donaldson at one o'clock.

"Hello, Mr. Sheppard," Claire said with a smile, rising to greet him before Mary could take over. She approached him, shook hands, and then took his hat and coat. "Coffee or tea?"

Sloane declined both. "Thank you just the same," he said. "Actually, before speaking with Mr. Donaldson, I'd like to ask both of you a few questions."

As she returned to her desk, Claire looked carefully at the man seated in one of the chairs for clients. He certainly was a looker, with his slicked-back hair, that vest and tie, pleated business slacks. She smiled and then realized Sloane had been speaking to her. As though he could read her mind, she blushed and asked him how she could help.

"Are you still working for George, Mr. Sheppard?" Mary asked before Claire could begin to speak. And before Sloane could answer, Mary told him all she had seen and heard at the Capital Club that afternoon. And how dreadful it all was, too, she added dramatically.

Sloane thanked her and mentioned he was seeking information on Thomas Latimer, on George's behalf. He then directed his focus on Claire.

Claire collaborated with Mary's version; she was eating Thanksgiving dinner with Mr. Donaldson and his stepdaughter when a woman tried to attack them with a carving knife. She lunged for Miss Dupont first, then after Laura pushed her off, she attacked Mr. Donaldson and in the struggle over the knife, she was stabbed and fell to the floor, near their table.

"I didn't actually see when she was stabbed," Claire told him. "Mr. Donaldson's back was to me. But it was a horrendous sight. And the blood on the floor and on Mr. Donaldson's suit jacket and shirt was just terrible." She shivered slightly.

"Well, I saw it all, Mr. Sheppard," Mary said, rather proudly. "From where my husband I sat, I saw the attack from the beginning. I saw Mr. Donaldson stab that crazy woman."

"You saw him stab her?"

Mary hesitated. "Well, he did stab her. But not that he intended to, of course."

At that moment, the inner office door opened, and Reggie entered. He cast a quick glance at Claire and Mary and then his eyes rested on Sloane. He smiled in recognition.

"Mr. Sheppard, I do remember you. I met you several years ago during an investigation. A client of mine was under arrest, and you were at the police station."

Memories of past clients returned to Sloane, who had in fact remembered meeting Reginald Donaldson previously. He also smiled in recognition.

"Please come into my office, Mr. Sheppard. Claire, hold any calls until later."

He ushered the private investigator into his office, which Sloane thought was more like his own personal enclave. Looking around, he was surprised there wasn't a bed and bureau. It was a very personal space and mannish to the extreme. Bookcases overflowed with court records, law books, files, and other miscellaneous papers. A few scattered ties and two dress shirts were draped over a corner chair. Glancing at his desk, he noticed a small photograph of his stepdaughter but no other personal pictures. He sat in front of the desk while Reggie returned to his desk chair and abruptly asked Sloane what he could do for him.

"Sofia Bartosz was your client. Tell me more about her and what you helped her with."

Reggie fiddled with the candlestick phone and opened and closed a folder. He coughed and hesitated as though he changed his mind and didn't wish to speak.

"She was seeking citizenship," he told Sloane. "Her paperwork was a shambles and as a result, her naturalization was delayed. Her English was not particularly good, which also didn't help her case. She never paid her attorney fee and threatened me, quite openly, in the outer office in front of Mrs. Palmer and Mrs. Olson."

"What did she say to you?"

"That she'd kill me. She held me responsible for her citizenship papers not working out."

Sloane had been writing in his small notebook. "She attacked you and your stepdaughter, but she attacked your stepdaughter first, is that correct?"

Reggie nodded. "Yes, we were eating dinner and suddenly heard a loud scream. A rather large woman came rushing into the dining room, with a carving knife and headed for our table. She lunged for Laura, who happened to turn and saw her. She was able to fight her off. She then threw herself at me. You know the rest, Mr. Sheppard."

Sloane nodded. "Were you acquainted with Thomas Latimer?"

"Just informally, through the Drakes. I didn't know him personally."

"And Szymon Bartosz? He was Sofia Bartosz's son."

"Yes, I read about it in the paper and heard it on the radio."

"Do you know anyone who'd want to kill Thomas Latimer?"

Reggie shook his head and reached for his pack of cigarettes. He offered one to Sloane, who declined. He struck a match and inhaled deeply before speaking.

"No, I don't know of anyone who wanted to kill Mr. Latimer. Perhaps you should look closely at his family. His brother George isn't all he seems to be. Even his younger sister, Susan."

Sloane watched as he blew smoke and ruffled some papers on his desk.

"And what's this ridiculousness about an impostor posing as Thomas? Mrs. Olson mentioned George thinks that's the case. Do you believe that Mr. Sheppard?"

Sloane hesitated. "At this point, I'm not sure what to believe. Have you been to the speakeasies downtown, Mr. Donaldson?"

Reggie continued smoking and took his time before replying. "Well, Mr. Sheppard, speakeasies are illegal, are they not? So, if I answer affirmatively to your question, am I under arrest?"

"No, of course not. I'm trying to determine if you might have seen Thomas Latimer or Szymon Bartosz in a speakeasy and what you observed."

"The person you should ask is my secretary, Mrs. Palmer. You were just speaking with her. She's a regular patron of speakeasies here."

Sloane again nodded. Realizing he was not gaining anything much from Mr. Donaldson, although convinced he may know more than he was willing to admit, he stood and shook hands with the lawyer.

"Thank you for your time, Mr. Donaldson."

"You're welcome, Mr. Sheppard. I wish you luck in resolving the Thomas Latimer case."

An awkward silence ensued as Reggie came from the back of his desk and opened his office door. Claire and Mary were still busy in the outer office; Claire typing reports, Mary speaking to a client on the phone and taking notes. Reggie thanked him again, then closed his door leaving Sloane in the outer office to question Claire and Mary again.

"Mrs. Palmer, Mr. Donaldson mentioned you frequent speakeasies."

Claire looked up from typing, rather shocked that this Mr. Sheppard would be so blunt, especially in front of Mary Olson. And fuming that stupid Reggie would even mention that to him in the first place. That was her personal life, anyway, so what was the point?

"Yes, I do occasionally visit speakeasies," she admitted hesitatingly. As though that's any of your business. "Why do you ask, Mr. Sheppard?"

"Perhaps you saw Thomas Latimer or Szymon Bartosz at one of the local speakeasies."

Claire nodded. "On a few occasions, I remember seeing Thomas. He was quite a man about town, even at his age. He had an arrest record and had been quite a problem for his aunt and uncle." She tried to steer the topic away from herself, but Sloane persisted.

"Did you see Thomas doing anything—different—illegal while out on the town?"

Claire frowned. "I recall seeing him drunk, acting obnoxiously, especially toward girls. Maybe he was involved with something he shouldn't have been." She hesitated. "And I never knew Mr. Bartosz. Just his mother, who was a client of Mr. Donaldson's."

Sloane mentioned how Reggie told him about Sofia Bartosz, including her threatening him in the office. Claire nodded and elaborated.

"Yes, she did threaten him," Claire said. "She was a most unbalanced woman. But I don't think she wanted to kill Miss Dupont or Mr. Donaldson. Perhaps she meant to attack someone else."

At that moment, Mary finished with her call. She hung up the receiver on the candlestick phone and entered the conversation. "Sorry, I don't mean to interrupt, but I couldn't help overhearing. My husband

and I think Thomas was involved with bootleggers." She paused. "Sofia Bartosz threatened Mr. Donaldson here in the office."

"Did you see him with bootleggers, Mrs. Olson?" Sloane asked, turning to her.

"Well, no, not exactly. But bootleggers are all over the city, you know. Even closer than you might think." She cast a furtive glance at Claire. Like her boss, Sloane had the impression she knew more than she was letting on. The phone rang again, and Mary answered, busy with another client.

Sloane looked around at the rather drab office, realizing again that he had learned all he could, at least for now. He thanked Claire, motioned a thank you to Mary as she continued talking on the phone and walked out, his mind wondering about the three people he just encountered.

And who had the most to hide and why.

At almost four-thirty, Mary exited the Douw Building, rather hastily. After daylight savings time ended, when darkness arrived abruptly, Mary was always uncomfortable in the office alone. Mr. Donaldson was still in court but had returned briefly to retrieve some folders. Before departing, he told her he may return afterward to finish work on a few cases. He also told her she could leave early. Claire had left about an hour ago, so she tidied her desk, put on her fur coat and cloche hat, and happily left the office.

Crossing State Street at the light, Mary reflected what a fortunate woman she was and how opportune her life turned out. She was married to a wonderful man, she was making an excellent salary and, with the extra money on the side, she had no financial worries and perhaps could spend a little more, too. She glanced at her watch. She had time before meeting James for the trolley, so she'd stroll up North Pearl Street, on her way to the department stores. But first, she had a call to make.

She headed for a payphone on Steuben Street, just past Whitney's, where she knew it wouldn't be too noisy. Upon reaching it, she entered the booth, closed the door quickly and searched in her purse for a nickel. She deposited the coin and spoke to the operator who placed the call. She waited for the person she wanted to answer.

"Well, it's Mary. You know why I'm calling, don't you? The extra money. I could go to the police, but I won't, unless you make good on your promise, so don't be foolish."

She smiled contentedly as she exited the phone booth. She never kept secrets from her husband and confided her scheme, to which he merely nodded and said nothing. Dear James, she marveled, always confident in my plans and looking out for me, too.

She told Mr. Sheppard a few things to think about. She wouldn't reveal too much, of course. She had noticed how man-crazy Claire looked at him, as though undressing him with her eyes, thinking perhaps of how she could seduce him, she certainly was professional at that. Mary laughed to herself. Claire's former call girl days and Mr. Donaldson's bootlegging activities. Well, she had a field day ahead of her and the streets were paved with gold.

Mary thought the Olmsteads must have a few secrets, too, despite being good friends with the Drakes. She knew they despised Thomas Latimer, especially after he stole that antique vase. Maybe they knew more than they were willing to admit. After all, they saw that crazy woman attack Laura and Mr. Donaldson. She wondered if they put two and two together as she did. Well, they wouldn't use it to their advantage, unlike me, Mary thought devilishly. They weren't clever like me either, she laughed again to herself.

She took a left onto North Pearl Street and arrived at Whitney's. As she expected, it was busy with holiday shoppers. She stopped and looked at the store windows, decorated with Santa Claus, toy train sets and Christmas trees. It was a lovely time of year, Mary thought, with evening settling over the city, light snow falling, the air crisp and invigorating. She contemplated buying a new hat for Christmas. She entered Whitney's and before long, purchased a new cloche hat, perfect with the beige dress she bought last week. A new string of pearls wouldn't hurt either, but not now, glancing again at her watch. She had better start down State Street toward the railroad building.

The traffic was rather heavy, even for the after-work hour. At the corner of State and Broadway, she waited at the front of a rather restless group of pedestrians as cars and trollies bedazzled her from all directions. With the bright streetlamps illuminating the snowy street and sidewalks, the headlights practically blinding her, Mary momentarily lost her sense of equilibrium.

At that moment, a large truck was turning right onto State Street. So many people, impatient to cross, pressed forward. Impulsively, Mary hung back in the crowd, holding onto her hatbox, but found she could not go back. There was something—or someone—directly behind her, obstructing her escape from the truck's path.

Mary wobbled on the pavement and then felt a strong, purposeful shove. She tried to turn and thought she recognized someone behind her just as she fell headlong in the direction of the massive vehicle, its wheels crushing the life out of her.

CHAPTER SEVENTEEN

George poured coffee for himself and his sister and set the cups on a tray, along with the sugar bowl and a jug of cream. He carried the tray to the kitchen table, where Sue was buttering a corn muffin. He set the cups down, along with the sugar and cream.

It was early Thursday morning and still quite dark outside. George was in his robe and pajamas, barefoot and unshaven, craving coffee, and his first-morning cigarette. Sue also was in her robe and pajamas, not quite awake. Sophie and Arthur had yet to get up, so George did the honors of preparing breakfast.

He cut a corn muffin while at the same time unfolding the morning paper that he brought in from the doorstep. He handed his sister the classifieds and sales fliers, while he scanned the city and national news. Articles on the upcoming administration and predictions for 1929, newly elected President Hoover promising "a chicken in every pot and a car in every garage." He noticed articles about the popularity of *Steamboat Willie* starring Mickey Mouse and the new Al Jolson movie, *The Singing Fool*, playing at Harmanus Bleecker Hall.

He was about to light a cigarette when suddenly he gave a sharp cry, causing the cigarette to fall from his lips onto the table. Sue looked up from the sales page and asked if something was wrong. Speechless, he merely pointed to a small notice, at the bottom of the local news.

Albany Times Union
December 6, 1928

A terrible accident has claimed the life of Mrs. Mary Olson of Albany. Mrs. Olson was killed last evening while attempting to cross at the corner of State Street and Broadway in downtown Albany. At the height of rush hour, Mrs. Olson was struck and killed by a truck as it turned right onto State Street from Broadway. Bystanders said Mrs. Olson, carrying a Whitney's hatbox where she apparently had been shopping, slipped on the slushy pavement, lost her balance, and fell in the direction of the oncoming truck. Mrs. Olson, employed at the law firm of Mr. Reginald Donaldson, Attorney, was a life-long city resident. She is survived by her husband, Mr. James Olson of Albany.

Sue read the article several times in shocked silence, then looked up at the startled face of her brother. As she returned the newspaper to George, her thoughts turned to her aunt and uncle and how they would react to this tragic news.

"Mrs. Olson died last night," George said thoughtfully, lighting his cigarette and puffing heavily. "I saw her not long ago when she came to the bank!"

"She was close to Mrs. Olmstead and Aunt Sophie," Sue said, glancing toward the kitchen doorway, as though her aunt were standing there. "How terrible for Mrs. Olson!"

George agreed. "I spoke to Mr. Sheppard yesterday in his office, before lunch. He was on his way to see Mr. Donaldson. I'm sure he spoke to Mrs. Olson and Mrs. Palmer, too."

"It says it was an accident," Sue said, sipping her coffee and finding she no longer had a taste for either the coffee or the muffin.

Brother and sister remained silent, a multitude of thoughts running through their minds. George put his cigarette in an ashtray and finally found his voice.

"Of course, it was an accident! We work downtown, Sue. With the traffic and trollies, the slushy sidewalks, she slipped and fell in front of a truck!"

Sue shivered slightly. "How awful! I didn't know Mrs. Olson too well, but Aunt Sophie always spoke well of her."

It was at that moment the phone rang from in the hallway. George and Sue looked at each other, surprised at receiving a call so early. George got up from the kitchen table and entered the hallway, just as Sophie was descending the stairs.

"Good morning, George," she said pleasantly to her nephew. She reached the last step, tightened the belt on her robe and was about to walk into the kitchen when George, who had answered the call, held the phone out to his aunt, speechless, his face perplexed and clearly upset.

Sophie, not understanding her nephew's reactions, simply took the candlestick phone and was clueless as to what was happening. Upon answering, she was relieved to hear Marjorie at the other end.

"Oh Sophie, I'm sorry to call so early. I just read in this morning's paper about poor Mary!"

Sophie was not quite awake. "What about Mary?"

"She was struck and killed last night downtown!"

Sophie held onto the phone, tightly, not believing what she told her, but she knew Marjorie was always honest and straightforward, so it must be the truth. She looked at George, who stood beside her, his face a mixture of incredulity and sadness. She turned her attention back to Marjorie, on the phone, who filled her in on the details as she had read them in the paper. Sophie thanked her friend for calling, told her she had just gotten up and hadn't seen the article for herself and would call her later in the morning. She handed the candlestick phone back to George, immobile, too weak to talk. She sat down at a chair in the hallway, dumbstruck, while at the same time Arthur came down the stairs. He greeted his wife and nephew pleasantly and noticed Sue had joined them in the hallway. He could sense something wrong, unspoken, known to them but not yet to him. He asked what the trouble was.

"Why don't we have our coffee, dear," Sophie told her husband, not wishing to alarm him first thing in the morning. "Marjorie's muffins are delicious, too."

As though by mutual consent, it seemed the right thing to do. George went to the stove and poured coffee for his aunt and uncle, brought the cups to the kitchen table along with a tray of muffins and then joined them, along with Sue, as Sophie related to Arthur the news about Mary. At the same time, she asked George for the paper, so she could read the article for herself. She fought back tears and Sue reached over and placed her hand on her arm.

"I saw Mary just the other day, when I was walking home from visiting Mrs. Olmstead," Sophie said, deep in thought. "She was coming out of the library. She seemed so secretive, really unlike herself, as though she was hiding something. I bumped into Mrs. Palmer, too."

"Why didn't you tell us about it?" Arthur asked.

"Well, I didn't think anything about it. Mary lives—or lived—on Dove Street, just a block from the library. Strange I'd see Mrs. Palmer in our neighborhood, too."

"Maybe she just wanted to go to the library," Sue offered sensibly.

"Poor Mrs. Olson," George said, reading the article again. He frowned. "Strange that she was crossing State and Broadway and the truck was turning right. Wouldn't she have crossed State from the Douw Building, to meet Mr. Olson? They usually take the same trolley after work, in front of the railroad building."

"Maybe she went to North Pearl Street to shop," Sue suggested.

"Maybe," George said, unconvinced.

"George, please don't look into things," Sophie said wearily. "Mrs. Olson has died, and we must support Mr. Olson at this time. And just before Christmas, too!" She clutched at a handkerchief and tried her best to stop crying.

"The streets are full of snow and ice this time of year," Arthur said, also extremely disturbed. "The city needs to do a better job in cleaning to make it safe for pedestrians."

George agreed, although reluctantly. He thought back to when he saw Mrs. Olson at the bank recently; her furtive demeanor, almost secretive as though she were hiding something. And showing surprise that her husband had visited the bank earlier in the day. He wondered if Mrs. Olson was suspicious of someone. Maybe she knew about the murders but was keeping it to herself? But why would she do that? Was she blackmailing someone?

George addressed his aunt. "I'm worried about you and Uncle Arthur."

Sophie assured George she and Arthur would be fine during the day. She'd plan dinner and have it ready as always for when he and Sue arrived home. George realized Sue had already left the kitchen and was busy dressing in her room.

"Have you spoken to Mr. Sheppard lately, George?" Arthur asked him.

George shook his head. "No, but I plan to call him today. I spoke to him yesterday as he was getting ready to leave for Mr. Donaldson's office. He planned to speak to him, Mrs. Palmer, and Mrs. Olson." He paused, uncertainly, reluctant to say what was on his mind. "I wonder if Mrs. Olson knew something about the recent murders. Even Mr. Olson, too. Maybe Mrs. Olson saw something she shouldn't have."

"George, I wouldn't look into anything," Arthur warned his nephew. "I wouldn't think Mrs. Olson's death is anything but natural. We have to support Mr. Olson the best we can."

Sophie agreed. "I'll call James later to see how he's holding up."

"I'll get us a Christmas tree later today," George announced. "They'll deliver it here for us, too. We can decorate it this weekend. It'll go right next to the fireplace."

He poured himself more coffee, lit another cigarette, and continued sitting at the breakfast table with Sophie and Arthur, deep in tumultuous thoughts. As the grandfather clock in the hallway struck seven-thirty, he realized so much time had gone by and he had yet to shave, shower or dress.

Getting up from the table, he butted his cigarette in an ashtray, slurped his coffee, and then gave his aunt and uncle each a reassuring hug. He then hurried upstairs to prepare for the day.

In the Olson's pleasant brownstone house on Dove Street, James Olson sat on the sofa in the living room, in his robe and slippers, not quite fully awake, listening to Inspector Harris and Lieutenant Taylor of the

Albany City Police. His face was somber and morose, his eyes blood-shot. Out of courtesy, he listened to the policemen although he had little to tell them. The policemen sat in armchairs across from James, listening to what he had to tell them.

"She must've gone shopping right after work," he explained. "There was a hatbox found near her. She must've gone to Whitney's first."

"Did she usually go shopping after work, Mr. Olson?" Inspector Harris asked.

James shook his head. "Rarely, although we've been planning for the holidays, of course."

"Do you have a large family?"

James again shook his head. "No, Mary and I have no children, although I think there are distant cousins on her side in either Buffalo or Niagara Falls, I'm not sure."

"The patrolman who arrived at the scene came here afterward to tell you what had happened, is that correct?"

"Yes, that is correct. I waited for Mary as I usually do and as she didn't show, I decided to take the trolley myself, thinking she was already home, preparing dinner."

"What time did you leave work, Mr. Olson?"

"The usual time, just a little after five o'clock."

"Your wife's accident occurred close to four-thirty, at the corner of State Street and Broadway. You didn't see it while you waited for the trolley in front of the railroad building?" His voice held incredulity.

"No, as I said, I came out just after five o'clock. I wasn't aware that there had been an accident. I didn't see anything. It must've been cleared by the time I came out of the building."

"The policeman at the scene had also looked at the contents of your wife's purse to establish identity. He noticed she carried quite a bit of cash in her wallet."

"Well, it's Christmas time, Inspector. As I said, she must've decided to shop before meeting me for the trolley."

"What is your position at the railroad company, Mr. Olson?"

"I'm an executive. I've been with the company for over thirty years. I see to railroad operations throughout the state, in particular trains going south to Kingston, Newburgh, and Port Jarvis."

While Lieutenant Taylor was also speaking to Mr. Olson and taking notes, Inspector Harris had the opportunity to look carefully at the man seated before them. Certainly not a bad-looking gentleman, about sixty or so, tall, physique well-toned for his age, attractive to the opposite sex, for sure. Must meet all sorts of women, too, with secretaries and female assistants. Of course, from his experience, the inspector knew outward appearances may cover an entirely different façade. He'd speak to others in the neighborhood to get more of an impression in the days to come. He asked Mr. Olson the names of friends they could contact on his behalf.

"Mary and I are friends with Mr. and Mrs. Arthur Drake and Mr. and Mrs. Henry Olmstead. The Drakes live on Lancaster and the Olmsteads on State." He hesitated. "I can call them myself, thank you just the same."

"In light of the recent murders here in the city, do you think someone may have caused your wife's death?"

James was appalled at such a comment. "Of course not, Inspector. I don't see how the recent murders could be connected to Mary's accident. The patrolman on the scene concluded she slipped and fell in front of the truck." His tone held incredulity and even resentment, that the inspector would mention something so ludicrous.

Although understanding his state of mourning and somewhat defiant attitude, which the inspector recognized were common in cases of recent unexpected deaths, Inspector Harris was rather surprised at the man's apparent harshness, as though he felt bitter indignation at having been subjected to such a preposterous suggestion.

Inspector Harris then stood, shook hands with James, expressed his sympathy, and thanked him for his time. Lieutenant Taylor closed the notebook he was writing in and also shook hands with James. They then walked to the hallway and the front door.

"Let us know if there's anything more, we can do for you, Mr. Olson," the inspector said.

James forced a weak smile and thanked them for stopping by. He opened the front door, said goodbye to the policemen and watched as they walked out into the cold light of the morning.

At the Ten Eyck Hotel, Sue was at her desk on the second-floor administration unit, filling out an expense report before bringing it to her boss for his approval. It was another busy morning at the hotel business office, with phones ringing, meetings in progress, and reports to be typed.

She looked up from the expense report and across the room saw Laura, just concluding a call. She hung up the receiver on the candlestick phone and met Sue's gaze.

"That was Mr. Sloane Sheppard," she announced, in a rather annoyed tone. "He'll be here to speak to us soon. Or I should say primarily, me. He mentioned he's spoken to you before." She sounded as though she resented Sloane's intent to speak to her and not Sue, having spoken with Sue at an earlier time.

"Yes, he met with all of us at home," Sue commented. She picked up the morning edition of the *Albany Times Union* and asked Laura if she had seen the notice about Mrs. Olson's fatal accident.

"Daddy showed it to me this morning when I was having breakfast," Laura commented. "We heard it on the radio, too. Poor Mrs. Olson."

Sue couldn't tell if she was sincere or just putting on an act. Since her near-death experience at the Capital Club, she had noticed a slight change in Laura Dupont, as though she would think of other people for a change than just herself. But Sue didn't think that would be a permanent change in someone so egotistical as Laura.

Business continued at a rather hectic pace; new accounts opened, out-of-state hotel executives from other lodgings were welcomed, two large conventions were planning functions at the hotel and a New Year's party was already set in the ballroom, with caterers and music being arranged. Sue had just hung up with a client when Sloane entered the office.

"Good morning, Mr. Sheppard," she said in recognition. She welcomed him to the office.

Sloane smiled, also in recognition. "Hello, Miss Latimer. It's nice to see you again. I'd like to speak to Miss Dupont. Is she here? I spoke with her earlier this morning."

"I'm over here," a female voice called from the far end of the room.

Sloane turned to his right and didn't realize there was another desk closer to the windows overlooking North Pearl Street. Looking around, he noticed numerous file cabinets, adding machines, three typewriters, two additional telephones and a mimeograph machine. A water cooler stood by the door, alongside another file cabinet. Despite being a large room, it had a cramped feel to it, perhaps because of the scattered tables on which reposed a multitude of files and reports.

Sloane made his way over to Laura's desk. She invited him to sit at the chair in front of her. She looked approvingly at the handsome man who claimed he was a private investigator. She wondered if he was single, although he was rather too old for her. But who cared about age, Laura thought, sizing him up quickly? Certainly, well-dressed, and conservative appearing, his trench coat and Fedora which he had taken off his head, revealing more of his personable face and a fine head of wavy black hair. Strong features and rather intent eyes. Laura smiled and liked what she saw.

"Thank you, Miss Dupont, for seeing me," Sloane began, noting her obviously haughty air. He took his small notebook out of his inner jacket pocket. "I've spoken to your stepfather…"

"I know," Laura interrupted. "Daddy told me. I don't know what else I can tell you."

"Why don't you start at the beginning?"

"You mean at the Capital Club? My stepfather and I, along with Mrs. Palmer, were having Thanksgiving dinner, when this crazy woman came at us with a carving knife! She took me by surprise, but I fought her off. She then lunged for Daddy, but he fought back, too."

"And then what happened?"

Laura looked at Sloane wondering if he really knew but wanted to hear it from her. She also wondered why he'd ask since he was investigating the murder of Thomas Latimer. What did this attack have to do with Thomas's murder? She took her time in replying.

"Well, they struggled, and the knife stabbed that crazy woman. She fell at Daddy's feet and there was blood all over his shirt and jacket and on the floor, too. It was just terrible."

"Were you acquainted with this woman, Miss Dupont?"

Laura shook her head. "No, but Daddy said she was a former client or something like that. I'm not really sure. You'd have to ask Daddy."

"I already did," Sloane said, rather tersely. "Is there anything more *you* can tell me about the attack, Miss Dupont?"

Laura again shook her head. "I'm sorry, Mr. Sheppard. I didn't know the woman, but I thought she must have been anti-American. There's a lot of that going on, especially after the war." She paused. "If you don't mind my asking, what's the point of asking these questions? I thought you were investigating Thomas Latimer's murder?"

Sloane thought Miss Laura Dupont a clever young woman. "I am indeed investigating his murder, Miss Dupont."

"And you think there's a tie in with his murder, the other guy found at the port and this crazy woman who attacked us?" She hesitated. "What about Mrs. Olson's death last night? You think that she was murdered, too?"

"I can't say at the moment," Sloane said, resorting to a cliché, which he knew irritated arrogant witnesses, like Laura Dupont. "I read about Mrs. Olson's death in the paper. The police are investigating. Apparently, it was an accident as she slipped on the slushy pavement."

Laura was quiet, fiddling with papers on her desk, moving the candlestick phone from one corner to another. Sloane realized he wouldn't get anything more from Laura Dupont. He stood to leave and thanked her for her time. As he approached Sue's desk, he could feel Laura's eyes on him, wondering what he'd say to her and what more he wanted to find out.

"Thank you, Miss Latimer, for your time."

"George still thinks Thomas wasn't Thomas," Sue said, rather bluntly, keeping her voice low so Laura wouldn't hear. "Has he said anything more about it to you?"

"Yes, he has," Sloane admitted. "I'm afraid I can't divulge information on the case as I am working for your brother, but if you have questions, you can always ask him."

Sue smiled, looking pretty and young in her blue dress and pearls. "I understand, Mr. Sheppard. George can be rather stubborn, especially once he thinks he's right on something."

This time Sloane smiled. He admired young George and Sue Latimer, obviously a close brother and sister, who relied on each other, having lost their parents at such a young age.

He made his way out of the office and pressed the button for the elevator. In no time, it arrived, the attendant opened the gates and Sloane stepped in. As it began its slow descent to the lobby, Sloane realized this case was far from over. There was something he wasn't seeing yet, a connection that needed verifiable proof. And Mrs. Olsons's sudden death. That, of course, was an accident. Sloane wondered, deep in thought.

The elevator arrived at the lobby and the attendant opened the gates. Walking through the vestibule, toward the revolving door, he also wondered if his hunch about Lena Bartosz was in vain.

In a comfortable apartment off of Genesee Street in Utica, a middle-aged woman was pacing back and forth, smoking incessantly, looking at the telegram she held in her hand. She had read it several times since receiving it yesterday afternoon. She puffed rather angrily at the cigarette that she held between nicotine-stained fingers. She then sat in an armchair in her well-furnished and spacious living room, her mind too full of anxiety and even dread.

Who was this Mr. Sheppard? Lena Bartosz fumed about her privacy, that he'd contact her in the first place, prying into her business.

What did he want to speak to her for? His message was brief but to the point.

Her mind returned to the horrendous ordeal of her sister's recent death and the death of her nephew. It was less than a month that her sister's body and her nephew's body had been returned to Utica. She had made the arrangements, a painstaking process. Sofia and Szymon had been murdered. Apparently, her sister went berserk. According to the policemen, she attacked a man and his daughter at the club where she worked on Thanksgiving.

Well, that sounded like Sofia, she thought, rather angrily. Hot-headed, her temper flaring, holding a grudge against the entire human race. But why did she take her frustrations out on that poor man and his innocent daughter? Maybe she meant to attack someone else?

She then thought of Sofia when they first came to the United States, settling in Utica. Neither she nor her sister married, their English was limited, but Sofia soon had two children out of wedlock. She'd tell people her husband died but she was still shunned by the community. The father of her two sons, a gypsy from Romania, left Sofia high and dry. Eventually, she moved to Albany, seeking a better life. But few people knew of the kind-heartedness her sister exhibited, by taking in a child who belonged to someone else. She membered how she and her sister fought the odds to raise the children, slaving at low-paying jobs, working hard to make ends meet. The war ruined everything, of course. And then the devastating flu pandemic that wiped out thousands. Families ripped apart, children left with strangers or in some cases abandoned, or in Sofia's case the couple she served as a housekeeper, entrusting their child with her.

Lena sighed, pushed some gray hair from her forehead, finished her cigarette, and put the radio on to a station playing popular tunes. Her sister was fortunate that she had been employed as a nursemaid to that wonderful couple. But after their deaths, she decided to move to Albany, with Szymon. Lena planned to stay in Utica with the other child. A strange arrangement, she told her sister, but it seemed to work.

But it was difficult, too, for her sister to know that she had contact with only one of her two sons, who went with her to Albany. The other was already in Albany and Lena always suspected that that was why Sofia moved there, to try to see him, contact him and maybe even claim him as her son. She had written and told Lena she tried to become a citizen, but there were problems with her paperwork and for various reasons, it all fell through the cracks.

Lena sighed again, a long-tired sigh. She reached for her pack of cigarettes. Once, she was rather pretty but her beauty faded, more from harsh living conditions and constant anxiety. She was somewhat overweight, her dress clung to her stoutest body, her round shoulders indicative of years of hard work. She was employed as a secretary at an insurance company and worked part-time in the evenings as a waitress at a local diner, but she didn't complain. She knew it was better than no job at all. And she had gone through periods without work. When she and her sister first came to Utica from Poland, they practically arrived with the shirts on their backs. That was so long ago, and so much had changed, some things for the better and others for the worse.

She looked again at the telegram. Mr. Sloane Sheppard, a private investigator in Albany. He'd want to speak to her about Sofia and Szymon. Most likely he didn't know about Pavel. Impulsively, she got up, went to the kitchen, picked up the candlestick phone, and asked for Western Union. She would not ignore his telegram.

She'd answer Mr. Sheppard and tell him he could come here tomorrow.

It was just after five o'clock and darkness had already settled over Albany. Downtown was full of Christmas shoppers and office workers rushing to get home to someplace warm. Trollies ran up and down State Street, North Pearl Street, Broadway, and Washington Avenue, amidst persistent snow showers and gusty winds, making the evening commute rather difficult.

After speaking with Miss Dupont and Miss Latimer at the Ten Eyck Hotel, Sloane returned to his office, just across North Pearl Street. He hung his trench coat on the rack behind the door, took off his suit jacket, loosened his tie and the top buttons of his vest. He was set to finish work on a few cases, tidy his desk and get ready to leave when he heard a knock on his office door. Thinking it was a client and cursing himself for not posting his business hours on the door, he opened it and instead saw a Western Union messenger.

"Mr. Sheppard? Telegram for you, sir."

Sloane fished in his pocket for a dime to give the young man. He thanked him, took the telegram, and closed the door. He saw it was from Utica and eagerly ripped it open. He read it several times, returning to his desk chair, lost in thought.

So, Lena Bartosz is willing to speak with me, he thought with satisfaction. He'd learn if what he surmised was the truth. Perhaps she'd know nothing that could help him. That'd be a chance he'd have to take. He looked at his appointment calendar on his desk and fortunately did not have anything scheduled for tomorrow. He then needed to check the timetable for trains to Utica. He went to a file cabinet and extracted several train schedules of the New York Central Railroad. No sooner had he returned to his desk to review them when another knock came on his office door. Glancing at his watch and wondering who'd come to see him after hours, reluctantly he opened the door and saw George standing before him.

"Mr. Sheppard," George said, relieved upon seeing him. "I was going to call you but since I work in this building, I decided to stop here on my way home." George noticed Sloane was getting ready to leave. "Oh, I'm sorry if you were just heading out, but I wanted to speak to you to find out if you've learned anything more about Thomas."

Sloane invited George into his office, while he put on his trench coat and fedora hat. "I contacted Lena Bartosz in Utica. I'll be planning a trip there, soon." He tucked the railroad timetables in his inside jacket pocket. "I'll join you on your way home, George."

George smiled. "Yes, I'd like that. We can talk on the way. I meet Sue in front of the hotel."

Sloane locked his office door and then joined George in waiting for the elevator. Once inside, with the attendant closing the gates, and squeezing in what was already a cramped space with office workers heading home, Sloane mentioned briefly that he had received a telegram from her.

"And what did she say?" George asked, excitedly, once they were in the lobby and walking toward the exit. He could hardly contain his anticipation as he eagerly looked at Sloane.

They walked on North Pearl Street, battling the snow showers, the cold wind, and the heavy crowds, and waited at the light at the corner of State Street. Sloane took his time in replying, choosing his words carefully.

"She agreed to see me," he told George as they crossed at the light. "But instead of calling Utica to speak to her, I'll take the train there."

"Do you think she knows anything about Thomas?"

"I'm not sure, George. She may have nothing to tell me. I'm sure she'll mention things about her sister and her sister's son. From there, I'll see if there is a connection with your brother."

George nodded, although disappointed that Sloane didn't seem to share his enthusiasm. Just then he spotted Sue, having come out of the hotel, bundled in her coat and cloche hat. She smiled and came up to them.

"Hi, George. Mr. Sheppard, fancy seeing you again!" She waited for an explanation as to why her brother was with the private investigator. "Is there something wrong, George?"

George shook his head. "No, Sue, I went to see Mr. Sheppard but he was leaving as I arrived. He told me he'd leave with us."

"Where do you live, Mr. Sheppard?" Sue asked him.

"On Madison Avenue," he answered. "I'll take the Lark Street trolley and get off at the corner of Lark and Madison and catch the Madison trolley from there."

"That'll give us time to talk," Sue suggested.

"Mr. Sheppard said he contacted the Bartosz woman in Utica," George told his sister, trying to keep the excitement out of his voice.

Sue also was excited. "Well, why don't we wait for the trolley," she told them, her teeth almost chattering. "The sooner I'm inside a trolley keeping warm, the better I'll feel!"

Sloane smiled at the young people and joined them in walking up North Pearl until they came to the trolley stop. A sizeable crowd of office workers and Christmas shoppers boarded at the same time, making it difficult to find three empty seats. George and Sue managed to find two seats, while Sloane stood briefly, before a rather heavy-set woman, loaded with a day's worth of Christmas shopping, got up, clumsily, dropping two bags worth of presents. George reached down and helped her retrieve them, enabling Sloane to sit in the seat she vacated.

As the trolley continued up State Street, turning left onto Washington Avenue, George turned to Sloane again and asked him about Lena Bartosz. Sue also looked at him carefully, not wanting to miss a word of what Sloane had to tell them.

Sloane related what little he knew of Lena Bartosz. As the sister of the deceased Sofia Bartosz, she may have information to impart that could draw light on the attack at the Capital Club. He told them he'd go to Utica tomorrow, once he figured out the train schedule. He added nothing more and saw two blank faces staring at him questioningly.

"But what does that have to do with Thomas's murder?" George asked, rather irritably. "Or I should say the phony Thomas."

"George, please don't say that," his sister implored. "There's no proof of an impostor, so you can't assume anything. Isn't that correct, Mr. Sheppard?"

Sloane noticed the trolley was about to turn onto Lark Street. He looked at George and Sue, again avoiding saying anything to cause hope or possible distress. He observed a large group exiting at the corner of Lark and Washington and at Lark and State, more people got on.

"I don't know if the murders tie in," he told them honestly. "She may have something to tell me. On the other hand, she may not, but at least she can tell me more about her sister."

"It's unfortunate what happened to Mrs. Olson," George said. "Did you hear about it?"

"Yes, I read about it in the paper," Sloane said and added nothing more.

George and Sue lapsed into an awkward silence, as the trolley continued its snail-like path up Lark Street. George still didn't see what this Bartosz woman had to do with Thomas, but he didn't pursue it any further with Sloane, at least not at the moment. Upon reaching the corner of Lark and Lancaster, he motioned to his sister that they should get off.

"Thanks, Mr. Sheppard," he told Sloane, as he stood, clutching onto the guards hanging from the roof. He put on his cap and got ready to brave the cold. "Please let me know if you learn anything when you're in Utica."

At the corner of Lark and Madison, Sloane descended and then soon boarded another trolley, heading north on Madison. While sitting between a large older man, absorbed in the evening paper, and a mother with her small son, Sloane thought over and over the facts of the case as he knew them.

Three vicious murders and the death of Mrs. Olson, her death ruled an accident. Sloane knew it wasn't that simple. It was close to six o'clock by the time he reached his apartment. Upon entering, he took off his hat and coat and then sat at the kitchen table and looked at the timetable for trains going to Utica. He'd purchase a round-trip ticket, returning in the evening. A long day, he knew, but to resolve this case, he felt it was necessary.

He'd send Lena Bartosz another telegram, letting her know he'd be there tomorrow. He picked up his candlestick phone and asked for Western Union. After placing the telegram, and marking it important, he felt satisfied as though the answers he sought would soon be within reach.

He then went to the sink, filled the kettle with water, and lit the gas stove. While preparing a cup of tea, he reviewed his plans. Tomorrow he'd leave on an early morning train for Utica.

And, he hoped, his trip to Utica would prevent another unexplained death in the case of Thomas Latimer.

CHAPTER EIGHTEEN

O n Friday morning Claire was busy in the office, finishing reports she had not completed on Thursday. It was business as usual at the law office of Reginald Donaldson, but not quite as normal as before. Sitting at her desk, she paused momentarily from her work. She took a sip of coffee and glanced out the windows.

A weak sun shone through the windows of the Douw Building on Broadway and State Street. It was still cold with occasional snow showers, but not nearly as windy as it had been. There was a definite feel of Christmas in the air, as Albany was prepared to welcome the holiday and the New Year. There were banners in store windows declaring 1929 the year of continued prosperity. With the Hoover administration ready to take office, Albany, like other cities across the country, was jubilant and optimistic about its future.

Claire had taken an early trolley downtown and arrived well before Reggie, to start work as she planned to leave early. She hoped it'd be a good day. She tried to get into the holiday spirit but found it difficult. She looked forward to a dinner date this evening that she had planned with another politician, this one from Yonkers, who she had met at a speakeasy recently. She was dressed to the nines, in a sleek black dress, highlighting her excellent figure, her bobbed hair combed and fashionable, an alluring scent of Chanel No. 5 and a long string of pearls hanging rather provocatively down her chest. She planned to meet her dinner date at the DeWitt Clinton Hotel. There was a band tonight at the hotel and a few twirls around the dance floor wouldn't hurt.

She looked around the empty office and rather liked being alone. She smiled to herself, reflecting that her access to all parts of the office had been extremely useful over the years. But she had never had access to Reggie's locked desk drawers, she thought bitterly because if she had, she'd have noticed her notebook which he somehow managed to obtain. As foolish as Reggie undoubtedly was, he was also clever and manipulating.

She sat back on her chair and was deep in thought. Well, no need to worry about interfering Mary or stupid Reggie, either, she thought rather smugly, lighting a cigarette. She didn't plan to attend the wake this evening, although Reggie told her he'd go, which surprised her. Certainly, Reggie couldn't have felt any compassion, as dense and shallow as he was. Even his selfish stepdaughter had more sense than he did.

We'll have to start looking for a new court reporter and secretary, Claire lamented. That'd take time, especially before Christmas as it'd be difficult to find a suitable secretary. But for now, she'd have to do Mary's work, which meant putting in overtime. She'd ask Reggie for more money, and he'd give it to her because he knew if he didn't, she'd expose his bootlegging activities. Did she really care if he spread the rumor of her former life in Elmira? Who'd believe him, anyway? Besides, she was firmly established in this city. She knew the right people and had the right connections. Politicians, businessmen, well-heeled society women who gave lavish parties. What did Claire care if Reggie told people she was a former call girl?

Well, I do care, she thought morosely. Her former life could destroy her and if she wanted to secure a new position, who'd want to hire a former call girl to work in a business office? Especially in a city like Albany, conservative and rather close-minded.

She had seen the article on Mary's tragic accident in the paper yesterday morning. Foolish Mary, galivanting around Albany, instead of watching for the heavy traffic. She must've been at Whitney's or doing something stupid. Well, she was out of the picture and need not pose a threat to her any longer.

No sooner had she finished typing a report when the office door opened, and Reggie walked in. Glancing up at him, Claire thought he looked worse than ever. His glasses halfway down his nose, his shirt wrinkly, he hung up his trench coat on the rack behind the door and addressed Claire with a weak smile.

"I'm going to Mary's wake this evening," he told her as though she didn't already know. "Are you still leaving early Claire?"

"About a half-hour earlier," was all she told him and didn't volunteer information. She didn't feel like discussing poor Mary or making small talk with him. As he proceeded to his office and was about to close the door, Claire cleared her throat.

"Reggie, do you plan to hire a new court reporter and secretary? I'm doing Mary's work and my own too and I think I should get compensated for both."

Reggie looked at her with a mixture of contempt and anger. He knew she was serious, and he also knew the consequences if he didn't give in to her.

"We called a truce, Claire, don't you remember that?"

"That has nothing to do with additional work." Claire didn't back down by his rather threatening tone. "I'm busier now than ever. I came in earlier than usual to get caught up. Someone has to complete

Mary's work. So, I believe I'm entitled to more money." She was blunt in her approach. "Wouldn't you feel the same if you were in my shoes, Reggie?"

She looked at him carefully and waited for his reply. When it came, it both surprised and pleased her, although she knew from experience not to trust anything he said.

"Well, I'm not in your shoes, Claire," he said, almost mocking her. "I'll give you an extra five dollars a week. That should suffice."

Before she could add anything further, he told her he didn't want to be disturbed and then closed his office door firmly.

She sat back on her desk chair, puffing away at her cigarette, a satisfied smile on her face. She'd taken care of Mary, putting that nosy, interfering woman in her place. Now she had put brainless Reggie in his place, too. Claire smiled to herself. She knew extremely well which side her bread was buttered on.

She crushed her cigarette in the ashtray on her desk, bent over a court report, and continued with her work. It'd be a good day after all.

In her clean and comfortable kitchen, Marjorie finished icing a vanilla cake and then placed the glass lid on top of the serving tray. The cake looked delicious. She planned to bring this latest confection to the Drakes as she and Henry were invited for lunch. As always, Marjorie insisted on bringing the sweet. She wiped her hands on a dishtowel and then went to the living room, where Henry was listening to the radio and reading the morning paper.

"We should leave for the Drakes soon," she told him, taking a seat on the sofa. "Frankly, I'm surprised Sophie has the strength to make lunch for us."

Henry agreed. "Perhaps she wants the company."

Marjorie agreed. "Have you spoken to James?"

"I haven't," Henry said. He buttoned his sweater, still chilly despite the warmth from the coal furnace. "I assume he returned to work. Probably the best thing for him."

Within fifteen minutes, Henry was locking the front door and ushering his wife outside. Bundled in heavy coats and scarves wrapped around their necks the Olmsteads left their charming brownstone, walking steadily up State Street, past the state capitol on their way to Lancaster Street.

They reached South Swan Street and turned left, soon arriving at Lancaster Street, amidst a heavy snow squall and snarled traffic. Upon arriving at the Drake's house, Marjorie rang the bell and waited patiently. Soon the door opened, and Sophie beamed happily at her friends.

She welcomed them inside, where Arthur stood behind his wife, greeting them in turn. He led them to the living room, where a fire danced brilliantly and warmed the room comfortably. Sophie stood at the living room entrance and announced that lunch was ready if they wanted to eat now.

"Have you heard from Mr. Sheppard?" Henry asked.

"No, thank goodness," Sophie said, much to her own surprise. They looked at her, wondering why she'd make that comment. "I mean, for George's sake. He keeps thinking Thomas wasn't Thomas. Just because there were differences in their appearance, doesn't mean he wasn't his brother."

"Well, Thomas did look different, Sophie," Marjorie admitted as she helped her set the table. "He certainly wasn't like George in temperament." She paused. "We have to get through Mary's wake this evening."

Sophie nodded. "Arthur and I are going, too. George and Sue will love this pot roast." She tried changing the subject, standing by the stove, lowering the temperature in the oven.

At that moment, the doorbell rang. Arthur went to the front door. He saw a young man, his face red from the cold, smiling and holding a beautiful spruce tree. A van was double-parked on Lancaster, with numerous Christmas trees loaded onto it.

"Is this the home of Mr. George Latimer? He bought a tree from us over at the tree market on Central Avenue. I told him I'd deliver it. Where should I put it?"

Arthur opened the door wider and led the young man into the living room, where he stood the tree against the far wall. George had already set boxes of decorations and garland on the floor. Henry tipped the youth, thanked him, and saw him to the door. Upon returning to the living room, he noticed Sophie, Henry and Marjorie were already there, with their coffee, admiring the pretty tree.

"George and Sue will decorate tomorrow evening," Sophie said, sitting on the sofa next to Marjorie and admiring the beautiful tree. "First, we must attend Mary's wake."

Although Arthur, Marjorie, and Henry continued talking about Mary and the wake set for this evening, Thomas's murder, and the events of the Bartosz's murders, Sophie sat quietly, saying little. Perhaps George is right, she thought, as though arguing against her own inner beliefs. Who was the young boy who came to this house ten years ago, who she raised, clothed, fed, and loved? And who did they bury a month ago if it wasn't Thomas?

She blinked as she realized Arthur was speaking to her. She joined her husband, Marjorie, and Henry at the card table for bridge, her mind momentarily forgetting the recent tumultuous events and the nagging suspicions clouding her mind.

With Christmas fast approaching, the Home Savings Bank was busier than usual, especially in the late afternoon. As the five o'clock hour arrived, George was about to leave for the day when the candlestick phone on his desk rang. Hoping it would not be a customer at this late hour, he was surprised to hear the voice of Mr. Sloane Sheppard.

"George, this is Mr. Sheppard. I'm still in Utica but will be taking a later train back to Albany." He mentioned he wanted to stop by tomorrow, Saturday, at their house to see him and his family. George could hardly contain his excitement.

"What did you find out, Mr. Sheppard? Is there a connection with Thomas?"

Sloane took a deep breath, not answering George's question directly. "I'll be bringing some people to your house, George. People I've met here in Utica. So, perhaps you can prepare your aunt, uncle, and sister for some revealing news before I arrive." He chose his words carefully without adding more detail. George was still delighted to know Sloane had made progress.

"Certainly, Mr. Sheppard. Thank you so much for calling."

It was planned then that Sloane would come to the house tomorrow afternoon, about one o'clock. George promised he'd relate this news to his aunt, uncle and sister and then hung up.

Outside on the sidewalk, crossing at the light and then waiting at the corner of State and North Pearl in front of the Ten Eyck

Hotel, George thought back to the conversation he just had with Mr. Sheppard. He'd tell Sue about it, of course. But there was something he said that came back to him. The more he thought of it the more it bothered him. *So, you can prepare your aunt, uncle, and sister for some revealing news.* He continued standing in front of the hotel, snow showers swirling around him, deep in thought. What did Mr. Sheppard mean? He realized he foolishly didn't ask what sort of news. And prepare for what?

At that moment, Sue exited the hotel. Together they walked to the trolley stop, conversing between themselves, unaware of the pandemonium they would endure the next day.

CHAPTER NINETEEN

I t was Sophie's habit to stay in bed a little longer on weekends, knowing George and Sue didn't have to leave for work. But with the news George imparted last evening about Mr. Sheppard's discovery in Utica, she found herself unable to stay in bed. Fitfully, she got up, put on her housecoat and slippers, and went downstairs. As she reached the hallway, she glanced at the grandfathers' clock. She saw it was only seven o'clock and already feeling wide awake, she decided to make the coffee and get breakfast ready for when Arthur, George and Sue came down. She could smell the freshly cut pine tree still in the living room, waiting for George and Sue to decorate it. She entered the kitchen, turned on lights and proceeded to the sink.

With the coffee pot on the stove, she went to the hallway and the front door to retrieve the morning paper. She noticed it had snowed again during the night. It was calm outside as though all life had ceased to exist. Closing the door and returning to the kitchen, she poured a cup of coffee and sat at the table. She was about to unfold the paper when her thoughts returned again to what George told them upon returning from work last evening.

Mr. Sheppard had been in Utica and must have met that Bartosz woman. Why in the world would he bring her here? How horrid, Sophie thought and took a rather large gulp of coffee. And she's coming from Utica just to see us?

And the phony Thomas, an issue in which George was so stubbornly adamant. Did this woman know something about it if it was really true? But how could it be, Sophie cried to herself. Wouldn't her brother and sister-in-law have known? Wouldn't they have told her when she and Arthur took the children in?

Well, not necessarily, she thought. Her mind went back to the tumultuous days ten years ago when her brother died overseas, and her sister-in-law died from that awful flu. She remembered before the war the homeless children in Utica and Albany, abandoned by their families, starving in the streets, begging for food. She read in the papers about unwed mothers, giving their babies to strangers, in exchange for money just to survive. She had heard first-hand from Marjorie, a nurse at Albany City Hospital, and had heard on the radio and read in the paper about the deprivation of starving children. Some were taken in by the state, others by strangers. Then the war only made conditions worse. It had created difficult if not unsavory conditions for families. But how did that relate to Thomas? George, Susan, and Thomas were born before the war, but it was during the war that they lost their parents and could have been homeless, just like thousands of other children.

Her reverie was broken by the sound of footsteps on the stairs. She looked up and saw George in his pajamas, robe, and slippers, unshaven, his hair tousled, sleep still in his eyes.

"Aunt Sophie," he exclaimed, entering the kitchen. "You usually sleep late on weekends."

He sat across from her at the kitchen table and immediately could tell something was deeply troubling her. He waited for his coffee but took his pack of cigarettes out of his robe pocket and was about to light one but decided to hold off.

"I'm concerned about this Bartosz woman," Sophie told him.

"She may have known mother and father," George said.

"I don't see what that has to do with us," Sophie said wearily. "George, dear, I wish you'd stop this insistence about Thomas. I know you mean well, but you're upsetting Uncle Arthur."

George lit a cigarette and then deposited the match in an ashtray on the table. "I don't mean to, Aunt Sophie. But I have my doubts which is why I went to Mr. Sheppard. It's been a month since Thomas was murdered, and the police haven't found who's responsible!"

"Do you suppose Mrs. Olson's death is connected with this?" Sophie asked him.

George was about to get up and retrieve cups, cream, and sugar when he looked carefully at his aunt. He took his time in replying, not wanting to upset her any more than she already was.

"I don't know. I asked Mr. Sheppard if he knew about Mrs. Olson's death, and he mentioned he read about it in the paper. But he didn't say anything more about it."

Sophie nodded. "He may not know anything else." She paused. "Mr. Sheppard is bringing that Bartosz woman?"

George hesitated. "Well, he didn't say who he was bringing but I assumed that's who he meant. He was still in Utica when he called me."

"When do you intend to decorate the tree?" Sophie asked, changing the subject. "Perhaps I'll help you. It'll take my mind off of things."

"I'll wait for Sue to get up and then start to empty the ornaments out of the boxes. And the garland, too. Maybe Uncle Arthur can help if he wants."

The morning wore on, George and Sue helping Sophie clean the kitchen and then retreating upstairs to dress for the day. Arthur approached his wife and asked her what was wrong.

At the sink drying the dishes, Sophie took her time replying. She wiped a plate with unnecessary vigor. "This is insane, Arthur, the whole thing is just insane!" She stopped, put the plate on the counter and wiped away a few tears. Arthur put his arm around her and tried to console her.

"We'll hear what Mr. Sheppard has to say, Sophie. Maybe he's found out more about that woman who tried to kill Mr. Donaldson and Laura. It won't hurt to listen to him."

"But what does it have to do with us?"

Arthur fumbled, seeing the point of her comment. "I don't know, dear. I really don't know."

They stood by the sink, trying to put together the fragments of a puzzle that had too many loose ends, too many unanswered questions. At that moment, the doorbell rang. Thinking it was Mr. Sheppard, Sophie heaved a heavy sigh, but then glanced at the kitchen clock and realized it was still early for his arrival. George answered the door and greeted Marjorie and Henry.

"Hello, George, dear," Marjorie said pleasantly.

George welcomed Marjorie and Henry, took their coats, and left them on the hallway chair. He then led them down the hallway to the kitchen, where Arthur and Sophie stood by the window. By the look on their faces, George could tell his aunt and uncle were still preoccupied and confused.

"Marjorie, dear and Henry," Sophie said, coming forward to greet her friends. "What a pleasant surprise on a Saturday morning! What brings you here at this time?"

Marjorie explained that she and Henry were going Christmas shopping downtown and stopped by to see if she and Arthur would care to join them.

"Well, we would, but we're expecting a visit this afternoon from Mr. Sheppard."

Marjorie looked questioningly from Sophie to Arthur and then back to Sophie. Even Henry had a puzzled look on his face. They waited for Sophie to continue.

"He called George yesterday from Utica. He's bringing people here to meet us."

Marjorie was at a loss for words. "Well, maybe it'll help to clarify everything, Sophie."

Sophie smiled weakly and then led her friends to the living room, where they could talk. Arthur put the radio on to a station playing Christmas carols, while Henry and Marjorie admired the beautiful tree waiting to be decorated. Marjorie mentioned they planned to visit James Olson later and Sophie commented she and Arthur would do the same.

At that moment George appeared at the living room entrance. He mentioned he wanted to take a walk, to clear his mind. Sophie told him as always to be careful.

"Why don't you wait for Sue?" Arthur asked before he turned to leave.

George shook his head. "No, she's getting dressed and it always takes her a long time. So, I'd rather go alone. I'll be back soon."

Sophie, Arthur, Marjorie, and Henry glanced at one another, each realizing the toll the murder of Thomas, the Thanksgiving murder, the death of Mary Olson and the possible impostor who they knew as Thomas had had on George. His face, usually upbeat, was now downcast. He excused himself and headed for the front door.

Once outside, George breathed in the fresh, cold air. He pulled his cap lower on his head and headed north on Lancaster for Lark Street.

As he expected, it was full of shoppers, heading to the specialty stores and the market. With his hands in his pockets, he walked along the busy street trying not to appear disgruntled. But he knew that was exactly how he felt.

He reached the intersection of Lark and State and then crossed at the light. Upon reaching Lark and Washington Avenue, he looked across at Harmanus Bleecker Hall. He hoped the Mary Pickford film Sue wanted to see was still playing. They had planned to see it but with all the turmoil they'd been through, they didn't have time. He crossed Washington Avenue at the light and was about to approach Hamanus Bleecker Hall when he almost collided with a tall man, walking hurriedly down the street as though in a rush. He apologized and then George realized who it was.

"Mr. Donaldson," he said and caught his breath. "I didn't recognize you."

Reggie smiled. "Hello, George. I'm just Christmas shopping. Laura always likes perfume and pearls, so I might get her those this year." It was a rather uncomfortable meeting, as Reggie towered over George, looking rather menacing in a trench coat and fedora pulled low on his head. George wondered why he felt he needed to explain what he was doing. Reggie made a few more words of small talk and then went on his way.

George looked after him as he walked on Washington Avenue, heading south toward the state capitol. And strange too that he'd walk to North Pearl Street instead of taking the trolley on such a cold morning. He seemed preoccupied, too, almost as though he was disturbed about something. Of course, the attempted murder was too much for him and for Laura, too.

Out of curiosity, he decided to follow Reggie down the street. It wasn't hard to spot him, as he was quite tall and stood out among the other pedestrians. At the corner of Washington and Swan Street, he noticed Reggie turned left, heading past the Cathedral of All Saints. Amidst the pedestrians and the snow showers, George saw Reggie talking to two men on Elk Street. He then noticed they got into a car, parked on the side of the cathedral, and drove off. He was about to turn to walk back up Washington Avenue when he was suddenly hailed.

"Well, hello, George," said a deep female voice. "What brings you here?"

It was Claire Palmer who stood in his path. George noticed her well-made up face, lipstick, and cloche hat. Her fur coat clung to her shapely figure. He had never actually spoken to Mrs. Palmer, although he had seen her plenty of times, but at the moment he wanted nothing more than to get away from her.

"Oh, I'm out for a walk," he told her although he'd prefer telling her to mind her own business. "What about you? Christmas shopping?" His voice had a tinge of sarcasm to it.

"No, just out walking, like you," Claire said and smiled. "It's such a nice day. It's invigorating, don't you think? I might stop at Whitney's later, to look at the Christmas sales."

George nodded. "Soon it'll be Christmas." He paused, not knowing what to say and feeling rather overawed by this over-dressed middle-aged woman. "Well, I have to get going, Mrs. Palmer."

Claire smiled again. "Nice to see you, George."

George continued walking up Washington Avenue and this time stopped at Harmanus Bleecker Hall. He noticed *My Best Girl* with Mary Pickford was held over. Sue would be delighted to hear that.

He crossed Washington at the light and thought of the people he just encountered, both rather strange and foreboding in their own right. Mr. Donaldson certainly acted peculiar, but then George had always considered him rather an odd character anyway. He glanced at his watch and saw it was close to eleven o'clock. He promised Sue they'd decorate the tree this morning before Mr. Sheppard arrived.

Walking briskly up Lark Street in the cold sunshine, heading toward Lancaster Street, his young mind wondered about Mr. Donaldson and Mrs. Palmer; certainly, unusual seeing them at practically the same time on a Saturday morning. He gave it no more thought as he arrived home.

"Oh, it's so beautiful," Marjorie exclaimed. "The perfect tree, George!"

It was after twelve o'clock and George, upon returning from his walk, eagerly began to help Sue decorate the Christmas tree. Sophie had convinced Marjorie and Henry to stay for lunch, although she didn't have much to offer, except sandwiches and salad. Marjorie and Henry told her they'd love to stay. Marjorie helped Sophie prepare the sandwiches and even assisted in decorating the tree with George and Sue. Inwardly she wondered if Sophie wanted them there while Mr. Sheppard paid them a visit. Henry helped George with the garland, while Arthur and Sue affixed ornaments on the tree limbs. Arthur had found a radio station playing wonderful Christmas carols. The time passed peacefully, with everyone caught up in the holiday spirit, humming and singing along to the carols.

They had enjoyed the sandwiches, salad, and coffee and after Marjorie and Sophie washed up in the kitchen, they joined them in the living room, helping to decorate. They stood back and admired the ornate tree.

"It's beautiful," Marjorie repeated. "Simply beautiful."

George thanked her, straightening up from looping the garland from the top of the tree to the bottom. He then climbed a step ladder and placed the silver star on top, making the tree complete. Sophie also admired the beautiful spruce, looking at it while standing next to Marjorie.

"Now we need to wrap the gifts," Sue said, also standing back and looking at the tree.

"Well, I haven't finished shopping yet, dear," Sophie admitted. "So, I'm afraid mine aren't ready yet. But you can put yours there, of course."

"We'll have the best Christmas ever," Henry said, putting an arm around his wife.

Marjorie and Henry always spent part of Christmas Eve with the Drakes. They exchanged gifts and enjoyed Sophie's fish dinner, along with Marjorie's desserts.

They were still admiring the pretty tree, George straightening some of the ornaments and parts of the garland when the doorbell rang. It was as if they had forgotten about their early afternoon visitor, so relaxed and intent on decorating the tree. Even George had momentarily forgotten, as though the soothing effects of decorating, along with the peaceful Christmas music, had obliterated the thoughts of the murders and Sloane's visit from his mind.

Nobody moved as the doorbell rang again. Although the head of the house, Arthur, rather than answering the door himself, sat rather tiredly in an armchair and allowed Henry to answer it. Sophie lowered the radio and then joined Marjorie on the sofa. Only George and Sue remained standing, by the tree, not sure what to expect.

They could hear Henry talking in the hallway, where he took hats and coats, leaving them on the hallway chair. He soon returned followed by Sloane Sheppard. Behind him were a middle-aged woman and a young man, peering anxiously into the living room, unsure of what they were doing and perhaps even regretting being there. Sloane cleared his throat and addressed the Drakes, the Olmsteads, George and Sue.

"Hello, George, Sue, Mr. and Mrs. Drake," he said, looking at them each in turn. "And Mr. and Mrs. Olmstead, nice to see you again." He was dressed professionally, his appearance neat and clean. He paused, while everyone tried to look past him at the two strangers. Aware of their probing eyes, he continued. "I returned yesterday from Utica and convinced these people I met to come here. They're staying with me and will return to Utica tomorrow." He hesitated. "I think it's imperative they meet you."

He moved so they could see the woman in the back of him. She was of medium height, and although perhaps only fifty, her face appeared as though she had endured many difficulties over the years and had not weathered them well, which therefore gave her the semblance of being older. She wore a black dress with pearls, no make-up and her brown hair was combed back, not fashionably, but adequately. She introduced herself to Sophie, Arthur, Marjorie, Henry, George, and Sue.

"Hello," she said, rather demurely. "My name is Lena Bartosz." She paused, uncertainly, rather nervously. "Thank you for allowing us into your home."

Sophie smiled briefly and welcomed her, unsure how to proceed and unsure why this woman was in her home in the first place. "And who is the young man behind you?" she asked, trying to look behind Lena.

George had yet to fully take in the scene before him. He moved forward to see better. And then he almost crumpled to the floor, feeling his legs weaken, holding onto the sofa next to Sophie. Sue noticed as her brother's face became ashen white as though he'd faint. Her gaze then returned to the two people standing before them.

The young man moved forward as Lena Bartosz stepped aside. He addressed them; a trifle embarrassed with so many eyes looking at him at once.

"Hi, everyone," he said with a boyish smile. "I'm Thomas Latimer."

CHAPTER TWENTY

I t seemed as though time stood still, and all life ceased to exist. No one moved or uttered a sound. The only sounds were the radio turned low, playing Christmas carols and the ticking of the grandfathers' clock from in the hallway. The peaceful Christmas music was in stark contrast to the tense atmosphere occurring at that moment.

Sloane looked at the people seated around the living room, realizing the extent of the sudden shock. Sophie sat transfixed, too horrified to speak, her eyes practically bulging from fright and disbelief. Arthur had gone completely ashen white, staring straight ahead, also unable to talk. Marjorie and Henry were dumbstruck, trying to formulate words, stuttering in confusion, and finally giving up the effort. Even Sue found she couldn't speak, aghast at the sight before her. After a few moments, George regained himself. He spoke, hoarsely, his voice a mixture of elation and astonishment.

"Thomas, it's you! I'm George, your brother! And this is Sue, your sister!"

Thomas smiled again. "Hey, George! And Sue! I've heard about you from Mr. Sheppard! It's great to meet you guys!" His demeanor was casual, as though meeting long-lost relatives was an everyday occurrence.

Now that he was in full sight of everyone, George could see him more clearly. He was of medium height and dressed casually in dark slacks, shirt and tie, his brown hair combed back from his forehead. He bore a striking resemblance to George. Even dressed unpretentiously, he gave a dapper appearance, like his older brother. Everyone continued staring at Thomas and he continued staring back at them.

There was an awkward, stunned silence until Sophie found the courage to speak. She cleared her throat and addressed Sloane and Lena Bartosz. In casting a quick glance at his aunt, George was surprised she didn't pass out from the shock. He was even more surprised she was able to speak at all. Her tone was firm and to the point.

"Is this some sort of joke, Mr. Sheppard? What is the meaning of this intrusion? Is George paying you for fabricating such a farce?'

Sloane shook his head. "No, Mrs. Drake, this isn't a joke or a farce. This is your nephew, Thomas. He's been living with Miss Bartosz in Utica." He paused. "He's a student at Hamilton College and eventually wants to go to law school."

Thomas smiled rather sheepishly, his face flushing, not used to such praise or attention bestowed on him. He stood next to Lena Bartosz, looking at everyone in astonishment.

"I believe you owe us an explanation, Mr. Sheppard," Arthur said, also rather firmly.

Again, Sloane nodded. "May we sit down? I think Miss Bartosz would like to tell you about herself." He paused. "I apologize for the shock this has caused each of you."

"I don't think shock is the correct word," Sophie said, still overcome by the news.

George had gone into the kitchen to retrieve extra chairs, allowing Sloane, Lena, and Thomas to sit. Lena looked first at Sloane and then at the family, tears almost welling up in her eyes. She took a handkerchief from her purse and dabbed at her eyes, trying to compose herself.

"Please forgive me, Mrs. Drake," she said. "This has been quite a difficult time. My sister and nephew were murdered recently, and I've had to provide the funeral arrangements in having their bodies brought to Utica. It's been an expense I wasn't counting on." She paused, looking at the faces before her. "I can't speak for my sister, only what I know to have happened many years ago."

Sophie encouraged her. "Yes, please, tell us." She glanced at Thomas, still not believing that she was looking at her nephew. She patiently listened to what this Bartosz woman had to tell them.

"When my sister and I came to Utica from Poland many years ago, we hoped to make a better life. It was hard finding work since we didn't speak English well. In 1898, Sofia became pregnant and gave birth to Szymon. The father left Sofia and Szymon never knew him. He used our last name, to avoid problems, but people in our neighborhood caught on. We were treated like outcasts, especially Sofia, as an unwed mother. The only people who were kind to Sofia and I were Max and Lydia Latimer, who entrusted the care of their youngest son, Thomas, to her."

"I still don't understand," George said, rather impatiently.

Lena cast a tired look his way. "No, I'm sure you don't, George because it is hard to understand. An unwed mother had few if any rights over her children. My sister had two children out-of-wedlock and little money to care for them. We worked day and night to keep food on the table. Sofia found work as a nursemaid to Thomas, who she loved and cared for as her own."

"Please continue," Sophie said soothingly.

Lena sighed. "Well, Max and Lydia died within the same year, leaving three homeless children. Lydia promised Sofia she'd take in Pavel, the boy you believed was Thomas, and raise him as their own, even naming him Thomas. Pavel never knew his real name or his father and believed that Max and Lydia were his parents. When Max and Lydia died, you and your husband took in the children, including Pavel."

"Who we thought was Thomas," George added, casting a glance at his real brother.

Lena nodded. "And Sofia and I kept the real Thomas."

"But why?" Sophie stammered. "Why would my brother and sister-in-law agree to this charade? Why would they give up their son to you and your sister?"

"Your brother and sister-in-law saw how well Sofia had cared for Thomas. When Max was killed in the war and Lydia came down with that terrible flu, there was nothing more they could do for their children. Sofia and Lydia were close, confiding in each other, that Lydia would raise Pavel as her own to take the stigma of an illegitimate birth away from her. Sofia told people she was married but Szymon's and Pavel's father, a Romanian, returned to his country." She paused. "I never knew the children's father, but nobody questioned it and it worked for Sofia."

"Do you mean that when my wife and I went to Utica to get the children," Arthur said, clearly astonished at what he was hearing, "that we had a child who didn't belong to Max and Lydia?"

Lena slowly nodded. "But they didn't see it that way. They loved Pavel as their own and provided him with the best care until Max died overseas and Lydia was so sick with the flu. Sofia and I continued living in Utica, caring for Thomas." She cast a glance at Thomas who smiled in return.

"Didn't having Thomas live with you also cause problems?" Arthur asked.

"No, not really," Lena continued. "We had moved to another part of Utica, where no one knew us. In the new neighborhood, no one knew Max and Lydia. And nobody knew the Latimer name, so we decided to let Thomas keep his last name. George, Sue, and Pavel then went to Albany to live with you while Thomas stayed with us." She spoke as though it was that simple but knowing full well it wasn't. She paused as if she had not gotten to the worse part. "In time, Sofia decided to move to Albany with Szymon, to make the new start she so desperately wanted as she didn't feel she had found it in Utica. There wasn't much for her in Utica and her English skills were getting better. She also hoped to see Pavel, although she knew that'd be difficult since he was living here as a Latimer."

"And did he know he wasn't a Latimer?" Marjorie asked in disbelief.

Lena shook her head. "No, he thought he was Thomas Latimer. He was an infant when Lydia took him in and cared for him. Sofia was an excellent mother. She loved and cared for Thomas, from infancy. That's why Lydia didn't want to separate them. She knew she was dying and entrusted the care of the real Thomas to Sofia. When Sofia moved to Albany, Thomas and I told her we'd stay in Utica. She left over a year ago. We'd stay connected through letters." She paused. "But I think she really wanted to move to Albany to see Pavel."

"And did she see him?" George asked, clearly mesmerized by this story.

"I don't know," Lena said. "But Mr. Sheppard wanted proof of his identity." She reached in her purse and took out a fingerprint card, dated 1908. "These are Pavel's fingerprints."

Sloane leaned over and took the fingerprint card from her. "I'd like to bring these fingerprints to police headquarters. From his numerous arrests by the Albany City Police, they'll make a comparison. I don't think there's any question that the prints will match."

"My brother and sister-in-law were very caring people," Sophie said tenderly. "Although I find this story difficult to believe, I know who's involved and therefore, I do believe it. Lydia never told me about the real Thomas staying in Utica. If he had a good upbringing with your sister Sofia, then Lydia knew that was the best for him. It can be difficult to separate an infant from its caregiver."

Lena wiped away a tear, then addressed George. "My sister never worried about Pavel, the phony Thomas, because she knew he was safe with your aunt and uncle. She hoped someday to see him again."

"And Thomas stayed with you and your sister?" Henry asked.

Lena nodded. "Yes, Max and Lydia didn't want to take him away from Sofia. She loved him as though he was her own son. Sofia and Thomas had a natural, nurturing bonding that Lydia didn't want to separate, especially after she became so ill. When Max and Lydia died, no one questioned why a Thomas Latimer was in our care. We'd tell people he was a relative we took in when his parents died." She cast a glance at Thomas and placed her hand on his. "Utica was full of homeless children then. It got even worse during the war. On the other side of the city, the Latimers weren't known, so our story was accepted." She glanced at Thomas, sitting next to her. "And I still love and care about him, too."

"What a courageous story," Sophie said, sadly.

Lena wiped away more tears. "We did it to help Max and Lydia as they helped my sister. It was hard being a refugee. But Sofia and I were lucky to know your wonderful brother and sister-in-law. During those difficult years, they were really the only people who were nice to us. You must've been proud of them."

Sophie nodded. "Yes, Max was a proud man and Lydia loved us all very much. And she loved helping others. So, your story doesn't come as much of a surprise."

"And now we have Thomas with us," Arthur said, looking at his handsome young nephew.

"Yes sir, for good!" Thomas said jovially. "This is the bee's knees, having a new family!"

"We have to thank Mr. Sheppard," George said in admiration, looking at Sloane.

Sloane shook his head. "No, George, your insistence led me to Utica." He looked at the Drake family, reeling from the shock of Thomas Latimer sitting in their living room, alive and well.

"Thomas's name is on the tombstone," Sue said, rather awkwardly.

Thomas showed surprise. "Well, I'm still here, Sue. I'm not dead yet!"

This comment brought a few laughs and seemed to clear the tense atmosphere. Lena mentioned she and Thomas would return to Utica tomorrow, but George pleaded with them to stay, at least for a few more hours. George handed her a pad on which she wrote her address and phone number in Utica. She told George to contact them any time. She invited them for a visit.

"I want to get to know my brother," George said, looking at Thomas. "This is the best Christmas present ever! The cat's meow! Welcome home, Thomas!"

George, Sue, and Thomas got up, approached one another, and hugged affectionately, tears streaming down their faces. Sophie and Arthur also rose, joining them.

Sloane and Lena looked at the content faces of the Drake family, united together after so many years, with the real Thomas. Marjorie and Henry marveled at the scene before them, wiping away tears unashamedly.

George mentioned they were still finishing decorating the tree and Thomas said he'd love to help. Sue turned up the volume on the radio and the wonderful Christmas music filled the room, creating a light and cheerful atmosphere. Sophie and Marjorie asked Lena if she'd like coffee and cake, and soon the women were in the kitchen, preparing trays to bring to the living room. Arthur and Henry were talking between themselves, while Sloane watched George, Sue and Thomas decorate the beautiful Christmas tree.

He was surprised no one mentioned Sofia's murder and the attack at the Capital Club on Thanksgiving. Perhaps the discovery of the real Thomas was all they could handle for now.

With Pavel Bartosz most likely Thomas (and the fingerprints would confirm this), that'd mean three members of the same family were killed. And then his thoughts turned to Mrs. Olson. Another strange death, too convenient. And too sudden.

It was as George, Sue and Thomas finished decorating that Sloane slowly recognized the truth. And then he cursed himself silently for not seeing it sooner.

It was later in the afternoon, almost five o'clock. Darkness had settled over Albany as it does so early in the winter. Shades were drawn, fireplaces were lit, lights were turned on. A cold night was ahead. Many people braved the chilly air to shop at Whitney's and Meyer's or attend one of Albany's magnificent theaters. To George the day was wonderful, and he didn't want it to end.

As the afternoon progressed, Lena and Thomas, along with Sloane, were encouraged to stay for dinner. Sophie, Marjorie, Sue, and Lena fixed a simple meal of chicken, rice, and salad, followed by Sophie's tasty chocolate cake, Marjorie's rich vanilla cake and plenty of delicious coffee. At the kitchen table, George sat between his brother and sister and had never felt so content. He looked across the table at Mr. Sheppard, who caught his eye and smiled. Mr. and Mrs. Olmstead and Aunt Sophie and Uncle Arthur were talking to Miss Bartosz, telling her about the Albany neighborhood and its many shops, restaurants, and theaters.

"I can see the resemblance," Sloane said, sipping his coffee, looking at George, Sue, and Thomas from across the table. "There definitely is a likeness."

Marjorie agreed. "You're part of the family, Thomas."

"Thank you for making me feel welcome," Thomas said humbly. "I've never had a family, except for Lena, of course."

Lena smiled. "We'll always stay connected, Thomas." Changing the subject rather abruptly, she addressed Sloane. "Do you have any idea what happened to my sister and nephews? The police told me they've been following leads but nothing so far."

Sloane put down his cup. "Your sister attacked Mr. Donaldson and his stepdaughter with a carving knife at the Capital Club, where she worked. She struggled with Mr. Donaldson and was stabbed, fatally."

"Yes, I know," Lena said, sadly. "I don't know what prompted her to attack strangers in a busy restaurant. And on Thanksgiving, too."

Sloane repeated what he knew of Sofia Bartosz; her previous encounter with Mr. Donaldson and Mrs. Palmer, her attempt at citizenship which was not successful and her unbalanced nature. These points were mentioned at the inquest and Lena acknowledged them.

"But that doesn't explain what happened to Szymon and Pavel," she persisted. "Do you have any leads as to who killed them and why?"

Sloane shook his head. "I'm not investigating their deaths. That's a police matter. George asked me to investigate his brother's identity." He explained again the circumstances under which he first met George and his subsequent investigation. "But it turned out to be a disappearance, rather than a murder inquiry. There are three murders the police are investigating."

"I remember my sister telling me she worried about Pavel and Szymon," Lena said. "In her letters, she'd mention she thought they were involved with criminals."

"Maybe that's why they were killed," Sue suggested.

"I've spoken to the police here in Albany and in Utica," Lena continued. She looked up at Sloane. "Do you think my sister's murder and Szymon's and Pavel's murder are related somehow?"

"I'm not sure," Sloane admitted. "I want to speak to the police about the death of Mrs. Mary Olson. She was struck and killed earlier this week."

"And you think Mary's death is related?" Sophie said, clearly taken aback.

"Again, at this point, I'm not sure," Sloane told her. "When I speak to my contacts at the police department, I'll have the fingerprint cards analyzed. If they match, and there's a good chance they will, then we'll know that the body buried as Thomas Latimer was actually Pavel Bartosz."

"In that case, I'd like Pavel's body returned to Utica for a proper burial, next to his mother and brother," Lena said. "That would involve an exhumation."

Sophie agreed. "We'll make the arrangements. You shouldn't have to face that alone."

"I've run out of cigarettes," Thomas said, realizing his pack was empty.

"Don't worry about that," Sue said, grinning. "Your brother's a smokestack!"

Laughter went around the table. Marjorie served her vanilla cake, while George poured more coffee. He lit a cigarette and mentioned he'd show Thomas around Albany tomorrow.

"Sorry, George, but tomorrow we return to Utica," Thomas told him, puffing at his cigarette. "I have classes at Hamilton, and I work part-time in a law office." He paused, seeing the disappointment in his brother's eyes. "I have a great idea! Why don't I spend the holidays here. Would that be okay with you, Lena?"

Lena looked across the table at Thomas. "Of course, dear. But you're my family, too."

"Then you'll come with him," Sophie said. "We'd enjoy having you for the holidays."

"Yes, we'd liked it very much," Arthur concurred with his wife.

Lena thanked them for the generous invitation. It was decided that she and Thomas would spend the holidays in Albany, getting to know their new family. As more stories were told and more coffee was drunk, Sloane mentioned that it was almost ten o'clock and they should return to his apartment. Marjorie and Henry also mentioned they needed to get home. George and Sue retrieved coats and hats while everyone gathered in the hallway. Sloane thanked them again for their hospitality.

"Thank you, Mr. Sheppard," Sophie told him warmly, "for making this a memorable Christmas for us."

George helped Thomas and Lena on with their coats and mentioned he'd meet them at Union Station tomorrow morning to see them off. Thomas wrote the time and train number on a pad Sue handed him, so George wouldn't miss it. Arthur then opened the front door, allowing Marjorie and Henry to pass through, followed by Sloane, Lena, and Thomas.

"I'll see you tomorrow morning at the station, brother Thomas!" George called as he watched them start to walk up Lancaster headed for Lark Street and the trolley.

Thomas turned to see George in the doorway. "See you tomorrow morning, brother George!"

George then closed the door and joined his sister, aunt and uncle in the living room, ecstatic over his younger brother returning to them, the best Christmas gift ever.

From the opposite direction of Lancaster Street, Laura had walked down Dove Street from Chestnut. Her first stop tonight was a speakeasy off of Lark, before heading to the Kenmore Hotel to dance the night away. From a distance, at the corner of Dove and Lancaster, she stopped as she saw quite a bit of activity at the Drake household. She thought she heard George calling after his brother. From her vantage point, huddled in the dark near a row of parked cars, Laura looked after the young guy, a middle-aged woman, and a man, who from a good way off looked like that Mr. Sheppard. What were they doing coming out of the Drake's house at this hour? Why in the world did George call him brother? And whoever the guy was he called George brother, too.

She shook her head, then continued walking on Dove Street with a firm step. She'd find out soon enough. She'd tell Daddy about it. Mrs. Palmer too.

CHAPTER TWENTY-ONE

G eorge arrived at the bank Monday morning, still astonished from the weekend. He had met Thomas and Lena yesterday morning at Union Station and saw them off, with plans for them to spend the holidays in Albany. Meanwhile, they would write to each other and even call long distance, too. The hell with the charges, George told Thomas jokingly, as they boarded the train. He had watched as it pulled out of the station on its way westward to Utica.

George, Sue, Sophie, and Arthur decided last night at dinner not to tell anyone about Thomas, not until the murders were cleared up, the tombstone was removed, and an exhumation took place. Sophie told George she'd handle those arrangements, so he wouldn't have to worry about it. He mentioned to his aunt and uncle that he wanted to go Christmas shopping after work, so he and Sue would be late arriving home. He wanted to buy gifts for Thomas and Lena when they came within a week. Sophie smiled at her nephew, admiring his warmth and dedication to his brother.

During a lull in his work, George decided to call Sue at the Ten Eyck Hotel. They had not met for lunch, as he was too busy to take a full hour, so he along with Alek went to the corner deli and bought sandwiches, bringing them to the bank and eating at a worktable in the back room. He asked the operator to call the hotel and once connected, asked for Susan Latimer in the administration unit. To his chagrin, it was answered by Laura, on almost the first ring.

"Well, hello George," she said, rather teasingly. "Sue? You just missed her. She's in a meeting taking shorthand, but they should be done soon." She paused. "What's new, George?"

George cleared his throat. He was always cautious in speaking with Laura. "Nothing really. What's new with you, Laura? Still going to the speakeasies?"

Laura laughed. "Of course, George. I love the nightlife." Her tone implied George wouldn't know since he never went to speakeasies. She waited for him to say something about his younger brother and the murders. She was disappointed that he offered no information.

George found his patience wearing thin as it usually did when speaking with Laura Dupont. He made an excuse that a client was waiting to speak with him and rang off. Just in time, as his manager approached and asked for his assistance. A busy afternoon for George, until the five o'clock hour came and to his surprise, his phone rang just as he sat down at his desk from attending a long and rather drawn-out meeting with the bank management. It was Sue, returning his call.

"Sorry, George. I was in a meeting pretty much all afternoon, taking shorthand that I have to type up. Laura told me you called. Is something wrong?"

George allayed her concern. "Don't forget the Christmas shopping we planned for tonight. I want to buy something for Thomas. And Lena, too."

Sue said she hadn't forgotten. "Whitney's is having sales on scarves. I'd like to buy one for Aunt Sophie and Lena."

George told his sister he'd met her outside and hung up. He realized the bank was about to close. He put on his plaid jacket and cap, said good night to colleagues and waited on North Pearl Street for Sue.

At that moment, Sue came up to him and soon brother and sister crossed North Pearl Street on their way to Whitney's Department Store. Once inside, they were jostled by a busy crowd of shoppers, hoping to find the perfect Christmas gift. Sue purchased two hats and scarves for Aunt Sophie and Lena. George bought a tie for Thomas and a pair of winter gloves for Uncle Arthur. Having spent more money than they had planned, George and Sue decided it was time to get home, Sue telling George she was famished and couldn't wait for her aunt's cooking.

It was as they left Whitney's and were on North Pearl Street, that George had a strange feeling they were being watched. He motioned to Sue to walk faster down the street, toward the intersection when they were soon stopped by Laura. She was behind them, bundled in her fur coat and expensive cloche hat. She looked at them sweetly and flashed her shiny teeth.

"Hello, George. Funny seeing you here, Sue. You didn't tell me you were going shopping after work. I would've joined you."

George thought that was the last thing his sister wanted. As though reading his mind, Sue glanced at him and then looked at Laura with venomous eyes, rather unusual for mild-mannered Sue.

"George and I decided at the last minute to shop," she said, and her tone implied it was none of her business. She noticed Laura looking at the hat boxes and the boxes of gifts George carried.

Laura smiled. "Shopping for lots of people, Sue? Tell all of your family hello for me."

Before either George or Sue could comment, Laura quickly continued walking, swallowed up in the crowd, heading toward South Pearl Street.

"What did she mean by all of your family?" Sue said, snow showers hitting her face and shoulders. She bundled her scarf closer around her and looked at her brother.

But George's attention was focused across the street, as he distinctly noticed Mr. Donaldson, walking on North Pearl Street. Didn't he know his stepdaughter was on the other side of the street? Sue was speaking to him, but he didn't hear her.

"George, what is it? I want to get home!"

"Look, Sue, there's Mr. Donaldson, across the street. I wonder where he's going."

Sue looked at her brother as though he was out of his mind. "He lives and works here, George. He could be going anywhere! Come on, I want to get going!"

"Wait, Sue," George said, not taking his eyes off of Reggie across the street. "Let's follow him and see where he's going." He started off without even waiting for his sister.

"George, I think you're mad," Sue said, barely able to keep up with him.

Brother and sister followed Reggie from the other side of the street, then noticed as he crossed at Sheridan Avenue. Amongst the crowds and a heavy snow shower, George reached the corner of North Pearl Street and Sheridan Avenue and saw Reggie steadily walking down Sheridan toward Broadway. He turned left and disappeared past Union Station.

Sue caught up with her brother, breathlessly. "Why are we following Mr. Donaldson?"

"He just bothers me, Sue, like he's up to something." He looked at his sister. "Do you think Laura knows about Thomas?"

"How could she?" she answered, rather irritably. "I haven't told anyone."

George continued looking down Sheridan Avenue, toward Broadway and the imposing architectural gem of Union Station, glistening in the distance.

"I'd like to get going, George," Sue said impatiently.

In steady snow, they started walking back up North Pearl to get the trolley to Lark Street. Brushing past crowds of shoppers and theatergoers, neither George nor Sue saw Claire Palmer, standing on the opposite side of North Pearl Street. She finished her cigarette, flicked it onto the sidewalk, crossed at the light and walked down Sheridan Avenue toward Broadway.

It was late when James Olson left the Delaware & Hudson Railroad Building on Broadway. After Mary's funeral, he found returning to work the best remedy. The Drakes, the Olmsteads and Mr. Donaldson along with his stepdaughter paid respects at her funeral. George and his sister were there, too. He noticed Claire Palmer didn't attend the service. He knew there was no love lost between his wife and Mrs. Palmer, so he wasn't really surprised. But he wouldn't think of that now.

Like his wife, James Olson was clever. He knew what his wife had been up to and the source of her extra income. She had seen more than he did at the Capital Club. She was able to put two and two together, he reflected. She had confided in him, rather than keep it hidden.

And why not, he thought, as he walked through the lobby heading for the exit, holding onto his briefcase, his Fedora hat low on his head, his winter coat buttoned up to brave the chilly air. He waited for the next trolley to take him uptown. As the rush hour was ending and downtown was thinning of pedestrians, except for the crowds on North Pearl Street, it was a rather lonely spot. Another cold night, he observed, with snow showers increasing, blanketing the sidewalks and streets.

He wondered about the Drakes and the Olmsteads, certainly an odd bunch. He had thought Claire Palmer odd too, from what Mary had told him. But secrets always abounded. Of course, he and Mary had their share of secrets. A little money on the side never hurt, he told himself, as though justifying their surreptitious activities.

James then impulsively decided to walk. But at that moment he felt the pressure of a small hard ring in his back, menacingly, which prevented him from crossing Broadway. Someone had crept up behind him and he wasn't even aware of it. A harsh voice ordered him to keep still. He couldn't tell if it was a male or female. It was over in less than a minute.

He was not discovered until a half-hour later when a policeman on patrol noticed something on the ground near the railroad building. Someone who drank too much at a local speakeasy? He noticed the bullet holes embedded in the back of the man's jacket. He then saw dark red stains on the snow-covered sidewalk.

The policeman knew what he saw. Red was for murder.

CHAPTER TWENTY-TWO

O n Tuesday morning, Sloane reached his office early as usual. He had plenty of cases to finish before the new year. He was visited by Lois as always, leaving him fresh coffee and a warm smile.

"Here's this morning's paper," she added, handing him the *Albany Times Union.* "There was a shooting last night on Broadway. A man who worked at the railroad building."

Sloane thanked her for the paper. He had removed his coat and suit jacket, settling himself at his desk, preparing for the busy day ahead. After Lois left and before his first client arrived, he unfolded the paper, noticing the city and world headlines; the continued prosperity projected for 1929 and the new president, Herbert Hoover. Turning the page to local matters, he saw the article Lois referred to.

Albany Times Union
December 11, 1928

Police are investigating a homicide that occurred on Broadway, near the Delaware and Hudson Railroad Building. Mr. James Olson, who was employed for the railroad, was shot and killed last evening. Police have determined robbery was not a motive. Anyone with information is asked to contact Albany City Police.

Sloane read the article several times. Mrs. Olson had died last week and now Mr. Olson was killed, near the building where he worked. But should he question it further? He realized his work for George had been concluded, with the finding of the real Thomas Latimer in Utica. The other murders were a matter for the city police. But Sloane knew he had one more card to play in this case. He knew there was a connection. He had to find it and fast before another murder occurred. He reached over for the candlestick phone and asked the operator to dial Albany City Police.

On Monday, he had gone to see Inspector Harris, with the fingerprint card Lena Bartosz had given him of her nephew, Pavel. If the fingerprints matched those they had on file of the young man arrested as Thomas Latimer, then it was apparent that Pavel Bartosz was the impostor. He knew the outcome of the comparison was crucial to the case. Inspector Harris told Sloane he'd contact him as soon as he had information.

But Sloane found he couldn't wait that long. After speaking to the operator, the call was connected with Albany City Police. The officer who answered put through the call to the inspector, who greeted Sloane, rather irritably as though he resented his call.

"Well, Mr. Sheppard, I was going to call you later this morning. We did have the fingerprints analyzed and yes, there is a match. The young man arrested multiple times as Thomas Latimer was Pavel Bartosz. The prints are the same."

Sloane sighed in relief. "I figured as such, Inspector. Thank you for this information." Before hanging up, he asked the inspector about Mr. Olson's murder last evening.

"That's under investigation. We don't have any leads, but we're asking people who work in the area, including railroad employees. So far, we haven't been able to produce anything solid. It wasn't robbery, as his wallet was still in his coat pocket."

"Do you know anything about bootlegging activities near the river?"

Inspector Harris sighed. "Of course, Mr. Sheppard. But the bootleggers are clever. We patrol the river area nightly and haven't arrested anyone, yet." He paused. "Why do you ask that?"

"Because it's possible that Szymon Bartosz and Pavel Bartosz were involved with bootleggers, which may be why they were killed. Bootlegging can be a profitable business, especially for refugees desperate for money."

Sloane thanked him for his help and ended the call. So now there were five untimely deaths, he thought. Pavel Bartosz and his brother, Szymon. Then their mother, Sofia. Mrs. Olson fell in front of a truck and was killed and just last evening, Mr. Olson was shot and killed. Related deaths or separate? Sloane knew he had finished with the Latimer case, but the murders of the Bartosz family were nagging at his mind. Pavel Bartosz, the phony Thomas Latimer, had last been seen at a speakeasy off of South Pearl Street. Quite possibly Pavel and Szymon had gotten in with bootleggers.

As it was close to the noon hour, Sloane decided to lunch at a diner on North Pearl Street. He grabbed his coat, took the elevator to the lobby and once outside, lit a cigarette, walking past Whitney's. He entered the diner and found it wasn't too crowded.

While partaking of a roast beef sandwich, cups of coffee and several cigarettes, he wondered if George was content with his real brother, alive and well in Utica. He also wondered if George realized the case was far from over.

Sophie had invited Marjorie and Henry for dinner that evening. For some holiday cheer, she told her friend on the phone. Marjorie and Henry gratefully accepted. Sophie was busy in the kitchen when they arrived.

"It smells delicious," Henry said, handing Arthur his coat.

"Roast beef and potatoes," Arthur told him, smiling. "George and Sue should be here any minute from work. They'll be glad to see both of you."

Arthur had turned up the radio in the living room to a station playing Christmas carols. Henry sat by the fire with his friend, conversing about the holidays and Thomas visiting soon at their house. "We're looking forward to his coming here," Arthur said. "Of course, the shock of it hasn't worn off, not yet anyway. But in time, I imagine it will. George is the happiest I've ever seen him."

The front door opened and in walked George and Sue. Their faces were red and flushed from the cold. Hanging their coats in the closet, Sue then heard Mrs. Olmstead in the kitchen with her aunt. She joined them while George entered the living room to greet his uncle and Henry.

"Hello, Mr. Olmstead," George said, shaking hands with Henry. "It's nice to see you. Are you staying for dinner?"

Henry smiled, admiring the handsome George, always the gentleman. "Yes, your aunt invited Mrs. Olmstead and I for holiday cheer." He beckoned George to sit near the fireplace to get warm. "Have you heard from Thomas in Utica?"

"Yes, he called me last night," he told Henry. "We've spoken twice since they left. He'll be here to spend the holidays with us."

"You must be happy about that," Henry said. "He's welcome to visit us, too."

George smiled broadly. "Happy isn't the word, Mr. Olmstead. The bee's knees!"

Sue entered and announced dinner was served. She greeted Henry and the men followed her to the kitchen, where a warm and gracious meal was awaiting them. Sophie served the roast beef, along with the mashed potatoes and vegetables. It was a delicious and hearty meal, and everyone ate plenty. Afterward, Sophie made coffee and brought a tray containing Marjorie's sugar cookies.

"I feel bad for James," Arthur said. "He was murdered last night on Broadway. What is this city coming to? Unless it was just bad luck."

"You think otherwise, Arthur?" Henry asked him. "Mary had an unfortunate accident and James was shot and killed, most likely by some hooligans."

Sophie agreed. "That's why George and Sue travel together on the trolley."

"The good news is that Thomas is back in our lives," George said, puffing at a cigarette.

"I have a good idea," Marjorie told them. "We have tickets for *Hedda Gabler* at the Grand Theater for tomorrow night. Why don't we all go?"

"Ibsen is one of my favorite writers," George said, enthusiastically. "I didn't know *Hedda Gabler* was playing locally. I haven't looked at the theater section in the paper lately."

"The Grand on Broadway is a beautiful theater," Marjorie told them.

"It'll do us good to get out," George said, as though making up everyone's mind.

"Maybe we'll bump into Mr. Donaldson," Sue joked, sipping her coffee but then regretted it as an awkward silence ensued and everyone looked at her.

"Why would we see Mr. Donaldson?" Arthur asked his niece.

Sue mentioned how she and George had seen Mr. Donaldson last evening before getting the trolley. "He was walking toward Broadway."

"Meeting a client most likely," Henry said. "He keeps busy with his work."

Sophie recalled seeing Mary and Claire Palmer recently on Lark Street, near the library. George commented he had seen Mr. Donaldson and Mrs. Palmer on Washington Avenue just last week, although no one saw any significance in seeing Reggie or Claire around town.

"Well, who knows," Sophie said light-heartedly, getting up and retrieving the coffee pot from the stove to refill everyone's cup. "Maybe we'll see these mystery people tomorrow night. Seems like a small world in Albany, after all."

CHAPTER TWENTY-THREE

B y mid-morning the next day, large, ominous clouds were threatening at first with intermittent snow showers. By afternoon, the low clouds unleashed their fury upon the city, depositing steady snow along with a cold, gusty wind.

It was early evening and George, Sue, Sophie, and Arthur sat in a trolley, steadily making its way along Lark Street, on its way downtown to Broadway. George glanced out the windows as the trolley passed Harmanus Bleecker Hall, the Capital Club, the Harmanus Bleecker Library and the Albany Institute of History and Art. Despite the snowy weather, it was a busy evening with shoppers, theatergoers and families dining out. The holiday spirit contributed to the bustling atmosphere.

George sighed contentedly, glad to spend the evening with his family. He looked dapper as always, in a shirt, tie and vest. He glanced at Sue, sitting next to him. She was more morose and withdrawn but George thought she still looked pretty, with a black dress, pearls, and a long winter coat, along with her chic cloche hat. Looking to his left were his aunt and uncle, also well-dressed in evening clothes, Sophie in a winter coat, a pretty blue dress, with pearls and a fashionable hat. Arthur was in a trench coat, suit, and tie, quite debonair with a Fedora hat.

It seemed forever until the trolley reached the end of State Street, before turning left onto Broadway. Along the way, it stopped to pick up more passengers and drop others off. Several groups boarded, some with shopping bags and boxes, excited over their Christmas purchases, others headed to Albany's many fine restaurants and theaters. The trolley finally reached lower Broadway and the theater district. George, Sue, Sophie, and Arthur got off in front of the Grand Theater and upon entering the beautiful lobby saw Marjorie and Henry. They smiled and went over to them.

"Hello, everyone," Marjorie beamed. "How lovely you look, Sophie! And Sue, you're pretty as always! I must say, George, you're certainly a handsome young man!"

George blushed. "Thank you, Mrs. Olmstead. It isn't too crowded here."

Sophie also commented on the sparse crowd. "Maybe the snow is keeping people away."

"Oh, they'll get here," Henry said sensibly. "There are always late arrivals at the theater."

"Thank you, Marjorie and Henry, for buying the tickets for us," Arthur told them. "It's quite a Christmas present. Sophie and I want to pay you for them."

"Nonsense, Arthur," Henry said, and his wife agreed.

"You're our friends," Marjorie said. "I just hope you enjoy the show."

Leaving their hats and coats with the young man at the cloakroom, they entered the majestic theater, richly decorated in cream white, lavish velvet seats, with a rich navy-blue curtain and soft lighting. An usher helped find their seats, located in one of the furthest rows. George and Sue were seated in the back of their aunt, uncle, Marjorie, and Henry.

Sitting comfortably in the plush seat, George looked around as the theater was slowly filling up. Most seats toward the front were already taken. He recognized people from the bank; businessmen and their wives, several assemblymen, and politicians were also in attendance. Sue noticed a few managers from the hotel with their wives.

Soon the house lights dimmed, talking ceased, the curtain rose and the intense drama of the first act of *Hedda Gabbler* began.

As the curtain descended on the conclusion of the first act, the house lights went up, signaling an intermission. Voices started in earnest, many patrons rose to stretch their legs, entering the ornate lobby. In George's case, it was to have a cigarette. Arthur, Henry, and Sue joined him while Sophie and Marjorie decided to stay seated to discuss their upcoming holiday plans.

In the lobby, George lit a cigarette and glanced at the other patrons, elegantly dressed women, and stylishly attired men. Sue joined her brother as he stood by the main entrance.

"What a show! I don't remember when I've enjoyed a play this much."

George agreed. "I hope Aunt Sophie and Uncle Arthur are enjoying it, too."

Henry asked if they wanted coffee or tea. A selection of cakes and pastries were also available. Realizing he had only one cigarette left, George wondered if cigarettes were sold there, although casting a quick glance at the concession area, he rather doubted it.

"None for me, thanks," George said, puffing at his cigarette. Sue also declined, but Henry and Arthur decided on a cup of tea. They soon began chatting amicably with other theater patrons. Sue was engaged in a lively conversation with a hotel manager and his wife. George was talking with a few employees he knew from the bank.

As the house lights began to dim, patrons started to reclaim their seats. Arthur and Henry were about to enter the seating area when they turned expecting to see George and Sue. Instead, they saw only Sue, trailing behind them.

"Where did George go?" Arthur asked, looking past Sue as the lobby began to empty.

"To a corner store to get cigarettes," Sue told him.

"Didn't he realize the second act is about to start?" Henry said.

"It's just around the corner, so he shouldn't be long," Sue said. "Besides, you know George and his cigarettes. He smoked the last one and left his other pack at home!"

Arthur, Henry, and Sue then returned to their seats to join Sophie and Marjorie. Sophie inquired about George and Sue explained where he had gone. Sophie started to protest, but at that moment the curtain rose. The actors returned to the stage and the second act of *Hedda Gabbler* began, enthralling the audience and holding everyone spellbound. Sue was so involved with the drama that she didn't notice the time that had gone by. It was during a change in scenes that she realized the seat next to her was vacant. George had not returned.

After acquiring his coat and cap from the cloak room attendant, George had hurriedly left the theater and walked south on Broadway to a small corner store, where he knew cigarettes and other sundries were sold. It was a blustery and cold night, but the snow wasn't as heavy as when they first left. Few pedestrians were on the dimly lit street. As he reached the small store, he entered and asked for two packs of Lucky Strikes. He handed the clerk the thirty cents and left.

As he was about to return to the theater, he noticed a large, old house, overlooking the Hudson River, not far from the theater. The streetlamps were dim on that part of Broadway, so in the obscure shadows, it looked rather forlorn and out of place. Two cars were parked nearby. Standing on Broadway, his eyes focused on two men, extracting what looked like crates and barrels from the trunk of the cars and carrying them to the back of the house. Oblivious to the snow showers hitting his face and shoulders and momentarily forgetting *Hedda Gabler*, George decided to investigate.

Coming closer to the dilapidated house, he saw more clearly what he had only seen from a distance. He looked around, at the deserted street, with few cars going by. He had been to lower Broadway many times but didn't remember seeing this ramshackle house.

From the darkness where he stood, he heard a low murmur of voices coming from behind the large house. Cautiously in the snow he made his way to the right side of the house and crept silently until he stopped behind a tree. As he peered through the branches, he saw a group of men hauling barrels and crates onto a truck. The murmur of voices reached him again clearly; rough, sinister, conspiring.

"We took care of it. That Olson fool isn't going to bother us anymore."

"But won't the cops get wise when they find the body?"

"Less interfering bastards, that's what I say, like the Bartosz idiot."

"Well, we don't have to worry about him. Or that Latimer fool, either."

A cackle of laughter and then more mumbling. As he stood silently behind the tree, George could see the men hauling the barrels and crates onto the back of a truck. George knew what he was seeing. Rumrunners! He had located an Albany gang, heard confessions of murder, and saw for himself their criminal activities. He looked closer through the branches and saw several large crates and at least five barrels near the back of the house, which he was sure contained illegal liquor. He thought he recognized one of the men, but in the snowy darkness, it was hard to distinguish who it could be. The men continued talking as George cautiously hid behind the tree.

"Where's the loot? Sure, you got it all taken care of?"

"Relax, man. The alcohol's in storage like we agreed."

He couldn't make out what else was being said as the conversation was reduced to mere whispers. But George didn't need to hear anymore. He realized he had located bootleggers who were illegally selling and distributing liquor throughout the city. And now he knew who was responsible for killing the Bartosz brothers and Mr. Olson, too.

He turned toward the sidewalk to return to the theater when suddenly he was grabbed roughly from behind. George fought with all his strength, but a large hand holding a rag firmly over his nose and mouth overpowered him until he lost consciousness.

It was the purest good luck that several people involved with the Bartosz-Olson murders were in the same place at the same time.

As George ventured out of the theater in search of cigarettes, Claire was enjoying a delicious meal and finishing her second glass of wine at the Valencia, a renowned Italian restaurant on Broadway. Her dinner companion was a politician from Brooklyn, in town for the general assembly at the state capitol. Claire had met him at the DeWitt Clinton Hotel, where he regularly stayed and she offered to show him the sights of the city. Having paid the check and gathered their coats, Claire and her companion came out of the Valencia and were about to catch the trolley when Claire stopped short. Before her, on the other side of Broadway, was Laura walking steadily in the light snow.

Of course, she was Christmas shopping, Claire immediately thought. But something wasn't right about the scene before her. She noticed Laura wasn't carrying shopping bags. She watched as she walked past Union Station, heading south on Broadway. The assemblyman was speaking to her, but she thanked him for a lovely evening, showed him where to catch the trolley and then crossed Broadway. The assemblyman looked after her wondering why she'd abruptly end their evening out.

Claire decided to follow Laura. The snow made walking rather difficult on the slushy pavement. She noticed Laura as she came upon a dilapidated, old house. From a distance, Claire thought it was one of the ugliest houses she'd ever seen. Almost slipping in the slushy ice, she tried to keep Laura in sight. In the whiteness of the snow and a few scattered pedestrians, she thought she had lost her. Then she almost bumped into her and cursed herself for not being more careful.

"Laura," she said breathlessly. "Funny seeing you here."

Laura looked at Claire gravely. "I could say the same for you." She paused, shivering in the cold and the nuisance of snow stinging her face. Her fur coat and cloche hat were becoming, and her face was made-up exquisitely as though ready for an evening out.

But she was alone, without an escort, Claire thought. Unless she had plans to meet someone. Then why was she walking down lower Broadway? Certainly not the best neighborhood in the city. Perhaps there was a speakeasy somewhere. But Claire knew the location of most of the speakeasies downtown, so she discounted that and looked intently at Laura.

"Do you know why I'm here?" Laura said, rather boldly.

Claire looked at her, then at the dilapidated house. "Yes, Laura, I think I understand now."

At that moment, a police car pulled up in front of the house. It had come from upper Broadway, its red lights swirling. Out stepped Inspector Harris, Lieutenant Taylor, and Sloane Sheppard. Claire looked at them and they in turn looked at her and at Laura.

Small world, she thought morosely and then waited to hear what they were about to say.

George blinked several times, trying to orient himself to his surroundings. Vision was rather dim. He brushed his hand over his eyes. He was lying on a cot in a cold, dingy and sparsely furnished room. There was a large man seated at a desk against the far wall, his back to George, a banker's lamp the only light on. He could hear men's voices from somewhere below so he realized he must be on an upper floor. The man at the desk got up and approached him.

"Mr. Donaldson," George gasped. "Wh-What's going on?"

Reggie looked grim but forceful, his eyes intent. He spoke hoarsely but to the point. "You know, don't you?" Before George could speak, Reggie continued. "You've always known. You knew what happened at the Capital Club. You knew I killed Sofia Bartosz. From your seat, you saw the look in that foolish woman's eyes as I plunged the knife into her."

"Like you did with her two sons?" George was surprised he had the courage to speak.

This comment caught Reggie off-guard. "Two sons? I killed your double-crossing brother and Szymon Bartosz. They worked for me as rumrunners. They planned to blackmail me by going to the police, so I eliminated them." He spoke as if it were that simple to get rid of someone as though he had every right to do so.

George started to sit up, but Reggie pushed him down roughly. He took a pistol out from the inner pocket of his jacket and pointed it directly at George.

"You'll stay here, George. I killed your lousy brother and I'll kill you, too."

"He wasn't my brother," George said, taking Reggie off guard again. He tried to stall for time, realizing the peril he was in. "He was Pavel Bartosz, Symon's brother and Sofia's son."

Reggie was infuriated. "What are you talking about, you stupid young idiot? I killed your brother Thomas. Don't want to face the fact, George?"

"Thomas is alive and well in Utica." He looked at Reggie's startled face in the dim light of the desk lamp. Finding himself at an advantage, he continued. "You killed Mr. Olson, too, didn't you? And was Mrs. Olson someone you did away with?"

"Snoopers get what they deserve," he said without remorse, still pointing the gun at George.

"You'll never get away with this," George told him.

"Who's going to stop me, George?" Reggie said mockingly.

"It won't pay to kill me," George breathed, clearly frightened.

"You were snooping around this house earlier," Reggie said, menacingly. "You've always been too nosy for your own good. You know too much about my bootlegging business now."

"I won't say anything, Mr. Donaldson, I promise," George pleaded, again stalling for time.

But Reggie had heard enough. He had no time or patience for this nosy, interfering, stupid young fool. And what was this ridiculousness about Thomas Latimer not being Tomas Latimer?

George tried to think of something to stall for time again. He realized Mr. Donaldson was not only an unscrupulous bootlegger but a killer—devious, unbalanced, and unrepentant. And he would be his next victim.

Reggie put the gun back in his jacket pocket. "I won't shoot you, George. Too noisy and messy." He returned to the desk and retrieved rope and several rags from a drawer. Then his deranged eyes rested on a trunk in the corner. "I'll kill you another way."

In the lobby of the Grand Theater, Sophie, Arthur, Sue, Marjorie, and Henry were standing in front of the concession stand, the only patrons in the lobby as the play had not yet finished. Arthur explained to the manager that his nephew had disappeared and asked him to call the police. Sophie was frantic with worry, while Marjorie tried her best to calm her.

Soon the front doors of the theater opened and in walked two policemen, wondering why they'd be called to such a magnificent theater. Arthur introduced himself, his wife, niece and Henry and Marjorie before explaining what occurred.

"Your nephew went to buy cigarettes and disappeared," the policeman, an older man who looked as though he had heard everything before, wrote on a pad. "And he didn't return?"

"No, he didn't," Arthur said, rather impatiently. "He went to the corner store, within walking distance. He should've been back by now."

"Something's happened to George," Sophie cried, clearly shaken. "You must find him!"

"Sophie, dear, try to be calm," Marjorie said, consoling her friend. "I'm sure they'll find George. Maybe he's deciding on a Christmas present for you."

"During the play?" Sophie cried. "He wouldn't do that without telling us."

"Please try to find George," Sue exclaimed, speaking directly to the policeman. "It's been well over an hour. He's been gone too long."

The policeman nodded to his partner, who exited the theater on his way to the corner store, while he continued speaking to Arthur. He asked what George was wearing, the exact time he left the theater and a description. He then told Arthur he would contact headquarters to send a message to other policemen on patrol to be on the lookout for a young man matching George's description.

Arthur placed an arm around Sophie, trying to restrain the fear and worry within her.

"Mr. Sheppard," Claire said breathlessly, looking at him in surprise.

Sloane looked at Claire and Laura, wondering what they were doing on lower Broadway on such a snowy night. As though reading his mind, Claire told him about her dinner date at the Valencia. Laura told Sloane and the policemen she was worried about her stepfather.

"This may be the house where he gets the liquor from the river," she said, shivering.

"We've been looking at your step-father as well, Miss Dupont," Sloane said, and Inspector Harris agreed. "Rumrunners usually are located near the river. This is one of the few houses here."

"Why didn't you contact the police?" Inspector Harris asked.

Laura hesitated. "Well, I wasn't sure Daddy was doing anything illegal."

Lieutenant Taylor nodded. "We've entered this building many times, day and night."

"And haven't found anything incriminating," Inspector Harris added.

"I didn't know how he'd get so much extra money," Laura said. She shivered again as the snow kept falling. "I just assumed his business was prospering. But I was suspicious and decided to see for myself." She paused. "I remember he mentioned a house by the river."

At that moment, two police cars came at an excessive speed down Broadway, stopping in the back of Inspector Harris's patrol car. Two policemen got out of each and came up to them. One of them explained they had been contacted by headquarters, that a George Latimer had disappeared in this area. Other patrols nearby were also alerted of his disappearance.

"George Latimer?" Laura said. "What could've happened to George?"

The policeman explained that he had disappeared from the Grand Theater after going to a corner store for cigarettes. Although they had passed the Grand Theater, neither Laura nor Claire had seen George around lower Broadway. Inspector Harris told the two policemen to check the back of the house, while they entered from the front.

"If George is in there, I want to help," Laura insisted.

"Miss Dupont, it could be dangerous for you," Sloane told her.

"I'll be with her," Claire said. "We can handle anything that comes along."

Without losing any more time, Sloane approached the front door of the old house and found it locked, which didn't surprise him. He then kicked the door open and entered followed by the inspector, the lieutenant, Claire, and Laura. From outside in the back, they could hear cursing and shouting as the policemen rounded up a group of men, bringing them to Broadway in handcuffs. From a side window, Sloane noticed the policemen settled them in the police cars.

Looking around, Sloane saw a sparsely furnished room, containing an old sofa, a few newspapers scattered on a rather large table against a far wall, thin curtains on the windows. A dim light in an old lamp on the table provided enough light to see by. It was cold in the room and Sloane could tell it was not a house that was lived in, but most likely a refuge for bootleggers.

"Look, there's a staircase," Claire exclaimed. "There must be rooms up there!"

Sloane and the policemen started to climb, the old wood creaking with every step. He told Claire and Laura to stay below while they investigated. They had no sooner gotten to the top of the landing when a shot rang out, barely missing Sloane by inches. Sloane and the policemen brandished their guns. They crouched down against a wall, to avoid being an easy target.

"Give it up, Donaldson," Sloane ordered. Getting no reply, he repeated his warning. "Surrender, you're outnumbered. You'll never get out of here alive."

"Oh, I believe I will, Mr. Sheppard," a voice spoke calmly out of the darkness.

Another shot rang out in their direction. Sloane returned fire as did Inspector Harris. They scurried to an open doorway, and stood silently, waiting. Sloane and the policemen then heard a quick rush of footsteps down a back staircase and then a door bang open and close somewhere below. Inspector Harris had his flashlight on, pointed toward the area where the voice had spoken. He motioned to Lieutenant Taylor to follow him down the second flight of stairs to the first floor.

Meanwhile, Sloane had also taken a flashlight out of his pocket and upon hearing cries of anguish from Laura and Claire, shined the light down the stairs.

"We're coming with you," Laura said and ran quickly up the stairs followed by Claire.

Without wasting time to protest, Sloane looked into three different rooms, shining his flashlight all around. He heard Claire and Laura also looking around. By a stroke of luck, he flicked a light switch that illuminated a bright ceiling light in a small front room, containing a desk with a banker's lamp, a well-worn cot, and a rather small trunk in the corner. Torn curtains were on the windows, overlooking Broadway. There was a damp feeling in the room.

From the doorway, Sloane could hear tapping, although he wasn't sure from what. With plenty of light, he walked around, followed by Claire and Laura. The tapping noises continued. From outside they heard more shouts and cursing as men were arrested and hauled off to the police cars.

Sloane approached the trunk in the corner and realized what he heard. He put the flashlight back in his pocket and then eagerly tried to lift the lid, but it was stuck firmly in place. Claire and Laura quickly joined him and with their combined effort, the lid gave way and clattered to the floor. Sloane reached into the trunk and saw George. He was bound, gagged and limp.

"Is he dead?" Laura gasped. "Daddy killed him!"

Sloane removed the gags from his mouth and around his eyes. He helped him out of the trunk, guided him to the cot and settled him, lying still. He heard breathing, although he was flaccid and cold. By this time, Inspector Harris and Lieutenant Taylor returned upstairs. Upon seeing George, the inspector cut the rope tying his hands and feet with a pocketknife.

"Take it easy, George," Sloane told him reassuringly. "You're safe now."

George blinked again and saw Sloane, Laura, Claire, Inspector Harris, and Lieutenant Taylor. He was confused, disoriented. There was suddenly an enormous sound of footsteps on the stairs. Within moments, Sophie, Arthur, Sue, Marjorie, and Henry entered the room. Upon seeing George, Sophie quickly moved forward, sat on the cot, got him to sit up and held him in her arms.

"Aunt Sophie," George exclaimed, feeling the warmth from her. "I thought I was going to die in that trunk," he said. "Mr. Donaldson put me in there. I tried to fight him, but he was too powerful. Stupid of me to come here in the first place."

"George, how did you get here?" Sue asked in a mixture of concern and disbelief.

George explained how he had gone for cigarettes but noticed this run-down house by the river. "And I decided to investigate," he added regrettably. "Fool that I am."

"No worries, George," Sloane reassured him. "We were on to Donaldson. You just happened to interrupt his business transactions."

Suddenly a gunshot was heard from outside, piercing the stillness of the night, in the back of the old house, near the river. Before anyone could react, footsteps were rushing up the back stairs. A policeman burst into the room. From the look on his face, Sloane sensed it was about Reggie. Claire supported Laura by standing next to her, as she could tell by the look on the policeman's face the news wasn't good. And she also assumed it was about Reggie.

"Donaldson shot himself near the river," the policeman explained, catching his breath. "He was dead when we reached him."

CHAPTER TWENTY-FOUR

It was close to midnight. The police, along with Sloane, offered to drive Sophie, Arthur, Sue, and George home, while another police car escorted Henry and Marjorie. As a nurse, Marjorie wanted to check on George. Laura and Claire were asked to join them. At first, Claire hesitated, then realizing the tumultuous events she had just been through, she agreed, helping Laura into a police car on their way to the Drake's house.

They were seated in the living room, each drinking hot chocolate that Sue made. Arthur had plugged in the electric Christmas tree lights and found a radio station playing relaxing Christmas carols. It helped alleviate the tension in the room and brought a smile to George, who was sitting comfortably on the sofa. Sue sat next to him, while Sophie and Arthur were in each of the armchairs near the fireplace. Sloane, Inspector Harris, Lieutenant Taylor, Laura, and Claire sat in extra chairs Henry brought in from the kitchen. Claire admired the comfortable living room and the wonderful Christmas tree, so nicely decorated. She commented on the lovely room.

"George picked the perfect tree," Sophie smiled at her nephew.

Sloane lit a cigarette and asked George how he was feeling after his ordeal.

"I'm angry at myself for going into that ugly house," he responded with a frown.

"When we came out of the theater, we saw the police cars at that house," Sophie explained. "We went there with the policeman." She paused, looking at George tenderly. "I'm glad we did."

"Why would Mr. Donaldson get involved with bootleggers?" Sue asked.

"He wanted the money," Sloane said. "And he was clever in his position as a city attorney to recruit men for the job. He hired Pavel Bartosz and his brother Szymon, but after a while, they decided to blackmail him."

"I told him about Thomas," George said. "He didn't believe me."

"What about Thomas?" Claire asked. She wondered what other shock could come her way.

Sloane explained the identity of Pavel Bartosz, who lived his life as Thomas Latimer, without knowing it. He told Claire about Max and Lydia Latimer, their close relationship with Sofia Bartosz who cared for Thomas since infancy and how Lena Bartosz, her sister, was raising the real Thomas in Utica after her sister moved to Albany with her son Szymon to seek a better life. Claire almost spilled her hot chocolate on her evening dress. Even Laura, now hearing it for herself, was astonished.

"Do you mean your brother is still alive, George?" Laura asked, still incredulous.

He nodded. "He's in Utica and will be here to spend the holidays with us."

"Reggie didn't kill your brother, he killed Sofia Bartosz's son," Claire said thoughtfully. "So that's why she attacked Laura and Reggie at the Capital Club. She must have recognized Reggie as the man who killed her sons and wanted revenge."

Sloane agreed. "We'll never know her exact motivations for the attack, but what you said is the most logical conclusion."

"I saw him kill her," George spoke, rather hoarsely. "At first, I thought it was a slip of the knife, like everyone else. But from where I sat, I could see the hateful expression in Mr. Donaldson's eyes. Sofia Bartosz was a big woman, but she couldn't overpower Mr. Donaldson."

"Why didn't you say something, George?" Sue asked gently.

"I wasn't sure what I saw," he admitted. "It wasn't until later that I put it all together."

"He also killed Mr. Olson," Sloane said, finishing his hot chocolate and putting the cup on the coffee table. "From their table, the Olsons had the same view as you, George. They saw Mr. Donaldson deliberately stab Sofia Bartosz. Like Mr. Donaldson, they were greedy for money and saw blackmail as a weapon. I can safely assume he pushed Mrs. Olson in front of the truck. It was risky for him, but he was desperate not to have the exposure of his bootlegging schemes ruin his life."

"I shouldn't have gone to that house tonight," George said again.

"The non-descript type," Henry offered. "No one would pay the slightest attention to it."

Inspector Harris agreed. "That's why it served as a good meeting place for the bootleggers. It had been abandoned for years and no one was living there. The city considered tearing it down at one time. We had been through it many times but found nothing to incriminate bootleggers."

"What made you suspect Reggie, Mr. Sheppard?" Claire asked.

"He seemed indicated," Sloane answered. "I needed proof. That's why when the inspector told me he and his men planned to check on the house again, I decided to go with them. I figured if Reginald Donaldson was a bootlegger, he needed a headquarters in the city, most likely near the river. He certainly wouldn't use his office. My hunch paid off."

"I was on to him, too," Claire said. Everyone looked at her questioningly. "That's why you saw me on Washington Avenue, George. I was following Reggie to see where he'd go. He was so furtive, despite his height, it was hard to keep up with him." She hesitated and then addressed Sophie. "When you saw me, Mrs. Drake, on Lark Street that evening, I was following him again."

"Why didn't you come forward with this information?" Inspector Harris said.

Claire took her time in replying. "Reggie had something on me that could destroy me, that could ruin my career in Albany. I had a difficult life when I lived in Elmira and somehow, he found out and decided he'd use it against me if I disclosed information about his bootlegging business." She hesitated. "I didn't know the extent of his illegal activity."

"He could've killed you, too," Laura said, looking at Claire. "It's better you kept it to yourself." She paused. "Sofia Bartosz must've been angry when she saw us at the Capital Club."

Sloane agreed. "She knew her sons worked for him as bootleggers, and she recognized him as the man who killed them. She wanted revenge and decided to kill him at once."

"In front of all those people?" Laura asked, astonished.

Sloane nodded. "When a mother loses her children to violence, at times her mental state may be severely affected. She wanted to kill you, too, Miss Dupont."

Laura shivered slightly. "I can't believe Daddy killed five people. All for money!"

"Not just money," Sloane added. "But security. He felt threatened by the blackmailing attempts the Bartosz brothers made on him, as well as the Olsons."

There followed an uneasy silence but the relaxing Christmas carols on the radio helped to diminish any awkwardness. Sophie cleared her throat and turned to Laura and Claire.

"We'd be happy to have you both for dinner on Christmas day."

"I'd like to spend the holiday with you, Mrs. Drake," Laura said gratefully.

"I've never really had a family," Claire said demurely. "I feel like I've gotten closer to everyone here." She hesitated. "Thank you, Mrs. Drake, I'd be happy to spend Christmas with you."

Sophie told them she planned to cook turkey for Christmas. "Since we're having extra guests this year." She mentioned Thomas and Lena Bartosz would be joining them.

"What will become of Mr. Donaldson's business?" George asked Claire.

"There are several lawyers who'd be interested in taking over for him," she answered.

At that moment, Sloane, Lieutenant Taylor and Inspector Harris stood and shook hands with George. He thanked Sloane, joining them at the front door. When they had gone, he noticed Laura and Claire putting on their coats, and Marjorie and Henry did likewise. Marjorie and Henry offered to walk Laura back to the house on Chestnut Street, before continuing to their own on State Street.

"I'd need to call a cab, Mrs. Drake," Claire said. "The trollies stop running by midnight."

Sophie offered to phone for her, while the Olmsteads and Laura said goodnight and walked out into the cold, still night. As she stood in the hallway with the others, Claire smiled at George.

"You put yourself on the line, George," she said. "You're a brave young man."

He smiled in return and opened the door again as he heard a car on the street. A taxi was waiting, and Claire wished them all a good night, waving as she walked outside to the taxi.

Closing the door, George hugged his aunt, uncle, and sister tenderly, then proceeded up the stairs, too tired to even think, entering his bedroom, a safe haven from the outside world.

Over the next week and a half, George was eagerly waiting for Christmas Eve, when Thomas and Lena would arrive. On that day, George and Sue met them at Union Station after work and were now contentedly seated at the kitchen table, having enjoyed Sophie's delicious fish dinner. Sue helped set the desserts plates, while Sophie brought out her chocolate cake and Marjorie's vanilla cake.

"The cakes look fantastic!" Thomas exclaimed. "I don't know which to choose from."

"You don't have to choose," George smiled. "Have one of each!"

Laughter went around the table as Sophie poured coffee and cut the rich desserts. The evening continued with conversation and more laughter as George, Sue and Thomas got to know each other. Sophie and Arthur couldn't remember when they had seen George and Sue so happy.

"Tomorrow, when I met Miss Dupont, I feel I owe her an apology," Lena said, sipping her coffee. "That's the least I can do for my sister's wrongful actions."

Sophie patted her hand encouragingly. "You have family in Albany now, dear. Let's put the past behind us. It's the future that matters."

Arthur suggested they listen to a Christmas concert being broadcast on the radio. While the men gathered in the living room, Lena helped Sophie, Marjorie, and Sue clean the kitchen. Sophie put their cups on a tray, and they then joined the others in the living room.

"When do you finish college, Thomas?" Marjorie asked him, settling in an armchair.

"Next year," he answered. "I hope to enter Albany Law School after graduation."

"That's great!" George exclaimed. "You can live here with us."

"We'll be a family again!" Sue exclaimed, tears coming to her eyes.

Sophie suggested they sing along to the wonderful Christmas carols. Arthur and Henry led them as George, Sue, Thomas, Sophie, Marjorie, and Lena joined in, singing along to *Silent Night*. They sang happily, enjoying each other's company and the joyful Christmas music. George smiled at his younger brother, who equally looked at him with affection.

"Merry Christmas and Happy New Year to everyone, and especially to Thomas!" he exclaimed, with a twinkle in his eyes. "I have a feeling it's going to be a great new year."

THE END

CPSIA information can be obtained
at www.ICGtesting.com
Printed in the USA
LVHW052312070722
722996LV00001B/42